"Halt this instant! You've been shooting at me!"

Gray swiveled toward the voice, which emanated from behind a large, two-trunk oak. "Shooting at you?" he shouted back, marching across the glade. "Stop spouting nonsense and show yourself. I'm here to guide you back. You've nothing to fear."

"I don't believe you." Neala Shaw, the bedraggled young woman with curly brown hair, brandished a tree limb in his face. "Who are you? You're trespassing."

Gray propped his shoulders against the tree. "You wouldn't deter a kitten with that twig, much less a man with a gun."

"Are you one of the sheriff's new deputies?"

"No! I'm Isabella Chilton's nephew. I just arrived for a visit. And I certainly didn't plan on rescuing any damsels in distress today."

"Well, what on earth are *you* angry for? You're not the one who was almost killed!"

Books by Sara Mitchell

Love Inspired Historical

Legacy of Secrets #5

Love Inspired

Night Music #13
Shelter of His Arms #31

SARA MITCHELL

A popular and highly acclaimed author in the Christian-fiction market, Sara's aim is to depict the struggle between the challenges of everyday life and the values to which our faith would have us aspire. The author of eight contemporary, three historical-suspense and two historical novels, her work has been published by many inspirational book publishers.

Sara has lived in diverse locations, from Georgia to California to Great Britain, and her extensive travel experience helps her create authentic settings for her books. A lifelong music lover, Sara has also written several musical dramas and has long been active in the music ministries of the churches wherever she and her husband, a retired career air force officer, have lived. The parents of two daughters, Sara and her husband now live in Virginia.

Legacy of Secrets

SARA MITCHELL

Steeple
Hill®

Published by Steeple Hill Books™

STEEPLE HILL BOOKS

Steeple
Hill®

ISBN-13: 978-0-373-82785-5
ISBN-10:   0-373-82785-7

LEGACY OF SECRETS

Jesus wept.
—*John* 11:35

For I am convinced that neither death nor life,
neither angels nor demons, neither the present nor
the future, nor any powers, neither height nor depth,
nor anything else in all creation, will be able to
separate us from the love of God that is in
Christ Jesus our Lord.
—*Romans* 8:38

For B.K. and Barry—neighbors and dear friends who not only walk the extra mile, but provide new shoes, food for the journey and umbrellas for all the storms of life battering our family these past few years.

Thanks for being there.

Acknowledgments

Many thanks to:

Dr. Robert S. Conte, historian, the Greenbrier at White Sulphur Springs, for his hospitality, help and endless patience with all my questions. Any historical inaccuracies fall solely on my shoulders!

Melissa Endlich, my editor, whose enthusiasm and insight warm the heart and energize the creative soul.

Janet Kobobel Grant, my long-suffering agent, whose belief in me never falters.

Prologue

Richmond, Virginia
September 1862

On a humid, chilly evening in late September, the boy finally reached his goal. His journey had lasted three terrifying nights and four equally terrifying days; except for the first night, when he'd stowed away on a northbound freight train, he was forced to evade swarms of soldiers, rebel and bluecoats alike. They roamed the countryside and main roads like the biblical plague of locusts his grandmother talked about, the ones inflicted upon the Egyptians.

For two of those nights the boy hid shivering in fear under cover of a forest, in a thicket of wild rhododendron, his nose filled with the ripe odors of leaves and wet earth while a hundred yards away the awful sounds of bloodcurdling battle rent the air. The thought of killing a human being twisted his insides. When he could no longer bear the cold and fear and uncertainty, he clapped his hands over his ears, choking on tears wept in desperate silence.

Swallowing hard against the memory, he focused on his present surroundings—a narrow alley on a busy street. Tall brick buildings engulfed him instead of trees; a cluster of wooden crates shielded him instead of bushes. Instead of the noise of battle, the sounds of a city filled his ears. Buggies and wagons rattled past in the street. Crowds of people choked the walkways. As the moments passed, gradually he crept onto the sidewalk and huddled in the shadow of the doorway to some kind of store. Directly across the street, a fancy hotel rose in lofty grandeur between two nondescript brick buildings. Inside that hotel, the man he had traveled over a hundred miles to see dined with his family, oblivious to the existence of the scrawny thirteen-year-old boy who was his nephew.

Time passed while he tried to decide what to do. He could feel his heartbeat clear up inside his ears. Dusk settled in, and he watched the lamplighter's progress along the street, lighting up the tall streetlights. Several times shiny carriages stopped in front of the hotel, collected and discharged men in top hats and expensive-looking suits, along with women in their hooped skirts wide enough for a flock of chickens to hide under. A colored man clad in a hideous purple uniform guarded the hotel entrance, nodding to arriving guests as he held open the door.

Several passersby glanced askance at the boy, and one frowning man in a greatcoat actually stopped, asked him what he was about, loitering on the walk.

"I'm waiting for my uncle."

"And where might your uncle be, boy, that he left you here on the street after dark?"

Sweat gathered on his palms and at the small of his back. "Oh, he'll be out in a few moments. He had to leave a message for someone in the hotel."

"Hmm. Well—" his voice turned brisk "—that's all right, then, I expect. How old are you, son?"

He stood straight, keeping his gaze open and earnest upon the gentleman. "Thirteen. You don't need to worry about me, sir. I'm perfectly fine." The cultured drawl of his proud North Carolina grandmother rolled easily off his lips, and he watched smugly as the lingering suspicion faded from the man's face.

"Very well." He touched two fingers to his top hat. "But you be careful, son. There's a war going on, and it's drawing closer to Richmond every day. I'd hate to see you conscripted into the army, though you've one foot in adulthood." Some emotion flickered in his eyes. "War's horrific enough for grown men. Don't believe anyone who claims otherwise, or fills your head with stories of the glory of battle. You tell your uncle to take better care of you, in the future."

"Yessir."

The man patted his shoulder, then walked on.

The longing boiled up, fast and ferocious, as it always did. He watched the stranger stride down the street, wishing so fiercely it made his teeth hurt that he had a father who cared whether or not he loitered alone on a city street. Who tried to shield him from the brutality of war. Before the fear could take hold again, he darted across the street and ducked inside the hotel while the doorman was busy handing some ladies down out of a dark green brougham.

The lobby was a maze of gleaming oak columns and red-cushioned chairs scattered between huge urns of potted plants. Mindful that his clothes were rumpled and dirt stained, he slipped from urn to urn, behind columns, making his way toward the dining room. The scullery maid at his uncle's imposing town house on Grace Avenue had been easily per-suaded to provide directions to the hotel; ever since he'd been a toddler he'd perfected the art of pleasing females.

Heart thumping, as a large grandfather clock dolefully

bonged nine times, he slipped inside the dining room—and saw them. Even when seated, his uncle was a commanding presence in his swallow-tail coat and blinding-white shirt, where a diamond stickpin winked with every motion he made. Next to him sat a pretty plump woman dressed in a deep red gown. Jet earrings and necklace decorated her ears and throat. That would be his aunt, and the two little boys dandified up in revolting little suits his cousins.

Everybody was smiling and talking, including the boys. He watched, still and silent as one of the wooden columns, while his uncle leaned over to hear something his wife was saying, a tender expression on his face the boy had never witnessed on another man's countenance, not in his entire thirteen years.

The longing intensified until it was a monster, biting into him in chunks of indescribable jealousy and pain.

Suddenly one of the sons, the one barely a toddler, knocked over a glass. His older brother laughed.

Across the room, the boy tensed, not breathing, while he waited for the father to reprimand his son, to perhaps even backhand him. Waited for the mother to deliver a shrill scolding, to lecture the hapless child on proper deportment.

Instead, the father calmly signaled for the waiter, righted the glass himself. Then he ruffled his son's hair, the expression of indulgence on his face visible all the way across the room.

Something snapped inside the boy.

That little boy should be him. He should have been part of a well-to-do family who dined in fancy hotels. *His* mother should be dressed in fancy lace and velvet, seated next to her husband. His father. His home should be the immense stone town house with the neatly manicured yard.

For years his mother and grandmother had filled his head

with stories and promises of a grand Mission that someday he would undertake, to right a Grievous Wrong. Now, unnoticed and invisible to the family that should have been his, he made a vow of his own.

Chapter One

Charlottesville, Virginia
Spring 1889

The funeral service was over, the mourners dispersed. A light breeze carried the faint scent of spring hyacinths, and the sound of the church bell, tolling its doleful message. Six blocks away, Neala Shaw followed her brother Adrian up the front steps, into a house devoid of light and life. Silently they hung coat and cloak on the hall tree, then just as silently wandered into the parlor. Unable to bear the shadowed gloom, Neala made her way to the windows to pull back the curtains before confronting her brother.

"Adrian…what you said, about leaving?" The silken threads of the tassels holding the curtains were tangled; she concentrated on combing through each strand with her fingers. "Tell me you didn't mean it."

"I did mean it. Every word." He tugged at his tie, yanking it off with quick, jerky movements. The stiff shirt collar followed. "Mother and Father are gone. Even if I wanted to, there's no reason to stay here."

Neala dropped the tassel and turned to stare blindly out the window, wishing just once her temperament would allow her the satisfaction of retaliating with equally hurtful words. How could Adrian behave so, when less than an hour earlier they had buried both parents?

She could still hear the sound of the shovels, still see the clumps of dirt pouring onto the coffins, signaling with brutal finality that, while Edward and Cora Shaw's souls were with God, their lifeless bodies were forever consigned to the earth. Until she herself died, Neala would never see them again, never hear their voices, never inhale the scent of Mother's honeysuckle toilet water or Father's sandalwood hair tonic. Never feel the warmth of their hugs.

All because of an accident. A tragic, deadly accident that shocked the community and devastated the few members left in the Neal Shaw family.

"Adrian, this is our home. I don't—"

"*Was* our home. The house and all its contents go on the auction block tomorrow, remember? Father may have been a respected university professor, but he knew as much about providing for his family as a squirrel finding nuts in a snowstorm."

Neala winced. "Where will you go?"

He shrugged, abruptly looking much younger than his twenty years. "I bought a train ticket for Newport News yesterday. Always wanted to see the ocean."

Curiosity overpowered caution. "Adrian, how on earth did you pay for the ticket?"

He avoided her gaze. "Sold Father's watch," he muttered after a minute. "I didn't have anything else." His voice rose in the face of Neala's silence. "It's not as though Father's here to care one way or the other. Besides, it's his fault we're in this mess. You could always sell Grandfather's legacy. I doubt if it's worth more than a few dollars, but that's more than Father left."

He could have slapped her face and not wounded her so deeply. "I will never part with the clan crest badge. Perhaps that's why Grandfather left it to *me*, instead of you." Neala watched her brother's face close up, but she was beyond placating him. "That crest has been part of the Shaw family for over three hundred years. Now it's the only legacy we have left. It's a shame I'm the only one who appreciates it."

"What did you expect? They named you after him, not me. He left the crest badge to you, not me. Not his only surviving grandson."

Silence gathered in the room, hanging like a damp fog. "I need to finish packing," Adrian finally muttered. "You'll be all right, won't you, sis? With the auction, I mean?"

"I'll manage just fine, Adrian."

"Um…do you know what you're going to do? Where will you live? The Johnsons'?"

"No, they don't really have room, especially with Hannah in the family way."

"Oh. What about the Marsdens?"

"Mr. Marsden suffers from sciatica. They're moving to Thomasville, Georgia, this fall."

Adrian hunched his shoulders, his expression sheepish but defiant. "Well, what about one of the boardinghouses where some of the teachers live?"

Neala folded her handkerchief into a neat square to give herself time to collect her sluggish thoughts. "Too expensive, I'm afraid, my dear." She managed with Herculean effort to produce a matter-of-fact smile. "Mrs. Hobbs told me about a school for women," she shared, the words dragging. "It's farther north, somewhere up in the Blue Ridge Mountains, I believe. She suggested I apply for residency there. I hadn't considered it because you were here, and this school is apparently only for women who have lost all their family connections. Mrs. Hobbs says tuition is paid through donations or trusts or something, since the only applicants accepted are those who find themselves without any resources." Carefully she kept her voice stripped of any hint of censure, but Adrian's cheeks turned a dusky red.

"Then you have nothing to worry about," he snapped. "This time tomorrow I'll be long gone. Tell everyone I'm dead, too. The way things have gone over the past few years in our family, I may as well be."

He stormed out of the parlor, and a moment later Neala heard the front door slam.

Philadelphia

The odors in the squalid alley would suffocate a buffalo. How could a human being survive, much less breathe here, Grayson Faulkner wondered as he and his partner picked their way down what seemed like a tunnel into perdition. A pack of snarling, slobbering dogs fought over the bloody carcass of another animal; Gray averted his gaze and breathed shallowly to keep his gorge at the low end of his throat. Rotting garbage, putrid food scraps and rusted tins formed piles higher than their heads. If he'd known what teaming up with a bounty hunter entailed, he'd never have let Marty Scruggs talk him into it.

When this job was finished, his old friend would have to hornswoggle a new partner. Seeking adventure all over the earth had been a satisfying way to explore life. But even Gray's years as a deputy marshal out in Wyoming Territory, where he'd seen plenty of depravity in the wild cattle towns, hadn't prepared him for the likes of a city slum.

Beside him, Marty gagged, then cheerfully cursed the dogs, the place, and the man they were looking for.

"I agree," Gray said. "So I hate to break it to you now, but after this job, my friend, I'm through."

"You and me both. But you lasted longer than I thought, seeing as unlike me, you're a gent born with a whole place setting of silver spoons in his mouth."

They passed a pile of steaming garbage, the stench so rank Gray's eyes watered. When he finished this job, he'd take a long-needed vacation, he promised himself. Somewhere green and fresh, where the air sparkled and he could hear birdsong. Somewhere nobody knew or cared about his prowess with a gun, or his family. Surely some little corner of this vast country could provide relief for a man on the verge of destroying whatever passed for his soul.

"Isn't this the one?" Marty hissed.

"Looks like it," Gray agreed after a moment.

They climbed several flights of creaking stairs lit only by a single bulb hanging from a long wire in the wretched foyer; the higher they climbed, the darker and more stale the air grew. Through thin, decrepit doors they heard voices arguing, babies wailing, smelled the stomach-turning odors of urine, sweat and mildew along with rancid food. Gray opened one flap of his shapeless sack coat, curling his fingers around the holstered Smith & Wesson revolver. It was a new hammerless model that had replaced his trusty Peacemaker; Gray was as proud of the New Departure model as a parent with a precocious child.

"I'm right glad you're along." Marty grinned slyly. "Still the best marksman east of the Mississippi, I hear."

Gray felt heat burn his ears and cheeks. "I don't know what you've heard, or read, but likely it's tommyrot."

They reached the top floor; in wordless accord they approached the door on the end, and Marty knocked twice. The churning in Gray's belly stilled, and an almost eerie calm descended—the falcon, poised to swoop upon its prey.

The door opened a crack, just enough for the two men to see a woman's pitted face and suspicious eyes. "Don't know ye," she snapped. "Go 'way."

Marty planted his foot in the door. "We're here to collar Kevin Hackbone. Please step aside, ma'am. We know he's in here, and we know there's no way out except through this door."

Gray watched a multitude of expressions streak across her face, unable to completely divorce himself from an uprising of pity. If she'd had a chance, a decent place to live and a man who took care of her... He stepped closer, crowding the doorway until reluctantly the woman stepped back. "He won't go easy," she said, jerking her chin toward a narrow hall.

"His choice," Gray returned quietly.

"If you help us, it'll be better for you," Marty added. He exchanged glances with Gray, then tugged out a pair of handcuffs and headed down the hall, to a closed door. "Come on out, Kevin," he called. "You're under arrest back in New York City, for robbery, assault and battery, and too many other crimes to waste more breath on."

"Come and get me, ya boot-kissing son of a sewer rat!" a nasal voice yelled through the flimsy panel.

"Now, Kevin, there's two of us out here." He shot Gray a quick glance, winked. "One of us is the Falcon himself. You've heard about him, right? Might wriggle away from me, but *you* know and *I* know you'll never make it past him."

"Got a knife, boyo. And I'll use it, I will."

"I've got a gun," Gray called back, glaring at his irrepressible friend. "And I'll use it."

The door opened. Looking like a mangy ferret, Kevin eyed the cuffs dangling from Marty's hand, then glanced down the hall where Gray waited by the door. After a long moment, Kevin heaved a sigh and held out his hands. "Knew it was just a matter of time," he muttered, all bluster gone.

Going too easy, Gray thought with a prickle of disquiet. He watched, every muscle tensed, waiting for Kevin to make a move as Marty proceeded to handcuff his hands behind his back.

"No!" the woman behind Gray suddenly shrieked, a demented scream ripping from her throat. She dashed down the hall before Gray could stop her, and there was a knife in her hands, a knife she lifted high above her head, a knife aimed for Marty's unprotected back.

It happened too fast. Even as he raced after her, shouting at her, Gray knew he was too late. Too late he screamed somewhere in the deepest recesses of his mind as he lifted the gun and fired but the knife had already plunged into Marty's back. Marty half turned, his eyes wide with disbelief. He shook his head, his gaze finding and holding Gray's even as his hands fell away from Kevin and he dropped to his knees, then crumpled on top of the dead woman—the first woman Gray had ever been forced to kill.

Gray scarcely noticed Kevin's escape. He gathered Marty in his arms, feeling the blood soaking his hands. "Hold on," he pleaded, pressing against the wound with all his might. "Hold on, Marty. You have to hold on…."

The friendly brown eyes, always so full of humor, full of life, were glazed now, staring vaguely up into Gray's face. Marty's mouth moved, and he coughed, blood trickling down his chin. "Gray…" he whispered, one hand fumbling aimlessly until Gray grabbed it, gripped it tightly. "Glad it wasn't you, Falcon…" The ghost of a smile flickered across his lips. "Would…ruin…your reputation."

His head lolled, and his body went slack.

His friend was gone.

Chapter Two

Isabella Chilton Academy for Single Females
April 1890

Drizzling rain accompanied a week of demanding examinations, but winter session at the Isabella Chilton Academy was finally over. Along with academic and home-management courses, graduates from the Academy were educated in every facet of etiquette and social skills in order to survive a world where a woman's role was no longer as rigidly defined. Since 1866, when Miss Isabella had converted her husband's family estate into a school in order to save it from Yankee carpetbaggers, every student who completed the four-year curriculum acquired either a husband or gainful employment with which to support themselves.

"God's design from the beginning was for marriage between a man and a woman," Miss Isabella liked to remind the students. "Regrettably, the world seldom chooses to abide by God's design."

Neala had spent the better part of the past year learning that painful lesson.

As was the custom, on the first day the capricious April weather cooperated, Miss Isabella treated students to a day trip. Today the destination was a shopping-and-luncheon trip to Berryville, which spawned a giddy atmosphere among all the women except Neala.

Restless, a trifle pensive, Neala had elected to stay behind to assist Miss Crabbe with school paperwork. An Academy fixture for years, Eulalie Crabbe was an excellent secretary, but the high-strung spinster could handle no more than two tasks at any given moment. "But it's not just the paperwork," Neala explained to Abigail Schaffer, one of her new friends at the Academy. "I, well, I need to take a long walk this afternoon. To think about…things."

"I understand." Abby gave a smile that belied the wistful tone.

"Why can't you help Miss Crabbe tomorrow?" Nan Sweeney interrupted from behind Abby. "You told me last week you were hoping to finally purchase a new ready-made wrapper, to replace the dress you ruined in the harness-room fire."

Would anyone ever forget that wretched imbroglio? It had happened over five months ago! All right, she could have perished—but if she hadn't tried to put out a fire she was responsible for starting, she would never have been able to look in a mirror again.

Violet Gleason, a farm girl standing next to Nan, chimed in, "Please do come. It won't be the same without you, Neala…"

"All right, my dears. Her decision's made, and I concur."

With the brisk kindness for which she was famous, the headmistress silenced the rest of the protests with a commanding wave of a gloved hand. Liam Brody, the school's coachman and stableman, handed the women into the coach, then shut the door with such haste he caught the ribboned hem of someone's gown. Muttering what no doubt were Gaelic imprecations, he rectified the mistake, jammed his top hat farther down over his forehead and swung up into the driver's seat.

Neala and Miss Isabella shared a smile. "Don't let Eulalie keep you past two," the headmistress ordered. She pressed her plump heliotrope-scented cheek against Neala's. "And don't forget to carry your whistle when you go for your walk. Mr. Pepperell is planting tomatoes this afternoon. I've told him to keep an ear out."

"I'll be fine."

"Hmm." The older woman idly stroked the side of her nose. "You haven't yet learned your limitations, have you?" A faint frown appeared between her eyes. "Don't let the new girls pester you so you miss your walk."

"They're never a bother," Neala murmured. "If I can help them know they're not alone, it's the least I can do."

"We all help one another here, it's true. But you are neither their mother, nor headmistress of the Isabella Chilton Academy. My students must also learn how to embrace solitude, and endure loneliness."

Heat crept up Neala's cheeks. "I just want to be a friend."

Miss Isabella's face softened. "Ah, Neala. My dear, I do understand. You are indeed a very good friend, to all of us. Even when you're trying to shoulder more than your share." She smoothed the row of ruffles on her basque. "While you go for that walk, remember that you do have a home here. People who care about you—simply because you're you. Think about that as well, hmm?"

At a little past four o'clock, Neala headed toward the thick forest that screened the Academy from fierce northwestern winds. Today, however, the wind was light, playful; spring bloomed in all its flagrant abandon. Neala loved this season of new birth, with the scents and colors of restored life bursting forth from the earth, reminding all mourners that death was never final.

Some time later she reached the sunlit glade she'd designated her forest chapel. Most of the students found hideaways like this, somewhere on the vast grounds where they could escape for a sip of solitude. Few of them… All right, only Neala and the mysterious widow Tremayne ventured this far into the woods. What *was* her name? Josephine? No—Jocelyn. Jocelyn Tremayne. Several times Neala had invited Jocelyn to join her. Though polite, the widow always refused, saying she needed time to adjust to her new life. If Neala pleaded, Abby occasionally joined her for a hike down to the river. But Abby preferred to spend most of her spare time in the stables, because she loved horses, so Neala tried hard not to be the infernal nag her brother considered her.

She kicked an acorn, then sighed, allowing the tranquil surroundings to purify her restless spirit. She hadn't yet grasped the notion of embracing lifelong solitude, but these walks seemed to help.

She would have made a wonderful explorer, like Lewis and Clark. Or perhaps an Indian. Yes, definitely an Indian squaw with beautiful long black hair. Long, straight hair worn in easy-to-manage braids. Not an infuriating head full of wispy brown curls that refused to obey hairpins no matter how firmly attached.

An hour later, pleasantly winded, mostly at peace, Neala started back for the school. She was humming a hymn whose words she had forgotten, absently stroking tree trunks as she wound her way back along the faint path her footsteps had created over the past ten months, when the resounding crack of a rifle shot rent the twilight silence.

Simultaneously the bark of the white pine inches from her face exploded outward. Neala leaped back, hands flying to cover her eyes even as realization slammed into her with the same force as the bullet struck the tree.

Some stupid hunter had almost killed her, thinking she was an animal.

She ducked behind the pine even as another bullet zinged past a mere two feet behind her. How stupid of her, to have worn dark mourning clothes for her walk, which made her far more difficult to distinguish from a deer or some other large animal. Neala scanned the direction from which the shot had been fired, but she could detect no sign of movement. She cupped her hands on either side of her mouth to create a make-shift megaphone like a ringmaster at Barnum & Bailey Circus.

"Don't shoot again!" she yelled. "I'm a person, not your supper!" Then, after two seconds of thrumming silence, she added, "And this is private property! One more shot, and I'll see that you're the one being hunted!"

A massive oak with two joined trunks offered more protection than the pine. Neala gathered up her skirts, hunched her shoulders and darted behind a thicket of mountain laurel, then raced for the oak's protection. She hunkered down, frustrated and angry because the oaf out there had spoiled the atmosphere.

Cautiously she peered around the tree. A hand's width from her nose, leaves and dirt exploded almost simultaneously with the echoing crack of a third shot. Stupid, careless hunter, she thought, a lump forming in her throat. If Adrian were here…

Impatient with herself, Neala smacked a fist against her palm. Right now she needed to extricate herself from a potentially dangerous situation, not wallow in maudlin longings. And if she didn't put in an appearance within two minutes of the coach's return, someone—probably an irate Liam—would set out to search for her. If the hunter were still in the vicinity, he might accidentally shoot Liam as well. What a wretched dilemma!

"Did you hear me?" she yelled again.

There was no response. For several vexing moments Neala sat, her mind searching furiously for a solution. Only when she crossed her arms did she remember the whistle dangling around her neck. All students, regardless of the length of time, were required to carry a whistle with them if they were out of sight of the main house. *Neala Shaw, you have nothing but a mess of day-old oatmeal for brains.*

Shaking her head, she lifted the whistle to her lips and blew.

Gray lay sprawled under one of the trees planted years earlier by new students, a charming if somewhat mawkish custom, to his way of thinking. Hands folded to pillow his head, eyes half-closed, he could almost hear Aunt Bella's crisp denouncement of such cynicism. From her perspective the trees were planted so newly orphaned students would have something to nurture, something they could claim, at a place she wanted them to regard as home.

Home.

Gray rolled and sat up, fighting the ever-present discontent with his life. Nothing assuaged the malaise, not women nor drink nor even a couple of shooting competitions where he'd reaped adulation and medals for pretending every shot he fired was aimed at Kevin Hackbone's heart. Sumner—no, it was not Sumner anymore. Now his only refuge from a stifling lifestyle was a school for females. Life was full of bitter irony.

Gray shuddered.

Why did Aunt Bella have to pick this particular day to hare off to Berryville?

He'd arrived an hour earlier, eager for a much-needed visit with the only female left on earth whose presence he could tolerate longer than twenty-four hours. Growing up, Gray spent miserable hours wishing Isabella was his mother, instead of the sweet but overprotective woman who refused to let Gray become a man. Even now, on his visits home, she treated him as though he were a perpetual three-year-old toddler. At fifteen, he finally rebelled and ran. Aunt Bella was the only family member with whom he'd stayed in touch. Understanding soul that she was, she'd waited out a year; when he turned sixteen she calmly told him to take his sorry carcass back home and mend fences, or she'd write his mother herself. And send Gray's two older brothers to fetch him.

A smile tweaked the corner of his mouth, remembering that first reunion. Aunt Bella had been spot on, of course.

He flicked open his watch, to discover only seven minutes had passed since he checked the time. Swearing beneath his breath, Gray stood up, scanned the winding drive again. It was going on five, dusk not far away. Why weren't they back home? He needed to talk, needed to hear her advice, soak up the love offered without chains.

When he heard the faint but piercing sound of a whistle, he whipped around, hand automatically going to the butt of his gun. Across the lawn, Mr. Pepperell had also straightened. He dropped his tools, his head swiveling back and forth as he, too, scanned the estate's southern woods. Gray loped over.

"What is it? Who's ruining the peace and quiet by blowing a blasted whistle?"

"I—oh, my, it most likely is Miss Shaw. She told me she was going for a walk." He paused to wipe a shaking hand across his brow. "I don't know precisely what—that is to say, I hadn't expected…"

"Why is she blowing a whistle?"

The gardener swallowed several times, his Adam's apple bobbing. Instead of a dapper gentleman politely sharing botanical tidbits, now he resembled an old man on the verge of collapse. "Distress." He peered dazedly up at Gray. "It's to be used only as a call for help. A—a safety measure, if you will. All students wear one when out of sight of the main house. They're most of them young women from towns and farms, not used to the country."

Clumsily he began untying his gardener's apron. "I must go. I'm the only one—"

"No, you're not," Gray interrupted. "I'll go see what the problem is. You stay here, alert the household to be prepared with bandages or whatever might be required."

Ignoring the gardener's halfhearted protests, he took off at a run in the general location of the last whistle call. When he reached the woods he paused, rapidly searched and discovered a path of sorts. Good. Jaw set, Gray plunged into the shadowed forest.

Chapter Three

Within two minutes, Gray was forced to slow his pace. Wet shrubs newly leafed slapped his sides; low-hanging branches tried to gouge his face, and he slipped twice on the narrow path that seemed to delight in its number of twists and turns.

After ten minutes he stopped completely. He swiped at his face, then tugged off his jacket and hung it on a dead branch. Irritation boiled through him. This whole day had been nothing but one infernal nuisance after another. And some timid female who couldn't find her way out of a potato sack… Well, this was just what he needed, tearing through unfamiliar woods like some stupid Galahad, only to wind up more lost than the equally stupid female. And she wasn't helping much at all.

"Where are you?" he roared. "Blow the whistle again!"

He waited, yelled again. Nothing. Very well. *Stay lost, then.* A chilly night in dark woods would teach a valuable lesson.

The whistle blew.

Gray ignored the quick tug of relief, turned on his heel, plunged off the narrow path and fought his way through yet another thicket of wet leafy shrubs, only marginally pacified when the whistle continued to blow at regular intervals. The young miss deserved a blistering lecture for getting herself lost—and he deserved to deliver it.

Of course, a remote possibility existed that she actually had hurt herself, along with getting lost. Aunt Bella needed to apply a firmer hand with her students, since these woods doubtless were home to bears, maybe even a wildcat or two. Trespassing hunters…

The skin at the back of his neck tightened. No matter how helpless or irrational a woman behaved, she never deserved to be mistreated. If this one had been harmed in any manner, or even frightened by some wandering weasel, Gray would track the vermin down and teach him a few manners.

He burst into a small clearing, and a feminine voice called loudly, "Halt this instance! You've been shooting at me, not a deer or a…bear!"

What—? Gray swiveled toward the voice, which emanated from behind a large two-trunk oak. "Shooting at you?" he shouted back, marching across the glade. "Stop spouting nonsense and show yourself." With an effort he moderated his tone. "You're safe now. I'm here to guide you back. You've nothing to fear."

He reached the tree, peered around, and barely avoided getting brained with a dead tree limb.

"I don't need a guide. And I don't believe you." A bedraggled moppet with curly brown hair and snapping brown eyes brandished the limb in his face. "Who are you? You're trespassing, and furthermore hunting is forbidden on this land." Her irate gaze fastened on Gray's revolver. The flushed cheeks paled.

Gray propped his shoulder against the tree trunk and crossed his arms over his chest. Her head scarcely reached his chin; she'd gotten herself lost, and she was alone in the middle of the woods with a man she'd never met. Yet she stood there, taking him to task without a shred of awareness of her helplessness. "Your stick wouldn't deter a tabby cat, much less a man with a gun. Even a man without one," he drawled, palm itching to slip the weapon from its holster to scare a modicum of common sense into her.

For a second the girl stared at him wide-eyed. Then she popped the whistle back in her mouth and blew. The sound at close range shrilled into Gray's unprotected ears, and he covered them in a reflexive action worthy of the greenest tenderfoot.

"Mr. Pepperell will be here any moment," she confidently stated after trying to deafen him. "Also a very husky Irishman. They won't take kindly to a trespassing hunter. You could have killed someone through your carelessness."

Disbelieving, for the first time Gray studied the woman objectively, without the haze of resentment fogging his mind. At first he'd pegged her for one of Isabella's youngest students, too naive to grasp her circumstances. Upon closer examination he realized she had to be in her early twenties, possibly a few years older. The wild tangle of curls and guileless eyes were nothing but a smoke screen.

She might be orphaned now, but he'd wager she'd had siblings at one time, all of them younger, poor saps she ordered about with the same officious superiority his sisters had inflicted upon his own miserable childhood.

"For your information," he finally said, mildly enough considering his mood, "I happen to know that your husky Irishman is only an inch taller than you, say, five feet six inches? And he's about as husky as a plucked rooster. As for Mr. Pepperell, he's nearing seventy. Had he come hunting you down, by now he would have expired from heart palpitations."

He lowered his head until their faces were mere inches apart. "Did you bother to consider the shock to his heart, the risk he'd face trying to race over a mile of rough terrain, to rescue you? I volunteered instead." He paused. "But turns out you're not lost. Or hurt. You're only supposed to blow that whistle if you're in danger, or dire straits. Ever read the fable about the boy who cried wolf?"

The chit searched his face with nothing but relief showing on hers. "If you know Liam and Mr. Pepperell, you couldn't be the irresponsible hunter, even though you are wearing a gun." She heaved a long, unladylike breath. "Are you one of the sheriff's new deputies?" With a quick flick of her wrist, she tossed aside the stick, then absently tucked wayward curls behind her ears. Her expression remained as bright and friendly as a puppy's.

"No!" Gray ground out, his back teeth snapping together in an effort to keep his temper from exploding full force. "I happen to be Isabella Chilton's nephew. I just arrived for a visit—a much-needed, *peaceful* visit. But my aunt wasn't there. So I didn't have anything better to do than chase through the woods to rescue an idiot girl who doesn't have enough sense to steer clear of an angry male."

"Well, what on earth are *you* angry for? You're not the one who could have been killed by a trigger-happy hunter."

A late-afternoon breeze dislodged more of her hair. Sighing again, she plucked out some hairpins and haphazardly stuffed the loose curls back into a slipping topknot. Despite his extensive travels, Gray had never encountered a woman so indifferent to her appearance. "Since you're not the hunter," she finished, "would you mind scouting the area before we leave? I doubt he's around, since I finally remembered to blow the whistle, but it wouldn't hurt to check."

"Are you seriously suggesting that someone was, ah, shooting at you?" He swept her disheveled form with another raking glance while the memory of Mr. Pepperell's worried eyes and trembling fingers filled his mind. "How about telling me what you're really up to, and save us both from a scene I'll probably regret. I despise liars, especially female ones who never consider the consequences to anyone but themselves."

She blinked, the self-assurance squaring her shoulders and tilting her chin fading. As rapidly as the sun disappeared behind the mountains, she transformed into an uncertain young girl whose aura of wounded dignity pricked Gray's conscience. "It's probably safe enough now," she murmured. "I'm going back this way." She gestured with her hand. "It's longer, but less strenuous." Without another word she headed off, her every step away from Gray a silent reproach.

He fought a losing battle with the nettles pricking his conscience. "Wait," he called, reaching her in half a dozen strides. It was a half-dozen more before he gathered the courage to speak again. "Listen. I apologize. I had no right to speak to you the way I did."

He yanked at his shirt collar, feeling stupid, petty—and a complete churl. Impossible to explain how her innocent query about his being a sheriff's deputy had ripped wide open a wound so painful to his soul he wasn't sure he'd ever heal. But he owed her something. "Will you stop a second, so I can at least offer a proper apology?" he growled.

She hesitated, then glanced up, her expression solemn. "All right."

"I'm sorry." He bit the inside of his cheek, then shrugged. "It's been a long day. I lost my temper. I'm usually not this boorish."

A shy smile flirted at the corner of her mouth. "It's all right. I shouldn't have accused you of being a careless hunter."

Gray still didn't believe her story, but finally had enough presence of mind to keep the thought to himself. "Well, we'd best make haste. By the time we return, Aunt Bella should be back."

"With my 'husky Irishman' driving the coach," the young

woman added dryly. "Not to mention all the others, who aren't going to be happy at all with my latest snarlie."

Latest…*snarlie?* Where had Aunt Bella unearthed this creature?

"Well, it's over now," Gray said, and managed what he hoped was a comforting smile. "All is well, hmm?" Ha. His need for peace was unlikely to be satisfied now, and the talk he'd yearned to enjoy with his aunt unfortunately would revolve around someone other than himself.

He started down the path, but the woman didn't budge. "What is it?" Regrettably, he was unable to erase the edge in the words.

For a few seconds more she stood there, her bottom lip caught between her teeth. Then she shrugged. "Yes. You're right. All is well. Thank you for…coming to rescue me." There was a pause, then she added in a wistful tone, "You're nothing at all like your aunt, are you?"

They didn't speak again. Thirty long minutes later, grateful for the excuse, Gray left her at the edge of the woods to return and fetch his jacket. Slanting sunbeams poured across the lawn, bathing Miss Shaw with a golden aura that contrarily enhanced her aloneness. Gray stomped back into the woods, and considered seriously the temptation to find a very large oak tree so he could bang his head against its trunk.

Chapter Four

Rutter, Virginia

Shoulders slumped, Will Crocker trudged down the dirt lane that led to his home. It was dusk, when light and shadow blurred surroundings into indefinable shapes. A man could be invisible at dusk, if he were careful. Will shrugged, vaguely uncomfortable with the thought, and hurried toward the four-room unpainted frame house where he and his mother had lived for the last fifteen years.

The hardscrabble community of Rutter, population 973, boasted few amenities, though one or two families made persistent efforts to achieve a level of civilized comfort—whitewashing the clapboard, planting a flower garden; one family had ordered an entire parlor set of golden oak out of the Sears catalog.

Momma always had a good word to say about their neighbors; she tried as much as she could to thank Will for his efforts to improve their own home, despite the disconsolation that plagued most of her waking moments. Life's unfairness had crushed her spirit; by the time Will reached his twelfth year her hair was completely gray, her eyes sunken in the once pretty face.

When Grandmother died, they had lost everything. Many a night when Will came home, the sound of his mother's bitter weeping seeped like cold fog through the thin bedroom wall. She seldom wept in front of him, and he allowed her to cling to the illusion that he didn't know how often she cried herself to sleep.

Mood bleak, he drew aimless patterns in the dirt with the toe of his shoe. No matter how bitter he might feel during these isolated moments, his mother loved him as much as she was able. Will was her only remaining relative. If he abandoned her, he knew she would die. Twice, in his late twenties, he'd gone so far as to move out. The first time his mother quit eating and almost starved herself to death; the second time she'd almost burned the house down. Will never tried living on his own again.

A vague shiver danced along his spine, one of fear and the longing he never quite knew what to do with because he couldn't remember a time when both emotions hadn't been part of his life, all forty-one years of it. When the Zuckermans' snug little house appeared at the bend in the lane, light glowing through the windows, he gave in to the longing instead of the fear. Silently, imagining himself invisible as a gray field mouse, he slipped up to a side window and peeked through the narrow gap in the curtains. Mrs. Zuckerman had died the previous year, but their oldest daughter, a horse-faced but congenial spinster everyone called Miss Leila, moved in to take care of her father. At the moment they were sitting at a small table, playing some kind of board game. A fire danced merrily in the parlor stove. Pretty crocheted doilies were scattered about on tables and the backs of chairs. Their old hound dog slept beneath the table, and as Will watched, Mr. Zuckerman reached down to give the fellow an absentminded scratch behind his ears.

The ache in his belly grew and spread. As silently as he'd slipped up to the window, Will backed away, then turned a resolute face toward his own home. Whatever he found when he stepped over the threshold, he would deal with it. He was no longer the mewling whelp of a boy prone to nightmares, or the scarecrow young man forced to work repugnant jobs for degrading wages so they wouldn't be thrown out into the streets.

Yet he could still feel the darkness inside, spreading like spilled ink. One day it would blacken him entirely, and he would disappear.

When he reached the door to their house, he paused, flexing his hands in a relaxing motion. Then he gave two brisk knocks and turned the rusting knob.

"Momma? I'm back!" Carefully he hung his bowler hat on the hall tree.

"William!" She rushed from her bedroom, her arms outflung. "Is it finished, then? Were you successful this time? Do you have it at last?"

He hugged her, savoring the welcome, the warmth that could transform so quickly into anguish…or anger. When he felt her stiffen, he released her instantly. "It's good to be home, Momma. But I'm very tired. Spent the last two days traveling, you know." He tried a laugh. "Had to walk the last fifteen miles."

She drew back, crossing long skeletal arms over her flat chest while her gaze seemed to devour him. "William? You look so tired, baby. And I don't see any excitement on your face." Vague fear swam into the pale brown eyes so like his own. "Something happened, didn't it? Something bad." Two bright red spots appeared on her cheeks. "William, please don't tell me you failed. Not again. No, not again. I've been hoping—praying for you. We're so close…"

Carefully Will gripped her shoulders, sat her down in her rickety old rocking chair he'd salvaged from the dump on the edge of town. "I promised to take care of us, and I will. Some things take a long time, remember? Listen, why don't we eat, and I'll tell you about the trip," he finished, hoping to divert her. "Let me hang up my coat, and—"

"Don't turn your back to me!" Her hand closed over his forearm, her fingers digging in. "You're lying…" She slapped him hard, right across his mouth.

As abruptly as the rage boiled up, it disappeared. Tears swam into her glittering eyes. "Oh. Oh, William, baby, I'm sorry. So sorry. I can't bear it." She choked on a sob that brought moisture to Will's eyes. "I didn't mean it, you know I didn't mean it. William, forgive me. Please."

With a final anguished, tear-drenched look at Will, she fled to her room and slammed the door. A broken stream of sobs and wails about how horrible a mother she was, about the unfairness of life echoed from the room, washing over Will in a seething flood.

His jaw throbbed from her blow, and he slowly lifted a hand to wipe away the trickle of blood from the corner of his mouth.

The unnerving attacks were becoming more frequent. Yet he didn't blame her. He couldn't. She was his mother. He owed her his life, and to a great extent, his future. But this last attack… He released a long, tired breath. Footsteps heavy, he headed for the stove. The squalor of unwashed dishes and unemptied slops pail, the odor of rotting food and musty ashes revolted his senses.

But on the grease-laden warming plate rested a dish. A neatly folded piece of cloth covered his dinner.

With stoic resignation, Will sat down to eat before he set about cleaning the kitchen.

Chapter Five

The cuckoo clock Mr. Chilton had bought her over forty years earlier on their wedding trip to Europe finished declaring the nine-o'clock hour. Isabella gratefully settled into the cushions of her favorite settee, and allowed a wisp of sweetly painful nostalgia to drift through her mind. *Everett, that clock always did make you smile….*

Unlike his previous visits, this evening Grayson ignored the clock's charming antics of woodcutter and wife chopping while the cuckoo warbled. Instead, as restless as one of the school toms on the prowl, he wandered about her private parlor, his hands idly drifting over the collection of objects given to Isabella by her students. His expression remained aloof, almost grim. She waited without comment for him to speak, though as always the growing hardness that surrounded him like a suit of medieval armor saddened her.

He swiveled suddenly, dropping back onto the game board one of the chess pieces he'd been fiddling with. "Aunt Bella,

I need to talk with you about—" A muscle twitched in his jaw; he lifted a hand to tug his earlobe, an endearing boyhood habit he'd never outgrown.

Calmly Isabella laid the piecework in her lap. "Talk to me about what? Perhaps your recent adventures over these past few months? Those, ah, shooting exhibitions? Don't scowl, dear. You had to know your mother would write to me when she read about you in the weeklies. Your father was kind enough to include several of the articles, one with a rather…interesting…photograph of you."

Grayson emitted an ungentlemanly snort. "Ah, yes. The photograph. The one where I was straddled with a foot on the back of two horses while I shot a bull's-eye at the target? Caused the gents to swear and the ladies to swoon. Doubtless Mother's was the only swoon not feigned." His laugh was short and bitter. "When I stopped by home for an overdue visit my 'reckless behavior that shamed the family name' provided fodder for three evening meals."

"I'm sorry your visit home was another difficult one."

He merely shrugged again, and looked away. "Never mind. It's not important."

"Come along, now." Isabella leaned forward. "Talk to me, my dear, about whatever you need to. But since it's after nine, doubtless there'll be a knock or two on the door soon." She paused, then finished matter-of-factly. "Ofttimes in the evenings, after chores, a student comes to me with her burdens, needing to share, or just needing a chat."

"There. That's what I want to talk about with you, Aunt." Her nephew casually scooped up the glass paperweight from the piecrust table and turned it round while he talked, his words increasing in volume along with velocity. "You run a school for orphaned women. But that doesn't mean you're their mother. No matter how many years they live here, they're not family. In truth you know little about them. Yet you take on all the responsibility for their misfortunes, not to mention their futures—and your own."

"My future, and that of my students, rests where it always has. In God's hands."

Isabella was not surprised when Grayson merely arched a brow, looking more cynical than ever. "The truth of what I'm saying doesn't change, especially after today's incident in the woods, with Miss Shaw."

Ah. Here then was the real purpose for this circuitous conversation.

"Now, really, Grayson. Someone shot at her. I think her reaction proved to be remarkably levelheaded."

"Ha! You wouldn't say that if you'd been there." He paused. "What do you really know about her background, Aunt Bella? I don't think you have ever fully appreciated the risk, inviting strange young women without any family connections into your life. I know Uncle Everett's family pretty much washed their hands of you after he died, and you turned Sumner into this school. But I don't think Uncle Ev—"

"Without the Academy's existence, I would have no home at all, Grayson. Not here, at any rate." Not for the world would she admit that his words jabbed, deep inside. "Tell me, are you more concerned about the fact that Sumner is no longer the beautiful Chilton family estate, or are your objections primarily all the 'strange young women,' Neala Shaw in particular?"

"Aunt Bella…" A band of red spread across his deeply tanned cheeks, but his expression revealed little. Somewhere over the years the boy had learned to screen his feelings from even his favorite aunt. "I'm not quite that much of a heartless cad. I'm sorry for her orphaned status—I know life is difficult, especially for…for women like Miss Shaw—but my first

concern is you. For your safety and well-being, especially
when you insist on maintaining such a small household staff.
What if I hadn't been here this afternoon? Your gardener would
have expired from the exertion had he been forced to traipse
through the woods, after an irresponsible woman old enough
to know better than get herself lost, then spin wild tales."

"Neala is neither irresponsible nor given to melodrama.
Really, Grayson. Last fall, for example, when she'd been here less
than a month, she saved the stables from burning down. She
almost died herself because she refused to run away. If you knew
her—"

"The point is that you don't *really* know her any better than
I do. She could have set that fire herself, Aunt Bella."

"Grayson! What a scandalous observation."

Her nephew shrugged. "Just staying objective. You seem to
think letters of introduction from solid citizens, detailed applications, and one personal interview are sufficient to protect
you. But I've seen—"

"As they have been," Isabella interrupted. She tapped her foot
several times, then forced it to stillness. "I've been operating this
school for almost twenty years, my boy. I can count on one hand
the students who had to be dismissed for lack of good character."

"All it takes is one," Grayson muttered darkly. "Women
have never been the 'weaker' of the species, regardless of how
you view them." For a nightmarish second an expression on
his face turned him into someone Isabella didn't know at all.
"Contrary to your quaint notions about creating godly wives
and 'Able Stewards of Society'—isn't that one of your
slogans?—a lot of females these days prefer to dump their
husbands completely, or marry a lonely old man in hopes he'll
die soon after the vows. They'd rather help rob a bank than
work in one. Sweet young things with innocent-looking eyes
can be ruthless, far more devious than most garden-variety

male criminals. Women kill, Aunt Bella. And smile at you while they carry out the deed."

Oh, my dear, my dear. He was still suffering, deeply. "You are referring to your friend's tragic death last fall, I presume."

Grayson had been in a very bad state, Isabella knew. He had written her a brief note explaining about the death of his childhood friend, asked if he could come for a visit—then spent the next months making a spectacle of himself with that dreadful pistol of his. Until the telegram two days earlier letting her know of his pending arrival, Isabella had not heard from him at all since the note.

"'Tragic death.'" He slammed the paperweight down hard enough to scratch the table and send several other knickknacks skittering toward its scalloped edge. "What an insipid description of the deranged woman who plunged a butcher knife in the back of an unarmed man. The partner I was supposed to be protecting. The friend I'd known for most of my life." His eyes glistened as he stared through Isabella, seeing frightful images she could scarcely imagine before he covered his face with his hand.

A knock sounded on the door. "Miss Isabella?" The door opened a fraction. "Can I talk with you for a little while? It's about this afternoon— Oh!"

Neala Shaw froze in the portal, her eyes flooding with dismay, guilt—and a smattering of outrage. "Mr. Faulkner. I didn't know you'd be in here."

Though her aching knees protested, Isabella managed to rise without betraying the effort it required. "Do come in, my dear. As it happens, my nephew would like to talk about this afternoon, as well."

"Yes. Do join us, Miss Shaw," Grayson echoed so mockingly Isabella almost swatted his arm. The mask was firmly in place again, all emotion smothered beneath the cynicism.

Small wonder that Neala walked across the room with the

aura of a condemned convict headed for the gallows. Isabella
started to speak, then caught herself as she watched the pair
of them size each other up as though they were the only two
people in the room. Hmm. She silently thanked the Lord for
His nudge, and waited for an appropriate moment to leave.

"Mr. Faulkner, since you're here, I suppose I should apologize for hitting you with a stick."

"Miss Shaw, no apology is needed, since in point of fact,
you missed."

"Yes, I did." Two bright spots of color turned her pale complexion the color of broiled salmon. "But it wasn't for lack of
trying. Perhaps I should extend an apology anyway, since in
God's eyes the intent of the heart, as much as the action, de-
termines one's guilt."

"Spare me your self-righteous homilies. I need them even
less than your contrived excuses." He stalked across to stand
in front of her, hands fisted at his hips. "My aunt, and Mr.
Pepperell—now, they're the ones who deserve your apology.
They're the ones who would have worried themselves into
early graves if I hadn't been here."

"Your aunt knows I would never—" Neala broke off, then
whirled around to Isabella. "Miss Isabella…are you all right? I
thought you looked…fatigued, at supper, but I thought it was
from the trip to Berryville. I didn't know, I mean I didn't
realize…and I haven't seen Mr. Pepperell since lunch. Is he—is
he—"

"Calm yourself, Neala." Isabella slid Grayson a reproving
stare as she laid a hand on the girl's rigid shoulder. "Mr. Pepperell and I are both right as rain. You've done nothing wrong,
and certainly nothing to cause me worry. Concern, perhaps,
because you still tend to assume more responsibility than is
appropriate. How fitting, isn't it, that my nephew seems to
share that very same trait?"

Grayson made a derisive sound, which Isabella ignored. Keeping her lips pressed together to keep a smile at bay, she squeezed Neala's shoulder a final time, then started for the door. "I'm sure the two of you can talk about me much more freely in my absence, so I'll go take care of a matter and return shortly."

"Aunt Bella..."

"Miss Isabella..."

"I trust both of you to remember what they say about the spoken word? Once allowed to escape, it cannot be recalled."

She closed the door behind her, and let out a soft chuckle. *Well, Lord, You wanted me out of the room. I leave them in Your far more capable hands.*

Gray stared at the closed door in consternation. His aunt had left him alone in the room with Neala Shaw. He didn't know which would provide more relief: tossing the conniving little baggage out the window, or exiting that way himself.

Neala cleared her throat. "Obviously she expects us to come to some sort of accord." Her fingers fluttered at her waist before she twined them together. "Mr. Faulkner, it would help tremendously if you believed me, about someone shooting at me, I mean."

"Why should I, Miss Shaw?"

"Because I'm not a liar!"

"Well, now how would I be knowing that, me darlin'?" he retorted in a perfect mimicry of the Academy's Irish stableman. Her obvious frustration pleased Gray more than was polite, but for some reason he couldn't seem to quit needling her. He folded his arms, rocking a little on his feet while he watched a barrelful of expressions race across her face. "This is only the second time we've met, after all. Why, for all I know your hunter might be lying in wait in my bedroom."

"Well, if he was, at least he'd be close enough to do the job! Oh!" The brown eyes rounded in dismay as her palm flew to belatedly cover her mouth. "I can't believe I said that! I can't believe… I don't know what came over me. I don't talk like that, I don't even *think* like that."

Abruptly she turned her back to him.

Deprived of the entertainment of watching her face, Gray's attention zeroed in on a long strand of curling hair that had escaped the pins to dangle down the back of her neck. She'd managed to stuff the rest of the mass into a twist of some sort; he thought it made her look dowdy, incredibly old-fashioned. Yet his fingers itched to twine that strand around his hand. He wanted to know if her hair felt as soft as it looked, if the curls were as untamable as the fire sparking in her eyes a moment ago.

And he hated the longing almost as much as he hated himself.

"Apparently you've not heard about my reputation," he observed coolly. "Even if you send a man with a gun after me, Miss Shaw, I'm not the one who'll end up in a pine box." When she turned back around, something in the dark brown eyes goaded him to add, "Well? Why don't you go ahead and say what you're thinking—that your headmistress's nephew is a dangerous fellow, and today he tried to shoot you out in the woods?"

She blinked, and the expression disappeared. "Mr. Faulkner," she began, then hesitated. Just as Gray opened his mouth to deliver another jab, she drew herself up and leveled a look upon him worthy of Aunt Bella. "Mr. Faulkner, do you enjoy intimidating people and insulting women innocent of any wrongdoing, or do you merely possess a misogynistic streak?"

"I only enjoy intimidating devious women," he whipped back without missing a beat. "Insults I save for conniving liars. As for an innocent woman, I can't remember the last time I encountered one, age notwithstanding. So you might say my…ah…misogynistic streak developed over years of exposure to various members of your misnamed 'gentler' sex."

This time she stepped back as though he'd just sprayed her with venom, but at least she didn't turn her back on him. "There's no use trying to talk with you, is there?" she whispered, half to herself. "You're just like Adrian…"

Adrian? "Who's Adri—"

"Tell your aunt I wished her a good night," Miss Shaw chirped in a voice women used with toddlers and small children. Without meeting his eyes she scuttled across the room to the door, where she delivered her parting shot. "I'd wish you the same, except I think you've forgotten how to have a good anything, which I find terribly sad."

The door opened and closed with a firm click. Gray stood, her words ringing in his ears. The desolation he'd been fighting for months pressed back around him, squeezing all the air out of his lungs.

Neala Shaw…

He closed his eyes, half lifted his hand as though reaching out for that dangling strand of hair. Eventually, moving as if he were fighting his way through thorns, he returned to the fireplace and sat down in the chair where Aunt Bella had been sitting. The faint scent of his aunt's toilet water wafted through his nostrils.

With a shuddering sigh Gray leaned his head back and tried not to think of anything at all.

Chapter Six

After completing morning chores, Neala grabbed her old corduroy jacket, a small writing tablet and a freshly sharpened pencil. As an afterthought, on the way out she retrieved a small magnifying glass from her desk. It was Saturday, and a brisk southwest wind carried the scent of rain and lilac through the windows. On her way downstairs, she debated whether or not to fetch an umbrella, decided the contraption would only be in the way and darted toward the back entrance off the kitchen, hoping nobody would stop her for a chat.

Grayson Faulkner's scowling image intruded into her mind as she scurried past the entrance to one of the school's informal parlors. What an infuriating man! Rude, unpleasant—a bully, he was. And he had hurt her feelings, which infuriated her even more. How could a saintly soul like Miss Isabella be kin to Mr. Faulkner?

Well, by the end of the day the rude bully of a man would be the recipient of a much-needed lesson. When Neala returned from her outing, she planned to be armed with enough proof of the hunter's presence in the woods yester-day to satisfy an entire room of Pinkerton detectives, much less Miss Isabella's nephew, who thought entirely too much of himself.

A small voice tweaked her conscience. All right, Neala conceded the point. Grayson Faulkner might be rude, unpleasant and arrogant, but last night, in the parlor, she'd sensed an undercurrent of emotion that, for the flicker of an eyelash, had almost prompted her to…feel sorry for him?

"Neala!" Judith Smithfield, her arms full of quilt scraps, interrupted the discomforting revelation. "We're quilting in an hour. Join us this time?"

"Not today, Judith." She waved an arm and grinned. "I'm off on a mission. I'll try to join the fun next Saturday." She ducked into the kitchen, almost tripping over a half-full pail of sudsy water.

"Oops, sorry, Neala!" Deborah McGarey sang out from beneath the huge island in the center of the kitchen. "I'm making pound cakes, but decided to break the eggs on the floor instead of the bowl."

Both of them laughed as Neala carried the pail closer. "Need help?" she asked reluctantly, relieved and guilty when Deborah shooed her on with a wry remark that only the guilty party should clean up smashed eggs.

Now *there* was the manner in which congenial people engaged in conversation, Neala thought, tossing her head. Stride determined, she crossed the grounds toward the forest. Civil people did not assume the worst about perfect strangers. Civil people did not act as though you had just perpetrated a crime of Machiavellian proportions, or accuse you of lying. And certainly a man who rushed to the rescue of a damsel in distress did *not* react like a churl.

The damp breeze swooped down, tugging several pins from Neala's hastily bundled hair. When a handful of curls blew over her eyes, she glared upward, then stopped long enough to untie a large kerchief from around her neck. In a few ruthless movements she covered her hair and retied the ends beneath her chin. She looked like a gypsy washerwoman—but since there was nobody to see her but birds and other woodland critters, what did it matter how she looked?

What mattered was unearthing evidence of the wayward hunter.

Over an hour later, Neala was ready to concede that the general populace afforded scant appreciation to detectives and officers of the law. Not only could she not find the exact spot where she'd been when the first shot rang out, she could not find the tree she'd ducked behind, from which she'd hoped to extract a bullet, or at least mark as evidence of being struck by a bullet. Thoroughly out of sorts, she finally collapsed beneath a stumpy pine tree, yanked off the kerchief, and rubbed her face with it. The wind had blown the clouds away, leaving behind sunshine and a watery, pale blue sky. Much preferable to a rainstorm when one was playing detective.

And playing detective was all she had accomplished, besides collecting dirt in her shoes and the remains of a spiderweb in her hair. On the other hand, the day had turned pleasantly warm, she was alone in one of God's forest cathedrals, and nobody was clamoring for her attention. All in all, perhaps 'twas best to send both hunter and Mr. Grayson Faulkner the way of the clouds. Neala lifted her sturdy nickel brooch-style watch to check the time, made sure the whistle around her neck was still within instant reach, then with a contented sigh opened her notebook and began to write.

Some time later, a flying pinecone landed smack on top of the notebook in her lap. Neala yelped in surprise and dropped her pencil. The pinecone scattered detritus along with her concentration as it rolled to a stop in the crease of her notebook. Neala gawked at the missile for a bemused moment, then leaned forward to retrieve her pencil. When she straightened, her eyes almost popped out of her head. Mr. Faulkner had materialized between the trees some twenty paces away. He strolled toward her, grinning like a mischievous boy while he tossed a second pinecone in his hand.

"You were so lost in your girlish scribblings I probably could have jumped from behind the tree instead of lobbing a missile before you noticed."

Neala ignored the crack about girlish scribblings. Based on her scant acquaintance with the man, it was not an unexpected remark. "You're fortunate I didn't scream louder than this whistle—" she glanced at his holstered gun "—which I might have if you'd decided to gain my attention by firing a bullet over my head."

The smug look on his face deepened. "But you're already accustomed to dodging bullets, aren't you?" He extended a hand.

Neala allowed him to help her up, but stepped back the instant she gained her feet. She ignored the strange squiggle that shivered through her from the firm warmth of his bare palm, focusing instead on irritation. "Mr. Faulkner, did you follow me just to bait me like you did yesterday?"

The smugness on his face darkened to disapproval. "Absolutely. And for the last ninety-six minutes I followed, you never so much as glanced behind you." One eyebrow lifted in a sardonic arch. "Too busy trying to scout out a likely spot to plant some evidence, I daresay." The forest stilled—no rustling leaves or twittering birds or even a stray breeze, as though nature held its collective breath while Mr. Faulkner scratched his chin and contemplated Neala. "If I wanted to shoot you dead, you'd be stretched out on the ground, with nobody the wiser. Tell me, Miss Shaw, do you enjoy tempting fate, or do you merely have a wish to expire in the woods, like some fairy-tale maiden?"

His phrasing replicated her accusation of the previous day, and the gleam in his eye told her he'd done so deliberately. All right, enough was enough. Neala returned his bold appraisal, though the weapon strapped to his side intimidated by its sheer presence. On the other hand, the bizarre prescience she'd experienced in Miss Isabella's parlor returned in greater force, the one where Mr. Faulkner very much reminded her of Adrian. Her brother also used to cover his unhappy restlessness with hurtful words and a facade of hatefulness. "Mr. Faulkner, it's plain that for some reason you don't like me very much. It's not necessary for me to understand why, but I'd like to. Miss Isabella's fond of saying that a few bruises on an apple don't mean the entire fruit's gone completely bad. It just means that—"

"I'm well acquainted with the concept, and its application." He ran a hand through his hair, took a long breath. A faint glimmer of humor washed through his eyes. "Miss Shaw, you look like a squirrel's nest."

Neala self-consciously lifted a hand to the unruly locks of hair dangling around her face and neck. "My hair has a mind of its own, especially when the humidity is high. But it's rude of you to remark on it, Mr. Faulkner. Didn't your mother teach you better manners?"

"My mother taught me many things, including manners. I've spent the past fifteen years trying to forget every one of her…lessons."

The rancor in his voice sent a chill along Neala's spine. "I better return to the school," she began with forced cheeriness. "Three hours is the limit for Saturday free time on your own, unless you're on the school grounds within sight of the house." She lifted her hand to cup the whistle and took a steadying breath. "I have no idea why you've chosen to think the worst about me, nor do I particularly care to defend myself against someone whose mind is closed to reasoning. But for your information, Mr. Faulkner, I came out here in order to find evidence of that hunter—not to 'plant' it, as you accused me of."

"Didn't find any, did you? I wondered how long you planned to wander around."

"In a war, spying is a hanging offense."

"Then it's a good thing we're not at war, Miss Shaw."

"Aren't we?" Neala retorted quietly. She turned her back and retrieved her notebook and pencil. "I'm going now, Mr. Faulkner. You can either follow along or choose your own path. Either way, you've made your feelings toward me obvious. I'd appreciate it if you'd ignore me in the same manner I plan to ignore you."

He frowned, then abruptly swiveled on his heel and hurled the second pinecone into the trees. "You understand nothing about my feelings, Miss Shaw. Toward you or anything else. If I'm wrong about you, I apologize. If I'm not—" the pause was loaded with thinly veiled threat "—and you cause my aunt or her school any suffering at all, even a moment's concern, you'll not be able to run far enough or long enough. I'll find you, and you'll think my behavior today saintlike by comparison."

"I...see." Neala tapped her pencil against her lips in a vain attempt to hide the smile threatening to burst free. Oh, but the relief flooding her insides was a heady sensation, the urge to reassure Miss Isabella's thunderous nephew impossible to ignore. "Mr. Faulkner, I think you're a lion with the heart of a kitten. Bless you for trying to protect Miss Isabella and the Academy."

She lost the battle with her smile. "At least I finally understand the source of your anger, misguided though it was. After all, yesterday I did try to wallop you with a tree branch. I know you don't believe me, but someone really was shooting out here in the woods yesterday. And when the bullet hits the tree trunk inches from my nose, I have to conclude that—albeit by mistake—they were shooting at me. I'll let the matter drop, however, since it's obvious I've been unable to produce any tangible proof." She shrugged. "You've also helped me realize that my actions might cause Miss Isabella more concern—of course, you know she doesn't 'worry!' I... Well, I've grown very fond of your aunt. Ever since my parents' deaths, I suppose I've come to regard her as—"

She stopped, belatedly aware that the hue of Mr. Faulkner's tanned face had turned a deep shade of red, and a muscle twitched the corner of his mouth. *Ninny,* she scolded herself. Few men were comfortable with sentimentality. "I'll hush," she murmured, then impulsively reached across to lay her hand on his forearm. "Don't worry, Mr. Faulkner. I know God is watching over Miss Isabella every breath of every day."

Mr. Faulkner snarled an ill-tempered curse. Then, without another word, he turned his back and strode rapidly into the woods, disappearing within seconds beneath the trees.

Neala remained a few moments longer, watching until she realized she must look like a moon-eyed girl gazing after her sweetheart. *Rubbish,* she thought. Idiotic, as well, gazing after a man who had just blistered the air with invectives. By the time she found her path back to the school moments later, however, she was forced to admit that loneliness was even harder to bear, after meeting a man like Grayson Faulkner.

Chapter Seven

May, 1890

Two weeks later, after classes on a lazy Thursday afternoon, Neala and Abigail decided to spend their free Saturday hiking down to the Shenandoah River. A picnic on the riverbank would be their reward for the muscle-stretching trek down the steep cliff. To be sure, a well-marked path had been carved out by some Chilton ancestor over a century earlier; more recently Liam had hammered out handholds on some of the steeper sections. The hike posed little danger as long as the hikers exercised due diligence.

"We're all of us adult women," Miss Isabella lectured new students. "Therefore I 'restrict the restrictions' here at the Academy, because I expect each of you to exhibit common sense in all your choices. Since fresh air and healthy exercise offer an excellent venue with which to strengthen our individual godly temples, it is my hope that all of you feel free to explore the five hundred acres surrounding the Academy. Carefully. Good sense is a gift from our Lord. Expend it wisely, my dears, and try to limit your *non*sense to games of croquet, bad-minton and the like."

"I enjoy Miss Isabella's sense of humor," Abby said around a mouthful of oatmeal cookie. "Did you hear her earlier today, pleading with Mr. Pepperell to stop talking to the tomatoes because she's afraid we'll end up with such a bumper crop the house might slide off the cliff from the weight?"

Neala looked up from the list of supplies she was writing down in her tablet. "'Tis very wry, is it not?" she agreed. "I remember when I first arrived I never knew when she was serious, or merely teasing. Um…shall we take lemonade in our canteens, or sassafras tea?"

"Better stick with tea. I don't believe we have many lemons in the springhouse right now."

Neala dutifully added tea to their list, and they spent several congenial moments discussing other particulars. Then Abby took a deep breath and began fiddling with the eyelet edging of her shirtwaist. "Neala?" she asked, her voice softer. "Are you… I mean, do you still…" She grimaced, her gaze touching on Neala's, then shifting to some place that bespoke of a pain more vast than the universe. "I had another dream last night," she finished in a rush. "It wasn't a nightmare—I don't have those as much anymore. But I was with my family, and it was so real…" Her hand reached out blindly and Neala grabbed it, wrapping reassuring fingers around it. "I didn't want to wake up, Neala. I didn't want to wake up, because then I would have to accept all over again that they're gone, and I'm not. I'm still here, scarred and disfigured and…and alone. I mean, alone because I know I'll never marry."

"Oh, Abby…" Neala swallowed hard, her own throat tightening against tears. "I understand. Sometimes I still think I need to tell Grandfather, or Mum…" Her voice trailed away. "But I do understand, completely," she finished. "Your heart sort of jerks when all of a sudden you remember they're gone. And it hurts so bad it's hard to breathe."

"At least your brother is still alive, even if you never see him again. Oh—I'm sorry, Neala. I didn't mean that the way it sounded. Truly I didn't."

"I know." Neala squeezed her hand once more and released it. They both sat back in the grass and smiled at each other. "Sometimes I dream that Adrian returns to Charlottesville, buys back our home, then finds me…" She stopped with a deprecatory grimace.

"Perhaps someday he will."

"Not likely." Neala chewed her lip for a moment, then waved a dismissive hand. "I'll always love Adrian, but I know I need to stop weaving fanciful tales that will never happen. Miss Isabella reminds me at least twice a week that I need to learn to accept how people are, instead of trying to nicely bully them into what I think they ought to be. I know she's right, but it's difficult."

She lifted her face toward the sky, soaking up the sunshine. "God planted a yearning in me for everybody in the world to get along, I suppose. But I must have a really hard head underneath all these wretched curls, because I keep trying despite the futility of it. My brother used to get so annoyed with me…"

Abby reached across to tug one of the infernal curling strands that was forever escaping the pins. "I love your hair. I wish mine had all that bounce and shine."

"Well, I've always admired yours because it's straight."

"What about Jocelyn's? Have you ever seen such a beautiful shade of red? She's very private, have you noticed? Even when I compliment her hair, she just gives me this sad smile. I wish she'd share her story."

"I'm sure she will, one day. Perhaps she's been able to follow Miss Isabella's advice better than the rest of us. 'Talking about the past can't redo it. We waste the present, and bore the listener…'"

"'…Because we all have a different past, and must walk a different path to overcome it,'" Abby continued, quoting one of their headmistress's most oft-repeated homilies.

They both laughed. Miss Isabella had a quote for everything—and never hesitated to trot an appropriate one out for a listener.

Neala pulled an annoying curl away from her face and wound it around her finger. "Well, I'll probably never accept that my brother's dead, but I have accepted that he…that he abandoned me." There. She'd finally stated the words aloud. "That's why I was allowed to come here. Miss Isabella decided I was enough of an orphan." She shrugged. "In all but the strictest sense, I am. I've heard nothing from my brother in over a year now."

"We both should remember that all of us here are only orphaned in bloodlines," Abby reminded her gently. "We have a home now, remember. And sisters?"

With a determined wave of her hand, Neala banished the hovering wisps of grief. "Absolutely. And now that I've come to know him, I might claim Liam as an uncle despite him being an Irishman instead of a Scot." They laughed again, and scrambled to their feet. "Come on, let's go inspect the kitchen and make sure our choice of picnic supplies is available."

"Don't forget to post our names on the list so everyone knows where we are. We may never have found your hunter, but when Nan and Alice climbed down to the river last week, they happened onto a pair of day-trippers, and I heard yesterday that someone else spotted either a hiker or a hunter—or was it some kind of animal?—on the edge of the grounds."

They commenced strolling across the grass as they talked. "The view over the river, toward the mountains, is breathtaking. With the Colonial Highway just at the bottom of the hill, I can easily imagine how a weary traveler would decide to break his journey, wander about. Sometimes I think I can almost hear God's voice in the river water, or the wind in the trees before a rain."

Abby only shrugged. Unlike Neala, her friend's faith in a loving God remained cautious, at times indifferent. Neala might not understand completely, but her imagination was vivid enough to realize that anyone's faith might be damaged beyond repair, when God allowed your entire family to burn to death.

Saturday morning dawned clear but chilly. A spring storm had swept through the previous night, followed by a refreshing northwest wind that plunged temperatures back toward February instead of May. Due to the chill, Abby and Neala decided to wear their cloaks, despite the awareness that it would hinder their progress down the cliff.

"But I'd rather watch my step a little more carefully than fall ill with ague," Neala cheerfully stated as she slung the cloak over her shoulders. "Besides, I've had this cloak since I was a child, and it's short enough not to trip me up."

Abby glanced ruefully down. Her own cloak covered all but the tips of her boots. "The pastor's wife gave this one to me several years ago, before I came here. She was taller than I am, but I was grateful to have a cloak at all."

"Hmm. I have an idea," Neala announced, fingers flying as she dumped shoulder satchel and canteen, then proceeded to unbutton her cloak. "We'll switch. I'm taller than you are, so my cloak will fit you better. Yours won't hang down to the ground, so neither one of us will have to worry about tripping."

"Neala, I didn't mean…"

"I know. But I do. So hurry up. We have to be back by three, remember."

Forty minutes later they paused for breath, giggling at each other because a strong wind had forced them to pull the cloaks' hoods over their heads and Neala announced they looked like a pair of phantoms floating down the cliff.

"Does add a bit of drama to our outing, doesn't it?" Abby said, giving a little shiver. "The wind creates all these rustling sounds, but we can't see anything much to the side, or behind us. There might be a bear about to pounce, or a wolf who mistakes one of us for Red Riding Hood."

"We'll wallop 'em with our walking sticks—oh, fiddle-faddle. My shoelace caught on these briars. Here—I'll sit on this rock and untangle it."

"Be careful. Those thorns are vicious. Want me to help?"

"I've got it. Why don't you go on ahead? This is the section where we have to go single file anyway. I'll be along in two shakes of a flea's whisker."

Abby nodded agreeably, and a moment later disappeared around a jutting boulder the size of a house. Neala only faintly heard the sound of her boots scraping over the stones. She hurriedly yanked at the laces, jerked when a thorn stabbed through her glove. Then her fumbling efforts caused the laces to knot. Several moments had evaporated by the time she retied her boots and set off after Abby. Impatient with the delay, Neala had to resist the urge to leap down the cliff like a mountain goat instead of exhibiting the common sense Miss Isabella prized so highly.

"Abby? Here I come!" she called, just as a gust of wind buffeted her back and shoulders. From somewhere above she heard a crunching, grating sound, like stone grinding against stone. Neala tossed her head in a vain effort to clear wisps of hair out of her eyes, at the same time fumbling for one of the handholds Liam had carved. Drat this wind, but it was difficult to see, between her wretched hair and the hood. "This wind is dread—"

An explosion of sound, as if a giant had just wrested one of the cliff boulders loose and hurled it over the side of the mountain, kicked the word back down her throat.

The path! Abby! Neala's heart lurched, pounded in sickening hard beats as she scrambled, slipping and reckless, down the trail, ripping her glove, tearing fingernails as she desperately fought to keep her balance on the steep, rock-infested path.

"Abby! Answer me! *Abby!* Did you see—" Gasping, she skidded to a trembling halt. "Father in heaven…Jesus, blessed Lord, help me." The agonized prayer died as Neala froze, not wanting to believe.

Abby lay sprawled in an unmoving heap on the only level part of the trail, her body completely covered by the rippling folds of Neala's cloak. All around her lay chunks of shattered stone. As though from a great distance Neala heard a faint splash—the remains of the falling boulder hurling itself into the river.

She didn't remember rushing to Abigail's side, didn't remember much of anything but the sound of roaring in her ears as she knelt beside her friend and with shaking hands pulled the cloak away from Abby's head. When Abby stirred, then moaned, breath and sound and color spewed through Neala in a flood tide. She gasped Abby's name, tears leaking from her eyes as she gently, carefully turned her over and stuffed Abby's cloak beneath her head. Sluggish blood oozed from a gash just above the other woman's eyebrow, but after a frantic search Neala found no other signs of blood, no other evidence of injury or a broken bone. Praise be to heaven above, but apparently she'd only suffered a glancing blow.

Abby's hand jerked, and her eyes fluttered open. She blinked several times, then winced. "N-Neala? Did…I… What happened?"

"Shh… You'll be all right. You're alive… Thank You, Lord! Oh, Abby…you're alive." One hiccupping sob escaped before Neala managed to throttle the wild emotion clamoring inside. Tenderly she laid her hand against her friend's chalk-white cheek. "The Lord worked overtime today, dearest. Somewhere above us, a boulder dislodged and fell. Probably loosened from all the rain we've been having." She struggled to catch a breath. "You s-seem to have been in its way. But you're alive. I don't know what I would have done… I couldn't have borne it, Abby… If you'd waited with me instead of going ahead…"

Abby's cold hand crept across to brush Neala's. "Do… hush," she whispered, her voice clear but weak. "I'm just glad it didn't…squash me like a bug." A faint smile barely lifted the corners of her mouth. "But I think—I think you better…blow the whistle?"

Chapter Eight

The Grand Hotel, Philadelphia

The rowdy bunch playing poker at a nearby table erupted into another argument. Gray and his friends, lounging up at the bar, turned to watch.

"My money's on the gent with a beard." Carl toasted his choice with his half-full glass of ale. "Looks mean enough to settle the fight with fists."

"Nah...too civilized here. We're not in Denver anymore," Dan said. "I'll go for the tall guy with the prissy middle part in his hair and too much pomade. Probably a lawyer. Fork-tongued pettifoggers can talk their way out of a hornet's nest after convincing the hornets to sting the innocent bystanders. Whaddaya think, Falcon?"

Gray clapped a hand on Dan's broad-as-a-barn-door shoulder. "I think I know better than to place bets on anyone about anything. How 'bout having the barkeep send a round to the winner of their... What's this one? The fourth shouting match?"

"Sixth," Carl replied with a sloppy grin. With his carrot-red hair and youthful face, he looked more like a tipsy leprechaun than Gray's old buddy. "It's the sixth altercation," he repeated. "But who's counting? I'll pony up an' send 'em a round, pal, but only if you pick the winner first. I wanna see if your luck's still as bad at wagering as it's good at shootin'."

Gray elbowed him in the ribs, causing Carl to stumble against the man on his other side. Everyone apologized and toasted each other…a companionable assembly of gentlemen enjoying a few after-dinner drinks in a high-quality tavern across the street from a quality hotel. No prickly sensibilities, no irrational reactions, or raucous tempers itching to explode like the ill-mannered foursome playing poker. Why couldn't females understand a man's need to fraternize with other men without feeling guilty about it?

"Quit stalling, Gray," Carl jibed.

With a good-natured snort Gray gestured across the room, toward the saturnine man holding his cards in a white-fisted hand. His unmoving silence presented a stark contrast against his arguing fellow card players. "I'll take the quiet one," Gray said. "Been my experience the ones who make the least noise wind up the most dangerous."

His two friends solemnly nodded. Ten years earlier they'd all signed on as army scouts at the same time, then maintained a deep if largely disconnected friendship after they'd left the army. Periodically they'd meet somewhere between Kansas City and New York—wherever each could travel within a day's time—to catch up on each other's lives. Gray mused with fuzzy sentimentality that he hadn't realized until now how lonely he'd been since Marty's death.

"I think we should consider establishing some kind of business together," he announced, smacking his palm against the bar with a resounding thud. "Settle down in one place. Get respectable."

"Settle down? Get *respectable?*" Dan swiped a strand of wheat-colored hair off his forehead. "You been letting your aunt sweet-talk you into giving up your sinful ways?"

"Not a chance. Aunt Bella knows better." Gray spread his arms wide, almost knocking Carl off balance again. "She just welcomes me home like the prodigal son." Then he scowled, for a brief moment remembering his motive for joining his friends in this saloon. "Sure wish I'd known there'd be a curly-headed little hornet in the jar this visit." He swore ripely over the subject, not for the first time, causing Carl and Dan to roar with fresh laughter.

"Never known you to react like this to any woman outside your mother," Carl observed between chuckles. "Some of 'em you treat like they're another man, and some a foul-tasting tonic you have to imbibe. Never understood why they all still flutter 'round you."

"Some young ladies seem to thrive on dreams of taming us wild ones." Dan nodded sagely. "Did I ever tell you about this schoolteacher I saved from a scalping when—"

"Yes!" Gray and Dan chimed in together.

Unabashed, Carl grinned. "So how 'bout when Dan brought his purty little cousin to Richmond, two years ago, wasn't it? Thought he'd finally found someone to pull the thorn out of Gray's woman-hating heart."

"Don't hate women," Gray muttered, feeling heat steal up the back of his neck. Not even the one who irritated his memories, with her thick mass of hair he wanted to bury his hands in, whose voice tantalized his thoughts with its soft Southern drawl. Neala Shaw was the only woman in years who didn't cower.

And Gray didn't want any part of her. Or any woman. He could enjoy a woman same as any other man—without allowing her to take over his life. "Just…don't ever want to be tied down to one," he finished, the words delivered almost defiantly. The clinging…the tears…the hurt looks calculated to instill permanent guilt—never again. No, sir, never again. He was a man, not a six-foot little boy, and he did *not* need mothering, or managing.

But he didn't hate all women. Fact was, he wanted to protect them, keep monsters from taking advantage, hurting someone weaker—no. If either of the species were weaker, it had to be the hapless male. Take himself, for instance. All he'd ever wanted was—

"Well, don't fret about Roberta chasing you down." Dan interrupted his sodden musing. "She married a train engineer last October. You're safe from her fluttering eyelashes—and me, having to pound your head, for breaking her heart."

"Ha! *You're* the one who's safe," Carl interrupted with an inebriated guffaw. "'Cuz you'd've been the one getting his head pounded, not our friend here. Good ol' Gray. Best man with a gun, best man with his stropped-razor tongue and falcon's eyes, and best man with his fists."

For some befuddled reason, the turn of conversation pricked Gray on the raw. Deep inside he knew his behavior toward women, and at times men, as well, could be disrespectable, and more often than he cared to admit, ventured perilously close to dissolute. The idealistic boy out to save the world from evil was long dead and buried somewhere west of the Mississippi River, and Gray told himself he didn't mourn over him. But surely at the advanced age of thirty-two Grayson Faulkner had not transformed into a misogynist, as that prissy urchin had accused him of. Surely he retained enough family honor to justify the moniker of gentleman.

When he wasn't three sheets to the wind, that is.

"On second thought," he abruptly announced, "let's call it a night." He waved toward the massive wall clock hanging between the stuffed heads of an elk and a ten-point buck. "It's after eleven. Closing up in less than an hour, anyway. To-morrow's Sunday, y'know. Can't have drunkards and carousers spoiling the Sabbath, remember."

"When's the last time you sat on a pew for a church service, Gray?" Carl asked.

Before Gray could answer, the quiet poker player across the room shoved away from the table and surged to his feet. "You there!" he called in a flat nasal voice, the tone belligerent. "You there at the bar with your pie-eyed friends. You been staring at me, and I don't like it."

Ignoring the angry blustering of the other men at the table, the man tossed down his cards and started toward the bar.

"Uh-oh." Dan glanced from Gray to the oncoming poker player. "Want us to take care of him for you, buddy?"

"Yeah, we'll settle it," Carl chimed in, slamming his drink down on the bar. "Shame for you to go visit your folks sporting a black eye."

Weary to the bone, eaten up with a bitter sense of shame that would not leave him alone, Gray was tempted to give in.

Pride, and a sense of fair play, wouldn't allow him. "I could go home wearing a blasted three-piece suit from Paris, with a carnation in the lapel, and the reaction would be the same as if I sported buckskins. And a black eye." As casually as he could manage given his none-too-steady knees, Gray stiffened his back and shifted his stance. "My family condemns me for my actions." Almost as much as he condemned himself.

The poker player stopped a yard away. "Got no use for rude drunks."

"Me either," Gray responded, flexing his hands. "Didn't mean to stare. Sorry to cause offense and all that."

Carl and Dan made a poor job of stifling laughter.

The stranger's face burned brick-red. "Seems ta me you and your drunk friends need someone to teach you a lesson."

"Ah...mm..." Gray struggled to retain a hold on his slippery temper. "Been out of school a while now." He tucked his thumbs into his waistband and propped his elbows on the counter behind him. "I don't want a fight, mister. Why don't you go on back to your table and try to teach *your* friends a lesson. From the looks of it they need schooling more than we do."

The man's head lowered and he took another step forward. "You don't want to make sport of me, you drunken lout."

"Nope," Gray cheerfully agreed. "Matter of fact, we were just leaving, weren't we, boys?"

Grinning like maniacs, Carl and Dan nodded.

"And," Gray repeated more softly, "I don't want a fight. This isn't the West, you know, friend. There are laws against public scenes."

"I ain't your friend. And if you weren't angling for a broken jaw, ya shouldn't have stared at me."

Without warning, the man swung, coming in with a left hook that might in truth have broken Gray's jaw if the blow had connected. But Gray read the action in the man's glittering eyes, and in a few swift moves rendered the astonished fellow immobile, sweating with pain. Both men knew the slightest pressure could break either a wrist or an arm; only Gray knew how thin the thread keeping him from losing control was. He blinked, fighting the tremors and volcanic emotion that stretched his body as taut as a man on a rack.

"When you live around pigs too long, the stench tends to cling." Sucking in a sobering breath, Gray released his victim except for a punishing hold that kept the man's right hand at an angle that ensured his continued compliance. "If you knew me, you'd know better than to provoke a fight I don't want. Now go on back to your poker buddies, and leave me alone." With a contemptuous shove he released him.

Silence hovered throughout the room as the routed card player slunk between tables. Men shifted their gazes as he passed by.

Feeling lower than a snake's belly in a deep pit, Gray muttered a curse beneath his breath. "Let's get out of here. I'm sick of feeding fodder to the Faulkner gristmill."

But as he stalked out, flanked by Carl and Dan, Gray lost the battle against the penetrating voice warning him that he was the perpetrator of the gossip, not the victim of it. For years he'd fought to free himself from suffocating familial chains, only to discover that in his determination to escape he'd trapped himself inside a cell without a door. He might as well wish himself on the North Star as to wish he could repudiate the Faulkner name, or change the person he had become.

Wouldn't it be a fitting cosmic joke if Neala Shaw were right after all? Grayson Faulkner, youngest son of a prestigious family whose honor and philanthropy dated back four generations, *was* a misogynist. And on the way to becoming a public punching bag as well.

Isabella Chilton Academy

Tucked fifteen feet up in the notch of a massive oak, screened by branches and a cluster of leafy maples, a man watched the wiry Irishman and the girl—*who should be dead*—explore the edge of the cliff. Still as a hoot owl, he watched them discover where he'd patiently chipped the base of the boulder until one hard shove sent it over the cliff. Of course he'd been canny enough to wipe away the boot prints, so he wasn't concerned with discovery. They would assume he'd climbed down the cliff and escaped in a boat up the river, or vanished into the forest. People were predictable and seldom thought their way beyond the obvious.

Nonetheless, the unpleasant truth scraped his mind like a

hacksaw blade: Neala Shaw was still alive. Instead of preparing for a funeral, someone had decided to investigate. And even a brainless dolt would realize the significance of their findings. Sure enough, moments later he clearly heard the windblown voices, heard them reach the inevitable conclusion. The Irishman—Liam, he heard her call him—vented his spleen in a loud mixture of Gaelic and English.

"…and ye can be sure as St. Patrick's cowl I'll no' be standing back fer that dunderhead of a sheriff. The black-hearted jackanapes who'd be after harming Miss Isabella's girls will be answering to me, see if he don't."

"Liam…"

"Now, missy. You got eyes, and a brain underneath all them curls. You know same as me the way of it, here."

Temptation cascaded through his veins; he wanted to finish her off now, right now, not even caring that he'd have to kill the Irishman as well. He wrapped his arms around the thick tree trunk to keep from giving in to the urge.

Frustration knotted his stomach and set his head to throbbing like a wound. *The boulder hadn't even struck the right girl.* All his careful preparations, every second of his meticulous planning, the dark nights he'd sweated through preparing the site to ensure the supposition of an "accidental" death…and *still* she was alive. She might as well be rubbing his nose in the dirt, gloating over his failure.

How could he have known they'd change cloaks? Why had they done so? It wasn't fair! *It was not to be allowed!*

He closed his eyes and struggled to remember his ultimate goal. Over the past several years he'd experienced other failures, but in the end patience and persistence always yielded success. Neala Shaw would be no different. And this time, the final act of retribution would bring about the final victory.

When he reopened his eyes, Neala and the Irishman had

vanished. He could hear nothing but leaves scuffling in the breeze, and his own ragged breathing. Panic raced over his skin, freezing cold, like sleet in January. Then his ear caught the faint sound of voices. Ah. They were returning to the house, then. Not searching the woods or the path down the cliff to the river. He was still undetected, still safe. Still in charge of destiny, theirs as well as his own.

Carefully he climbed down the tree, dropped to the ground, then set off after them. Through binoculars he watched as they crossed the lawn and entered the main house.

Nothing to do now but wait. And maintain the watch.

For the next two days he prowled, a silent onlooker stoking resolve with a blend of righteous anger and bitter frustration. They knew the boulder was deliberate—but was there enough evidence to point to Neala Shaw as his target? The sheriff hadn't put in an appearance, but that might be because the old woman who ran the school didn't want to broadcast such disquieting news: either a student had been singled out for elimination, or the intent had been to kill whoever was on the path at the time.

Every now and then he wanted to laugh. Delicious temptation goaded him to ignite a whispering campaign, for the pleasure of watching all the other students flee like roaches escaping a fire. The hoity-toity Isabella Chilton Academy's reputation would be as smashed to bits as the boulder he'd shoved over the cliff.

By the end of the second day temptation dribbled away. All he truly cared about was Neala's reaction. Would she finally run again? He passed delicious hours hoping so. He was weary of this place, especially since it only served to remind him of his failures to eliminate Neala Shaw. And he'd been sighted at least once, which festered inside, more of a worry than he liked to admit. The longer he lurked about, the greater the likelihood of exposure, questions. Speculations that would force him to have to kill an innocent bystander.

The possibility sickened him. Despite his skill at it, he had never enjoyed taking life. Such an act shouldn't be so easy, like swatting flies or squashing worms. Men who killed for the sport of it, or worse, for money, deserved the hangman's noose.

But when there was no choice, when duty and honor required it, he did what was necessary. Yet the responsibility weighed him down as heavily as the hundredweight sacks of flour he used to have to lift in one of his many jobs.

His job right now was to deprive Neala Shaw of life.

On the morning of the third day, he awoke in his cozy sleeping bag covered by leaves with tears dampening his face. Even peppermint drops could not soothe the sour taste in his stomach. It was with profound relief that shortly after the sun cleared the Blue Ridge he watched Liam-the-Irishman drive the coach up to the house; moments later Neala and the headmistress appeared. What an ugly old woman, he thought, shuddering. He'd hate having to arrange for *her* demise. The Irishman handed Neala inside the coach, then tossed several pieces of baggage and a large trunk into the boot.

At last! Neala had decided to flee. Finally he would depart this cursed school, which in his mind had taken on the personality of a brooding guardian, protecting Neala Shaw and thwarting his every effort.

Now that she was leaving, she would be more vulnerable. Wherever she fled, he would follow, as he had followed her here the previous year. And this time—he would finish the task.

He would not enjoy it, but confidence filled him as he watched the coach slowly clatter down the long winding lane toward the turnpike. This time *he* would emerge the victor instead of the vanquished.

Then he remembered: he had no horse. He did not have a horse, much less a buggy, or even a wagon. Without transportation he would never be able to track the coach to its destination.

He dropped to his knees, pounding the earth in helpless rage.

Chapter Nine

Like the shrouded boatman carrying departed souls across the river Styx, the night train swayed and rattled its way southwest toward the West Virginia mountains. All its passengers save Neala were asleep, no doubt enjoying blissful dreams of their destinations. Wide awake, hands clenched in her lap, Neala yearned in vain for blissful dreams, rather than the living nightmare of leaving the Academy—of the reason *for* leaving.

Why couldn't Miss Isabella understand that she hadn't wanted to go? She was compelled, by what she considered irrefutable evidence: someone, for some unknown reason, apparently wanted Neala dead.

Restlessly she shifted about on the seat, her mind as jostled as her body. Over the past endless hours of travel she'd forced herself to reexamine all the deaths in the family the past several years. The unhappy conclusion, at least for Neala, could neither be escaped nor ignored: every one of those deaths except for her grandfather's heart seizure could have been carefully arranged to appear as though they'd been accidents. Her uncle's drowning…one cousin struck by a runaway freight wagon, the other in a hotel fire…her parents.

And her own "accidents" at the Academy—the fire in the harness room. The hunter who had "mistaken" her for an animal. Then finally, the boulder that had almost killed Abby, because she'd been wearing Neala's cloak.

A spasm of grief tightened her throat, grief and the ever-present anxiety that now coated every moment. She couldn't stay at the Academy, of course. But what on earth could she have been thinking, scuttling off to hide at a place like White Sulphur Springs?

For over a hundred years the Old White, as it was referred to by long-standing guests, had enjoyed a reputation as one of the world's premier springs resorts. Presidents and politicians mingled with wealthy landowners, European aristocrats and Yankee industrialists. Old South debutantes—"the belles"—those young ladies of impeccable breeding and beauty, flocked to the Old White for the sole purpose of securing a husband and supplying guests and journalists with an unending store of gossip.

Even under the chaperonage of an old family friend, Neala would be a scruffy stray kitten amidst a bevy of pampered Persians. Fiddle-faddle. She huffed out an impatient breath. It didn't matter. She wasn't going to the Old White to fit in, much less cast lures for a husband, regardless of what her chaperone and family friend Mrs. Frances Wilkes might have "arranged" for her.

Neala was going there to hide, in a crowded, respectable setting. Surely the murderer would never consider searching for plain Neala Shaw among the elite guests summering at White Sulphur Springs.

Still, she would always have to be on her guard, not only for herself, but for everyone around her. She could not bear the thought of bringing danger upon dear Mrs. Wilkes, who had known the Shaws as long as Neala could remember.

An unacceptable lump swelled in her throat. She always

found herself longing for something she couldn't have. Losing. Leaving, having to let go. How much time would have to pass to assuage the grief of leaving the Isabella Chilton Academy?

Miss Isabella wanted her to trust in God's notion of divine protection. Neala would have appreciated a few words from the headmistress on precisely how one best manifested such trust in a non-corporeal Being, when nobody here on earth was inclined to believe her.

If only she hadn't insisted that Abby borrow her cloak. No, if Abby hadn't worn that cloak, Neala would still be a blind duck in an open field. And despite their refusal to countenance such a possibility, both Miss Isabella and Liam conceded that it had been a person who shoved that boulder, not nature. But like the headmistress, the wiry coachman considered it nothing beyond a nasty prank, unlikely to be repeated.

Without warning, a bucketful of terror numbed her limbs as though she'd plunged them into a frozen pond. Neala jabbed her scalp with a hairpin. The brief pain didn't help.

Nobody believed her. To be blunt, nobody wanted to believe her, and how could she blame them? She herself didn't want to believe her assertions. Not for the first time, Grayson Faulkner's image pricked its way willy-nilly into her mind. Now there was a man with little use for speculations. Yet despite his uncivil behavior toward Neala, for some inexplicable reason she found herself thinking about him. A lot. One moment she'd be immersed in fear and desperation; the next, her wayward brain dragged out an image of Mr. Faulkner.

Oh, he was a good-looking fellow, with his black hair and those blue eyes that… Well, mostly the expression in those blue eyes flayed her like a fish. But there had been a time or two, in Miss Isabella's parlor, and the next day, when he'd followed her in the woods, that she'd glimpsed something in his expression that made her skin feel too hot.

Quit behaving like a headless chicken, Neala. She would never see the man again and even if she did, more likely than not her skin would feel hot from anger or embarrassment. Flumagudgin. She didn't even understand why she kept thinking about Grayson Faulkner, when she needed to invest every scrap of energy in staying alive.

The sentiment seemed to echo in the crowded, stuffy coach.

Stiffly, with trembling fingers Neala dug around in her reticule and tugged out the only heirloom left to remind her that she had been part of a family, whose roots stretched back for centuries. After removing her gloves, she wrapped her fingers around the cool weight of Grandfather Shaw's crest badge.

He had so loved to talk about the badge. Originally fashioned from hammered silver, it had been worn on an ancient clansman's bonnet, held in place with a leather strap during battle. The present badge now sported a symbolic silver strap and buckle that circled the crest, along with some assorted colored-glass chips set in various places. Her grandfather had valued this badge more highly than gold. The central crest, he loved to remind her, had been given to Neala's great-great…well, a great many great-grandfathers ago, after he saved the clan chief's life. During the generations that followed, the eldest sons determined to distinguish themselves in similar fashion, to bring honor to their branch of the Shaw clan.

Yet as Adrian had reminded her throughout their childhood, it was Neala who had inherited Grandfather's name. And it was only Neala—granddaughter Neala—who was allowed to hold the crest badge. Growing up, the privilege had consoled her when Adrian kicked her shins under the dinner table or teased her about her curly mane of hair.

But they'd been family. Even now Neala liked to believe that, had Adrian been willing to take his place as the only remaining male child in the Neal Shaw branch of the clan, Grandfather would have bequeathed the badge to him.

But Adrian had scoffed at what he considered naught but sentimentality. He refused to be saddled with the antiquated notion of family honor, much less worship a stupid object that probably wouldn't fetch two dollars at an auction.

And he had run away. Neala's breath caught in her throat as a horrid possibility leaped into her mind. *What if Adrian had not run away after all?* What if the killer had discovered his whereabouts, and Adrian was not missing, but dead?

A fog of numbness shrouded her. Dead. Everyone in her family, everyone but her. All that remained of the Shaw family was Neala, a trunkful of letters, journals and papers—and the old crest badge that Neala had kept hidden from the auctioneers. And if she couldn't discover who was trying to murder her, and somehow stop them, that lineage would end forever, along with the fierce pride symbolized in the badge she clutched with desperate fingers.

White Sulphur Springs, West Virginia
August 1890

Sunbeams streamed through the trees, transforming the resort grounds into a multi-green patchwork of light and shadow. In striking contrast, all the buildings, from the four-hundred-foot-long Old White Hotel to the hundred cottages scattered over forty acres, glistened in their coats of blinding white paint. Greenbrier's White Sulphur Springs—"the Old White," longtime guests affectionately called it—lay nestled with the serenity of puffy white clouds in a deep blue sky between three gentle peaks of the ancient Appalachian Mountains.

Through the early-morning mist shrouding the trees just

beyond the rows of cottages, Howard's Creek threaded a silvery path along the upland valley that stretched westward between the mountains. Here was a magical place, where whispers of Indian legends mingled with Old South manners. The ravages of the War Between the States had vanquished neither its gentility nor the sulphur springs from which gushed forty thousand gallons of water daily.

Over the past weeks, for at least a few hours each day, Neala allowed herself to lay aside her circumstances, instead thanking the good Lord for such a peaceful place. 'Twas difficult to dwell upon threats of death when every breath filled her lungs with pure mountain air, and the sounds of nature rang through her ears. Birds warbled, squirrels scampered among the boughs of oak, sugar maple and pine, while chipmunks darted among the laurel and rhododendron; on this morning, the air was dew dripped with a nip of autumn just around the corner. It was a fairy-tale scene, complete with a doe and two half-grown fawn slipping through the trees behind the line of guest cottages dubbed Paradise Row.

Neala always suppressed a smile whenever someone referred to "the cottages." Most of the brick structures had been constructed fifty or more years earlier by wealthy Southern blue bloods out to impress, and it took a stretch of the imagination for Neala to equate any of them with her notion of a cottage. Some of the rows resembled miniature versions of the main hotel, with miles of stairs and endless rows of columns to support the long porches. Presidents and society's elite spent entire seasons in those "cottages," graciously mingling with guests of unremarkable stations. Lesser-known families, bachelors and more plebeian guests were housed, like Neala, in spotless but plainly appointed rooms either inside the main hotel, or in the smaller rows of one- and two-room cottages.

The atmosphere at the White was unlike any other resort hotel in the world, Mrs. Frances Wilkes often remarked. "The quality of its guests might be exclusive, but the atmosphere is most democratic," she liked to remind Neala in her cultured Southern accent. "Even those prattling publications acknowledge the sociability here at the Old White. I trust you'll find no cause to disagree."

Since her arrival Neala had befriended two housemaids and one of the groundskeepers, along with a shy debutante from Pennsylvania and an elderly Confederate general. On matters of democratic sociability she found it easy to agree with her status-minded guardian.

Unfortunately, in other areas she and Mrs. Wilkes remained perpetually at loggerheads. Neala refused to agree either to the elderly woman's matchmaking efforts, or to her insistence that Neala allow her to provide costumes "appropriate to the guests at the Old White."

To be sure, there were a number of debutantes who might cast a pitying glance at her simple day and evening frocks and lack of adornment in a place renowned for ladies' fashions. Since professors' daughters weren't accustomed to grand fashion, Neala ignored the glances with the same sunny indifference with which she faced down the autocratic Mrs. Wilkes.

A sensation of timelessness permeated the air here, a peacefulness that banished haste and softened the sharp edge of anxiety. Her sleep was more restful, less riddled with nightmares of an unknown murderer. It was as though life both past and future was restrained inside a stoppered bottle, allowing a freedom from "vexatious rules of etiquette which hem in fashionable life at home," according to one of the many treatises on White Sulphur Springs scattered about the hotel's various reading rooms.

For Neala, that meant the freedom to wander about on her own, another issue upon which she and Mrs. Wilkes disagreed.

"You've changed, in a most disappointing fashion, from the

accommodating child I remember," she liked to fuss, chin tilted imperiously. "The docile companion I anticipated seems to have grown into one of those disagreeable females who claim they wish to be emancipated. Stuff and nonsense. Intelligent women have always enjoyed the power they wield in their homes. This longing for emancipation, as though they were slaves, will lead to nothing but chaos, you mark my words. I daresay such notions on your part must be laid at your father's doorstep. Edward was always annoyingly progressive in his principles."

"Father was respected by everyone, because he treated people as Christ commanded," Neala responded, earning a rusty laugh and a pat on the cheek.

"There, now. That's the sweet girl I remember. You needn't defend your father to me, child. He may have been less than an adequate provider, but he was a good enough father and husband, despite his over-idealistic notions."

Neala forbore from trying to explain that her "emancipation" rose from necessity rather than inclination. She wandered alone in order to regain confidence. She refused to live the rest of her life cowering in her room because she was alone, without an escort, protector, or even a friend. If she could not achieve a semblance of serene independence here at White Sulphur Springs, likely there was no sanctuary this side of heaven she would find peace—until she discovered who was trying to kill her, and why.

Of course, like Miss Isabella, Mrs. Wilkes refused to believe that members of the Shaw family had been murdered, or that Neala herself was in fact hiding from the murderer or murderers. As far as the elderly widow was concerned, so many tragic deaths had weakened Neala's sensibilities; what she needed was a healthful dose of the waters, and a healthy focus on the living instead of the dead.

Sometimes Neala was almost tempted to believe her. Mrs. Wilkes's personality burned fiercely despite her almost eighty years. A quintessential matriarch of the Old South, her blood-lines included several senators, a governor and even European royalty. Her third husband had purportedly owned half the state of Alabama.

On this sunny morning in August, as usual she and Neala were on their way to taking the waters at the domed springhouse down the hill from the main hotel. Neala would have enjoyed the daily pastime more if the water didn't originate from a sulphur spring, which engendered a burned-match odor to the liquid. She could scarcely swallow the stuff without grimacing.

Today she was pensive, having spent until the wee hours of the night poring through the diary her grandmother Annie had kept the first year she and Grandfather Neal were married. Och, to have a love so strong as theirs…

"Must I be inflicted with a gloomy face this morning?" Mrs. Wilkes demanded, her walking cane thumping along the path.

"Sorry." Neala offered a wan smile. "I fear I stayed up too late, reading Grandmother's diary."

"Pish-tosh. You can be most vexing, my girl. Every Southerner since the War Between the States has a tragedy to share, grief to bear. You're only entitled to one life here on earth. Seems to me you could expend yours better than forever prattling about near-tragic accidents and untimely family deaths, and poring over a trunk of worthless papers. I've spent the better part of these past weeks introducing you, outfitting you properly, even instructing you on the finer points of a schottische so you'll be prepared for the Grand Ball tomorrow night."

She paused to nod regally to a couple strolling past in the opposite direction. "People come here to celebrate the joys of social intercourse, not wallow in their respective melodramas.

I lost my first husband after only seven months, my second one in the War, and poor Vernon to Kentucky bourbon. I told you about Vernon, didn't I?"

"Yes, ma'am. He drank too much, and one night tripped over a boot scraper, fell and cracked his skull."

"Died on the spot. I didn't carry on about it then, and you don't see me carrying on about it now. Nor did I ever concoct implausible stories of sinister goings-on." She slanted Neala one of her censuring looks. "Haven't had anybody attempt to toss you off Lover's Leap, or accost you on a walk up Prospect Hill over these past months, have you?"

"No, ma'am." But that didn't mean it wasn't ever going to happen.

After they finished drinking their glasses of sulphur water, Mrs. Wilkes led Neala away from the crowd of other guests, down another of the many walking paths that crisscrossed the grounds.

"My letter from Isabella yesterday was most interesting," she announced. "For some reason beyond good sense, she has decided to enlist the help of a private investigator to look into the matter of the dislodged boulder. Good heavens, the incident occurred over two months ago."

Neala failed to suppress a gasp of indignation. Mrs. Wilkes slanted her a look before continuing. "I do not pretend to know what she hopes to accomplish. Private investigator indeed! I plan to tell her of my profound distaste in associating with such a person."

"She didn't tell me, or I would have dissuaded her," Neala said. "Besides, if anyone hired a detective, it should be me." And she had considered doing so, but only briefly since she had no means of paying such a person for services rendered.

"Balderdash. I absolutely forbid it." Mrs. Wilkes nodded to a noisy group dressed in riding apparel, spoke severely to sev-

eral bright-eyed belles whose high-pitched giggles "offended
the restful atmosphere," then turned back to Neala. "However,
this…person has already agreed, and will be arriving here
within the week to interrogate you. You needn't look like that.
I plan to send the upstart packing myself. Now—no, you may
not interrupt me, girl."

Ruefully, Neala complied. Later on, she would telegraph
Miss Isabella, and—

"Neala! Are you paying attention?"

"Yes, ma'am." With considerable effort she forced her attention back on the widow.

"As I was saying, I noticed George Watlington—with that
equestrian party heading for the stables—sizing you up. You
could do worse. Only mark against him to my knowledge are
those ears of his—big as the handles on a soup tureen. One
could only hope the children would inherit yours." She in-
spected Neala's. "It's a blessing for a woman to have ears like
you, small, flat against the head. Too bad about your hair—
much too rebellious. We'll have to instruct Lallie to pin it up
securely for the ball, show off your ears. Made to wear earrings.
Speaking of that, I must insist you borrow my rubies tomorrow
evening."

"That's very kind of you," Neala offered meekly. "I promise
to look dazzling for you, Mrs. Wilkes."

"Bah! Matters not a whit to look dazzling for me, and you
know it. Far better to dazzle the Watlington fellow. Now, I'll
hear no more on the matter. It's time for breakfast. After that,
you will accompany me to the post office. I'm sending Isabella
a strongly worded reply about the inadvisability of indulging
the weak minds of vulnerable young women. Private investigator indeed!"

Chapter Ten

The following night a thousand guests milled about the grand ballroom and spilled outside, crowding against the large window bays opened to view the proceedings. Streamers of multicolored veiling hung suspended about the cavernous room; the grandstand, alcoves and door arches had been lavishly decorated with greenery and garden roses. Even the two rows of pillars that ran the length of the room had been festooned in the colorful streamers. Debutantes floated across the floor in colorful sweeps of heliotrope silk, pink satin and white chiffon, full of life and a certain awareness that all eyes were trained upon them from the toes of their dancing slippers to the carefully arranged hair piled atop their heads. Jewelry winked and sparkled in a dazzling display around their creamy necks and dangled from their ears. The gentlemen's formal black tie and tails and snowy white shirtfronts offered a perfect counterpoint to the rainbow of color.

Reporters from newspapers and magazines all over the country prowled among the guests like hungry alley cats—another example of what Mrs. Wilkes referred to as the "vulgarization of our way of life." In Neala's first week at the

White, an earnest gentleman with kind brown eyes had sidled up to her at the evening ball, inveigled her name before Neala realized his occupation, and was avidly peppering her with questions about Mrs. Wilkes when her mentor had steamed across the room and dispatched the fellow with a single look.

No member of the press had bothered Neala since.

Tonight, clad in a quiet plum-colored evening gown that muted even the Burmese rubies Mrs. Wilkes insisted she borrow, for the most part Neala watched the proceedings with a crush of other spectators. Mrs. Wilkes, along with a number of other habitués, held court from a row of chairs arranged for them at one end of the floor. The orchestra was in fine form, and several times gentlemen, including the large-eared Mr. Watlington, wove their way through the crowd to ask Neala to dance. She agreed mostly to please Mrs. Wilkes.

She also knew better than to confess to the matchmaking dowager how often wistful speculations about Grayson Faulkner continued to tease her heart. Now, if Mr. Faulkner suddenly appeared and asked her for the next dance…

Neala would turn him down flat.

The romantic atmosphere here must have affected her common sense.

She gave herself a mental pinch, then turned to the woman beside her and launched into an animated conversation.

By a little past midnight, the heat and noise battered at even the stoutest set of nerves, and the clash of perfumes and flowers and gentleman's hair pomade was making Neala's head swim. Over the hours more than one elderly guest had had to be escorted outside to inhale a reviving draft of chilly mountain air. Smashed into one of the window bays between a middle-aged couple from Ohio and a rowdy trio of young men making calves' eyes at the debutantes, Neala tried in vain to spot Mrs. Wilkes to see if the elderly woman needed to retire, though Neala's concern would doubtless be met with nothing less than a sharp rebuttal.

The dancers gathered in the center of the dance floor for another waltz, and with a stab of guilt Neala decided to savor her final moments of a sight she would never be part of again. Miss Isabella, and the rest of the students back in Virginia, would expect a detailed accounting.

Movement swelled outside the window as more onlookers seemed to converge behind her. Neala tried to wriggle forward on the window seat to escape the crush. Perhaps if she could stand…

Someone grabbed her arm; she glanced over her shoulder, but the lady from Ohio shifted just then, stumbling against Neala. Their gazes met in commiserating glances. But when Neala inclined her head to hear the proffered apology, she felt gloved fingers close around her arm again. She half turned, attempting with little success to discover who was trying to gain her attention—or haul her out of the way.

"So sorry," one of the young men to her left exclaimed as he was pushed sideways to collapse beside her onto the seat. "Odious bit of a crowd, isn't it?"

The fingers slipped away from her arm. Laughing, Neala started to warn the young man about the impatient onlookers outside the window who wanted them out of their way. At the same instant she opened her mouth, the orchestra struck the opening chords for Strauss's "Vienna Waltz." She waved him away instead and they both turned to observe the dancers. As she tried again to wriggle forward, she felt her arm clasped for the third time. Only now the tug was unrelenting, forcing her to lean her head back toward the window. Warm, bourbon-scented breath tickled her neck, just beneath her right ear.

"You couldn't hide forever," a hoarse voice whispered. "It's your turn now. You'll have to die. I'm sorry…"

Applause burst around her, the music soared, and the swell of a thousand conversations hummed through the ballroom as the dancers whirled around the floor.

Neala sat immobile, frozen in place, like a hapless butterfly pinned against a board.

For the first twenty-four hours after the ball, Neala barricaded herself in her room. After arranging for room service to deliver her meals, she sent word to Mrs. Wilkes that she was feeling poorly due to the excess activities of the ball, and planned to rest for a day or two.

Not surprisingly, the widow appeared at her door within an hour to personally demand explanations, and to change Neala's mind. Neala weathered the onslaught in polite silence. Then—equally politely—she promised to join Mrs. Wilkes at two the following afternoon, for a watermelon tea on the grounds. Hopefully, she reasoned, by that time she would be able to shore up her defenses adequately and behave with sufficient aplomb to mollify her irate sponsor.

At any rate, what would be gained by cowering in her room for the rest of the season? The murderer had discovered her whereabouts. He had approached her directly in the midst of a thousand oblivious guests. If he was determined to carry out his threat, a watermelon tea sufficed as well as her bedroom at the hotel as the site of her demise.

Miserably uncertain, Neala spent most of the day seated at her desk, reading through family documents yet another time, or wandering about the small room. Every so often she gazed forlornly out the window, where carefree guests strolled along the paths, lounged about on blankets spread over the long grasses, played croquet—all of them without a care in the world because *they* hadn't been told they had to die.

By the following morning, fear, restlessness and boredom

propelled Neala out of her hiding place hours before the two o'clock watermelon tea. Heart rattling her rib cage, she marched along the hall, down two flights of stairs and outside to the grounds. Then she sat on one of the wooden benches wrapped around several of the larger trees, where she was visible to *everybody.* Surely the murderer would not carry out the deed in view of several hundred witnesses.

Almost an hour passed before her heartbeat settled to a calmer rhythm and she didn't jump whenever someone strolled by or spoke to her.

"Miss Shaw?"

Neala whipped her head around, then smiled a genuine smile. "Mr. Crocker, how nice to see you. I trust you've had no more run-ins with a wasp's nest?"

The groundskeeper removed his cap and smiled back shyly. "No'm, no wasps lately."

The question had become a silly yet enjoyable ritual they shared each time they happened to meet. Neala had first encountered Mr. Crocker several weeks earlier; she'd been strolling along one of the paths behind Alabama Row that led to the footbridge over Howard's Creek when she spied Mr. Crocker frantically attempting to escape a swarm of wasps. Using her parasol, Neala leaped into the fray, swatting and shooing until both of them finally collapsed in relief on the steps of one of the cottages. Despite Mr. Crocker's protests, Neala had fetched some baking soda and water, made a paste and applied it to his myriad stings. He'd been panicked that his carelessness might cost him his job, since he'd only been employed by the hotel a week earlier. Neala assured him that nothing of the sort would happen, but she would speak to the head groundskeeper on Mr. Crocker's behalf. Ever since, whenever he caught sight of her, Mr. Crocker made a point of speaking to her, and Neala inquired about the wasps.

"Were you commandeered into helping clean up after last night?" she asked next.

"No'm. I've been over to the cottages, trimming the bushes. Um…did you attend? The Grand Ball, that is?"

The smile on Neala's face stiffened, but she answered readily enough. "Oh, yes. And it *was* grand."

"I imagine all the gentlemen asked for dances."

That startled a laugh out of her, and helped her relax back into naturalness. "Hundreds of them! Why, all those debutantes turned into wallflowers, I was so besieged by partners."

"You shouldn't belittle yourself," Mr. Crocker murmured. His sallow complexion turned red, and he wiped a grass-stained hand across the back of his neck. "Begging your pardon, Miss Shaw. I've no right to address you in such a manner."

"Pish-tosh," Neala retorted, borrowing one of Mrs. Wilkes's favorite expressions. "I'm not a wealthy debutante. Frankly, I never entertained hope of ever being one." Mr. Crocker's bony but not unattractive face revealed such bemusement a wash of friendliness swept over her. "In fact," she shared impulsively, "what I'd really like to be is an intrepid lady reporter for a New York newspaper, like Miss Nellie Bly."

The groundskeeper looked shocked. She realized belatedly that blurting out such personal information was perhaps not wise. Sighing, she waved a dismissive hand. "Don't mind me. I've a bad habit of speaking before I think. My mother is forever reminding me— Oh!"

The pain struck without warning. Stricken to silence, Neala could only stare at the groundskeeper while tears leaked from the corners of her eyes. Fumbling, she tugged out her hankie and dabbed at the moisture. "I—I beg your pardon, Mr. Crocker. It's just that sometimes I forget. My mother—she's dead, you see. Both she and my father were killed in a carriage accident. It's been over a year now, but sometimes…" Her voice trailed away helplessly.

Mr. Crocker looked extremely uncomfortable. After an awkward expression of sympathy, he announced that he should return to his work, crammed his cap back on his head and scuttled off across the lawn.

Neala berated herself for her blabbermouth. She should not treat a man she had met less than a month earlier as though they were lifelong friends. Worse than the sin of familiarity, however, in light of her circumstances she shouldn't presume upon the friendship of anyone. Her acquaintance with Mr. Crocker, along with the several guests she met with regularly, might already have placed them in danger.

What rattled her bones was the potential harm to Mrs. Wilkes.

Trains arrived and departed from the Old White daily. Come Friday, Neala planned to be on one of them.

At a little past one in the morning, the third night after the ball, she wandered over to the window because once again she was unable to sleep. Shoulders slumped, she gazed out at the moonlit night, scarcely aware of its silvered beauty. Never had Neala felt so alone, so conscious of the symbol of the heirloom momentarily cradled in her hands.

Abruptly she leaned forward, her attention drawn to a movement at the edge of some trees, a little ways beyond one of the gas-pole lamp fixtures that illuminated the path. That looked like… Yes. It was a person, a man, walking with the swift soundlessness of a wraith. Or a murderer? The crest dropped from her hand and fell to the carpet with a muffled thunk as Neala abruptly realized she had been standing in an open window, with a parlor lamp blazing away behind her, illuminating her silhouette. *Brainless peahen,* she railed at herself even as she braced her palms on the sill and leaned farther out, peering from her third-story perch over the moonlit grounds.

There was no sign of the shadowy figure. For all she knew, she'd conjured him up out of exhaustion, fear, and a fanciful imagination.

Muttering to herself, Neala turned out the lamp, retrieved the crest and laid it back inside the box with her mother's diary. Time she acknowledged the fear, accepted that her sleep would be riddled with nightmares, and climb into the wretched bed anyway.

Gray couldn't get over the changes. Of course, the last time he'd been dragged to White Sulphur Springs with his family, he'd been fourteen and miserable. Idly he twirled the walking cane Aunt Bella had thrust into his hands at the last moment. Made him look more the part of Harrison Faulkner's youngest son, she said, eyes twinkling because she knew his feelings quite well.

Breath spiraling upward in a chilled misty vapor, cane twirling, he stood on the edge of the Chesapeake and Ohio railway platform, listening to the fading creak-and-clatter of the train while he absorbed the changes.

For one thing, he was standing on a train platform. He recalled without fondness that years ago the trip from the family home in Richmond had been in their cumbersome coach, required six days of travel, and his sister—married and "in the family way"—spent most of the time whining, or emptying the contents of her stomach, once all over his new half boots.

"Evenin', sir. You be needing a buggy ride across to the Old White?"

Inexcusably inattentive, Gray spun halfway around in a crouch, one hand reaching for the gun, his other hand gripping the cane like a sword. *Blamed idiot.* He cudgeled instinct back into his persona as the "respectable son of Harrison Faulkner."

"Sorry," he apologized to the colored man dressed in the hotel's uniform. "You startled me. I was…miles away."

"Ah. Well, here's a better place to be for you, I'm thinking. Nothing clears a man's soul like a season at the White."

That, Gray thought, was a matter of opinion. "You may be right. I think I'll walk across instead of ride. It's a beautiful night, and I feel the need for some fresh air, after that train trip."

"I could fetch yo' bags over if you like, then," the porter offered, eyeing the pile of luggage stacked beside Gray. "Shame to spoil such a fine walk, totin' all those cases. Got a full moon tonight, big and round as a silver dollar."

Good killing moon, a cattle thief once told him. "Yes. Thank you. I'm staying in the third cottage along Baltimore Row." Gray effected the bored drawl of inherited wealth, while inside he cursed himself roundly for giving in to Aunt Bella's pleas. As for Neala Shaw… Well, he'd promised his aunt two weeks.

In a hundred yards, however, with a night sky lit by that full moon, and nostalgic aromas of wood smoke, meadow grasses, and the resiny tang of something unique to White Sulphur Springs flooding his senses, Gray felt a loosening inside himself.

Against all expectations to the contrary, he realized he was glad to be here. For over two hundred years weary souls had found their way to the springs in this secluded valley, and gone away refreshed. The worn slopes of the Appalachian Mountains more resembled blue-green forested hills compared to the stark soaring grandeur of the Rockies, but they offered something Gray had forgotten existed.

Peace.

He strolled at an ever-decreasing pace, past Virginia Row,

expanded now he saw by more than half a dozen cottages. All of them gleamed as white as the moon, their silhouettes illuminated by electric lights, courtesy of the group of businessmen who had bought the place up a decade earlier and transformed it back into a world-class resort.

When he reached the central hotel he stopped, studying the plain but dignified grandeur of its porches and columns. The owners who had refurbished the resort in the late seventies had built a four-story wing on the western flank. Just what the place needed. More fancy rooms to entice more guests.

Neala Shaw was inside the main hotel. Number 323, Aunt Bella had told him. Her windows overlooked the back lawn, and Neala wrote her what a pleasure it was to see the sunset behind the mountains. What was it about the girl that roused his aunt's fierce maternal instincts to such an intense degree? Gray had puzzled over the question for days, ever since she'd written, begging him to help. Isabella Chilton had always been protective of her students, but in all the years he'd known her, she had never laid aside that steely common sense, nor her resolute faith in a God Who was supposed to care when even a bird dropped dead.

His aunt's beliefs in a sovereign, all-loving, all-knowing God always made him feel as though he were locked inside a very small cage placed in the center of a very large city. Bad enough to be saddled with a set of inbred ethics he couldn't escape, but Gray refused to accept that every breath he drew was monitored by the Almighty. He'd endured plenty of that suffocating attention when he was growing up, thank you very much.

With a single head shake he focused instead on the unpleasant possibility that his aunt's concern for Neala might be justified.

"Mind you, I haven't informed her of my changed mind,"

Aunt Bella had wryly informed him. "Neala's possessed of a vivid imagination along with her overdeveloped sense of responsibility. I didn't want her charging back up here to nag the sheriff into an early grave."

All right, Miss Shaw, Gray challenged her silently. *Let's see how you prove your case to me.*

A reluctant grin tickled his mouth as he recalled her reaction on their previous meetings. Definitely not the sort to cower beneath the bedclothes, or cover her eyes and screech like a steam kettle.

Moonlight stitched a lacy pattern through the trees and across the vast lawn. Eyes narrowed, Gray thought for several long moments, then casually made his way around the main hotel, noting the darkest corners, the location of trees, shrubs, paths and lamplights.

A single window in the back glowed yellow against the ghostly white of the main hotel. Gray absently noted that it was a third-floor window; he was about to head for his cottage when a silhouette appeared. A slender but definitely feminine silhouette. When she leaned out, the golden lamplight behind her framed a head of riotous curls spilling over a pale face and tumbling down her shoulders. With the careless disregard of a coquette, she propped her elbows on the opened sill and stared out into the night.

Neala Shaw.

The woman possessed the self-protective skills of a lemming.

Gray's job as bodyguard commenced right now.

Chapter Eleven

A knock on the door echoed through the room with the resonance of a thunderclap.

Neala jumped, fumbled for the bedside lamp, then froze. If she turned on the lamp, whoever was out there would see the strip of light and expect her to open the door. If the room remained dark, they might go away.

On the other hand, if this was the murderer, he might conclude she was asleep, affording him the perfect opportunity to pick the lock and slay her in her bed.

Or it could be a frantic hotel clerk, alerting guests to a fire.

An urgent summons to Mrs. Wilkes—she was ill, injured. The guest across the hall needed immediate medical assistance…

Heart pounding in concussive thuds, Neala stood rooted to the floor. What to do, what to do—a weapon. She should be searching for a weapon, something with which she could defend herself.

The knock sounded again, this time louder, with an overtone of impatience. "Miss Shaw?" A man's voice carried through the panel. "It's Grayson Faulkner. I know you're in there."

There was a pause, as though he were giving her time to absorb his words. "Open the door," he finished, and it was not a request.

Lord, I know I told You I'd accept anyone, but did You have to send him as your chosen bodyguard?

She turned on the lamp, tightened the sash of her night robe with fingers that trembled, then marched across the room. "I certainly will not open the door," she managed to say civilly enough for having to raise her voice to be heard through the thick panel. "It's two o'clock in the morning. You scared the curls out of my hair, Mr. Faulkner. Go away and come back at a civilized hour."

There was no reply. Frowning, Neala took a cautious step forward, thinking to lay her ear against the door to see if she could hear the sound of retreating footsteps. Instead came the sound of a key rattling the lock. Even as she leaped to grab the knob, it turned in her hand. The door swung open, almost knocking her off her feet, and Miss Isabella's outrageous nephew stepped inside, shutting the door behind him. In his hand he held an odd-shaped key that bore no resemblance to Neala's room key, but before she could challenge him about it he'd tucked it away.

He scowled down at her, arms folded across his chest. "What were you thinking, standing in front of a lighted window? If the killer wanted to put a bullet through your heart instead of pushing a boulder over a cliff, you offered the perfect target."

So he'd been outside somewhere on the grounds, spying on her? *Again?* "I had already reached that decision myself." She waved toward the darkened room. "See? No more lights. There was no need to frighten me half to death by pounding on my door." She clutched the lapels of her bed robe more closely. "Besides, I'm already frightened enough."

"Good," he snapped. "Perhaps you'll be more inclined to obey me when I tell you what to do." His startling blue eyes wandered over Neala with an intensity that noodled her knees.

Annoyed, she stiffened the knees and ordered her spine to follow suit. "Why did you come, Mr. Faulkner? Surely you explained to your aunt that you, well, that you don't like me very much." Speaking the words aloud somehow gave them more power; instead of returning his glare, Neala stared just beyond Mr. Faulkner's shoulder. Between fright and humiliation, she was inches away from howling like a toddler.

"I'm here," came the sardonic reply, "because my aunt believes I can protect you. She also believes I might have more success tracking down the unknown person or persons who apparently will go to extraordinary lengths to dispose of you."

Despite herself, Neala's lips trembled. "I believe there's only one, a man. Two nights ago he, ah, spoke to me." She finally met his gaze. "I was sitting on a windowsill at the Grand Ball, s-surrounded by other guests. He grabbed my arm, pulled me backward, and whispered in my ear that he—" she scrabbled for breath, finished levelly enough "—was sorry, but it was m-my turn to die. By the time I was able to turn around to search for him…" Her voice trailed away.

Sparks seemed to leap from Mr. Faulkner's eyes, sizzling into air that all of a sudden crackled. He took a step forward, stopped, pinched the bridge of his nose and muttered something beneath his breath. Then, startling Neala so badly she flinched, he clasped both of her hands in his much larger ones and tugged her toward him. "All right," he murmured. "All right." Warm fingers gently stroked her taut knuckles. "I'm here now. I'll take care of you. Try to not be afraid."

Neala gaped at their clasped hands. "Mr. Faulkner, I don't understand you. I was expecting you to accuse me of making it up. Like you did the hunter… I don't understand."

He gave her hands a final squeeze, then released them with a short laugh. "Well, it's like this, Miss Shaw. I've come to realize you don't lie worth a— You don't lie well."

"Thank you so much. But—"

"Besides which every last soul at the school, not to mention Aunt Bella, praise you to the skies for your charming personality, your unassuming manner, and your 'laudable loyalty,' I believe was the way the school secretary—Miss Crabbe?—phrased it. And over the past couple of months I've—" He stopped, ran a hand over his beard-stubbled jaw, started to speak, grimaced. "I don't like being wrong, Miss Shaw," he finally admitted. "But I wish I'd searched the woods that day, instead of simply following you. You might not be in this predicament now if I'd done what I'm trained to do."

"If what I've come to believe is true, there's nothing you could have done." Neala fiddled with the crochet edging on the sleeves of her robe.

"Why do you say that? Go ahead, tell me whatever it is you need to tell me."

"What? I mean, how could you possibly—?"

"It's your eyes," he offered unhelpfully. "You've an easy face to read, Miss Shaw. So what is it you're debating whether or not to tell me?"

"Oh. Well. Um… I've been studying and thinking on things ever since I arrived here, back in June." She gestured to the large steamer trunk in the corner of the room. "Gone through all our family papers, diaries and letters countless times. I practically have them memorized. And…" She hesitated again.

"Tell me," Mr. Faulkner repeated, still with extraordinary patience.

Patience? From Miss Isabella's nephew? If he'd remained the churlish and disdainful man she remembered, Neala might have been able to stand her ground, insist that an interrogation wait until morning.

But she was exhausted, tired of the fear, tired of the sense of isolation. Weary of shouldering a burden crushing her beneath the weight of its sheer irrationality. "I think someone has been killing off everyone in my family," she blurted, then steeled herself for the response.

He merely inclined his head. "Why?"

Now there was a question. "I don't know." Her voice wavered. Heat flooding into her cheeks, Neala abruptly swiveled and escaped to the other side of the room, where the massive trunk offered at least an illusion of protection. "I don't know," she repeated. "I've thought and thought about it, but come up with nothing. I mean, my father was a professor at the University of Virginia. My uncle and grandfather owned a small freight company. It was successful, and highly respected. But we're just folks. Nobody famous or remarkable, much less wealthy. Yet after the man whispered to me the other night, I've had to accept that for some reason, he's possessed of a blind hatred for everyone in the Neal Shaw family."

"Neal Shaw? Your father?"

"My paternal grandfather. I was named after him. My mother lost two babies before me, so when I was born—" She blinked rapidly. "Mr. Faulkner, could we please continue this discussion later?"

"Certainly. Can I trust you to keep away from the window, and to remain in this room until I come to fetch you?"

"I don't see why I should—"

"In that case," Mr. Faulkner interrupted as he strolled across to the pegs on the wall and proceeded to unbuckle his gun belt, "I'll be remaining here, with you."

"You most certainly will not!" Tears forgotten, Neala stalked across to the door and flung it open. "I appreciate very much your—your kindness. But contrary to what you believe about me, I'm not some mealymouthed young miss to be manipulated or…or managed. You leave this instant, Mr. Faulkner. I will not be bullied, do you understand?"

"Then you have a problem, Miss Shaw. I will not be dictated to, particularly when it comes to honoring a promise to my aunt." His lip curled upward in a mocking half smile. "I think we can both agree you've little chance of tossing me out of here. And no doubt you've heard all the stories about Harrison Faulkner's infamous youngest son. I daresay your old family friend might raise a ruckus when she hears we're sharing a room, but—" he shrugged "—it's your choice."

For as long as she could remember, Neala had played the role of peacemaker, pacifier, placater. She tried to get along with everyone, particularly her brother. But as she sifted through Mr. Faulkner's insulting ultimatum, an alien urge to rebel, to call his bluff, swelled inside, propelling her back across the room. Hands fisted on her waist, she stopped directly in front of the infuriating man. "After I write Miss Isabella a letter to inform her of your behavior, I'm going to bed. If you insist on ruining my reputation that will be *your* choice. Not mine. My conscience is clear, Mr. Faulkner, in my eyes, and the Lord's."

For a moment he did not respond, and the air in the room seemed to pulse in rhythm with Neala's heartbeat. Then a muscle twitched at the corner of his beard-scruffed jaw and astoundingly, he laughed. "Game and set to you, Miss Shaw," he finally drawled. "I should have expected it, given your disposition."

"My disposition?" What about his? Neala pressed her lips together to keep from blurting the question aloud. First he held her hands and reassured her. Then he laughed. *He'd laughed.* No longer could she pigeonhole him as an older version of

Adrian to be placated, nor ignore him as an ill-tempered misogynist.

But since she could no longer anticipate his reactions, she couldn't bring herself to trust him entirely either.

"What *are* you going to do, then?" she asked at last.

"I'm going to leave you. No, not consign you to the jaws of a killer. You needn't look like that. I meant, I'm leaving you and your clear conscience to hopefully peaceful dreams." He paused, surveying the room. "However, since it's possible I'm not the only one who saw you silhouetted in the window…" in several long strides he crossed the room, fetched the cane-bottomed chair shoved beneath the small library table "…put a chair against the door. Like this." He demonstrated, then placed the chair on the floor beside the door. "Think you can manage?"

This time Neala could only nod.

"Good. Then I bid you good night." He swept her an obviously mocking bow. "Is ten o'clock this morning, in the main parlor, agreeable with you?"

Her ears tingled from his laughter, her mind's eye reeled from the warmth in his eyes and the reassurance in his voice, but Neala scraped together enough sensibility to answer with a simple affirmative.

"Fine." He rebuckled his gun belt, touched two fingers to his homburg and put his hand out to the doorknob. Then he turned back. "You're certainly a different—and I'll admit intriguing—kettle of fish. In fact, Miss Shaw, I think I've changed my strategy toward protecting you." One eyelid lowered in an unmistakable wink. "Sleep well."

The door closed quietly behind him. As Neala stood, motionless, she heard him use his odd-shaped key to lock her door.

Still dazed, she carefully jammed the back of the chair beneath the knob. Then she wandered over to the bench at the foot of her bed and sat bonelessly on its cushioned seat.

"Miss Isabella," she pondered aloud, "what have you done?"

At the moment, it felt as though her former headmistress had supplied a fox to protect the henhouse, and she couldn't help but wonder whether Mr. Faulkner or an unknown killer posed the greater threat. One to her life, the other—her heart.

He hated this place. He especially hated having to spend hard-earned money in order to blend in, though much of his wardrobe had been acquired through judicious robbery. Even that necessary endeavor angered him. He considered thieving beneath him, the dishonorable handiwork of ignoble riffraff.

Why did Neala Shaw choose this place? His initial elation at having finally tracked her down was completely negated by having to associate with people who represented everything he despised. Pompous jackanapes, every last one of them, with their puffed-up sensibilities, their aura of smug complacency. Probably not a single one of them able to tie his own shoelaces, much less survive in forest or factory for weeks on end. If one of them tried to blend in to his world… The mental picture amused him. Easier for a hurdy-gurdy monkey to sip tea in the Old White's dining room.

He, on the other hand, had perfected the art of the chameleon. An anonymous chameleon, that was him. In other circumstances he had been able to function more like a wraith, invisible and unsuspected.

Here, regrettably, invisibility would not serve his purpose. Thus, he'd adapted accordingly. Hiding in plain view while he waited for the right opportunity to carry out his mission was almost more exhilarating than years of careful, meticulous planning so that he could never be recognized. Fancy that. A magician as well as a chameleon, practicing finesse and sleight of hand.

People could be such fools. Other people, not Neala Shaw. From her he had come to expect more, because she had managed to slip through every one of his snares. He could privately admit to relief and, until now, a certain measure of pride in her.

But now… He plucked a large tulip tree leaf from an overhead branch and systematically shredded it to confetti. Now Neala had proven to be no better than any other weak-brained woman.

And it was all because of that irritating man. For over a week now he'd watched her succumb to every lure Grayson Faulkner cast her way. Why couldn't she see that his supposed courtship was a sham, a ploy where Neala would become just another fool in a ritual designed from the beginning of time to end in humiliation for either or both participants?

He was not a fool, however. Nor was he an out-of-control madman, both of which traits would result in his capture. Regrettably, Faulkner—and he hoped to find out more than just his name by dinner that evening—could not be disposed of. The man was a philanderer, but he had nothing to do with the Mission. Personal honor demanded that innocents, however despicable, be spared. More to the point, both his and Neala's deaths would bring a locustrian plague of authorities, all of them determined to unearth the person who had tarnished the Old White's impeccable reputation.

Therefore he must somehow find a way to separate them, or give in to the highly risky solution of suffocating Neala in her room.

There they were. He fixed an urbane smile on his face, and as they passed he tipped his ridiculous straw boater. The moment they were out of sight he paused to strike a match on the sole of his shoe, turning to light his cigar so he could watch.

They walked closer together than they had a week ago, and

Neala's expressive face had lost some of that pale, drawn look. She actually looked pretty this morning, with a spring to her step never present when she strolled the grounds with the old widow woman, or by herself.

He viciously ground the match beneath his heel. This was what happened when sentiment was allowed to sway one's will. All those times when he'd followed Neala on her solitary strolls, he'd watched the faces of people light up when she was with them, watched her friendliness to lowly hotel employees as well as illustrious guests. And he'd decided to grant her this one last pleasure. He'd waited for years. He would have waited for her to finish out her last season on earth, here at White Sulphur Springs.

No longer.

He'd thought Neala Shaw different, almost worthy of redeeming the name bequeathed to her by the man who had ruined it through his betrayals.

With a shake of his head he realized he was staring after them more than was wise. Cigar clamped between his teeth, he strode off across the deep grass, for the first time eschewing the path. There were plans to be made. He no longer felt regret for having to kill Neala Shaw. And he never should have warned her, never should have allowed his emotions to sway him.

That was one mistake he planned never to make again.

Chapter Twelve

For the first time in the two weeks since he'd arrived, Gray found himself simply enjoying the role of hotel guest, and suitor. The latter was a role he'd never expected to embrace, much less entertain passing fantasies of turning pretense into reality. Pretending to court Neala in the grand fashion of White Sulphur Springs suitors had simply offered the most plausible way to remain constantly in her company.

No wonder Aunt Bella had given him that cat-in-the-cream smile when he'd shared the plan he'd devised to protect Neala.

Gray shook his head. Contrary to all his expectations, Neala had turned out to be an entertaining companion, curious about everything, with an unself-conscious friendliness to which even a cynical Gray was not immune.

She was, unfortunately, a nightmare to protect, even as her suitor. Friendly, curious young women always spelled trouble. But Neala's impulsiveness added a volatile element to the mix that left Gray perpetually feeling as though he were trying to tie back a pair of butterfly wings without irreparably tearing them.

Thus far she'd climbed a tree with the giggling twelve-year-old daughter of a state senator; innocently insulted an elderly Yankee colonel by informing him that the North's victory did not absolve them of blame, since it was Yankees who had purchased and transported all the slaves from their African homes; and cajoled Gray to help gather a bouquet of wildflowers for a sick chambermaid.

This morning they were walking along Howard's Creek, one of Neala's favorite pastimes and thus far the most benign of her pursuits.

"Oh, look, Grayson!" she exclaimed, pulling him back into the present. "Over there, a pair of Canadian geese. Aren't they beautiful?"

"I don't think you've pointed out anything in the last week that you haven't considered beautiful."

She gave him a sunny smile. "That's because nature is part of God's creation. Of course there's something beautiful in everything."

"Algae?"

"It's a pretty shade of green."

"Dirt?"

"Things grow out of it."

Enjoying teasing her, Gray tucked her hand through his arm as they walked. She'd almost stopped jumping whenever he did so. He smiled to himself. "Mosquitoes?"

"Food for frogs."

"Ah. And no doubt you find frogs beautiful?"

"Oh, no you don't!" She laughed, pulled free and skipped ahead of him a few paces. "You just want to lure me into a comment about toads turning into princes from a kiss."

"Well, I'm no prince, but hopefully you no longer— Neala! Watch out. You're too close to the edge!"

Even as he spoke, the bank crumbled beneath her feet. Gray lunged forward as Neala, arms flailing, tilted toward the creek.

He grabbed one delicate wrist, hauled her backward, then—because he couldn't resist—gathered her into a close embrace. The smell of violets, starched linen and warm woman filled his head.

"Oh, my!" Neala's hands fluttered against his chest. "Thank you. I…um… G-Grayson? You can let go of me now."

The feel of her lissome form awakened in Gray a waterfall of feeling that caught him off guard. He knew how it felt to desire a woman, but tenderness? A longing not merely to satisfy a physical urge, but for the simple joy of holding her close?

He all but shoved her away, yet even as he struggled to distance himself from her, watched his hand lift, felt the warmth beneath the index finger he lightly brushed across her rose-hued cheek. "You need to watch your step," he murmured absently.

"Yes," Neala agreed.

For several seconds they stared at each other, while all around them insects darted about the long meadow grass, the creek water bubbled gently beside them, and the summer sun bathed them in peach-toned light. Somewhere in the woods a bird trilled.

"Mrs. Wilkes would peel me like a grape if I'd showed up for lunch dripping wet," Neala said eventually, the words breathless and hurried.

The reminder of their luncheon engagement with Frances Wilkes effectively wiped the smile from Gray's face. The bizarre emotion that had turned his blood the consistency of syrup dissolved in a welcome rush of irritation. The old woman was about as subtle as a stick of lighted dynamite, and more than once even Neala had remonstrated with her about her heavy-handed matchmaking. Unfortunately, Frances Wilkes had met Gray's parents some years earlier, when her third

husband was still alive. To the matrimonial-minded dowager,
the challenge of taming the infamous Grayson Faulkner, with
his impeccable family pedigree, was irresistible.

"We better head back to the hotel." Without touching her
again he swiveled and started walking back the way they'd
come. "You might have been spared a dunk in the creek, but
you'll want to freshen up." Half-angrily he scanned their surroundings, realizing that a man with a rifle and reasonable aim
could have bagged his bird, and Gray to boot, all because of
Gray's inattention. Some bodyguard he made—and it was
Neala's fault.

Either do the job, or find someone else who will.

He paused, sucking in a deep breath while he waited for
Neala to come abreast. When she smiled up at him as though
nothing had happened, he didn't know whether to be relieved or
miffed.

"Why won't you teach me how to shoot your gun?" Neala
asked then, not for the first time. "Yesterday one of the maids
loaned me a Sears Roebuck catalog. Did you know there are
small derringers a lady can carry inside her purse? Think how
much better protected I'd be."

"Do you realize that the more you pester me about it, the
more determined I am to refuse?" Unlike his mother and
sisters, or most other women, Neala didn't pout or invest significance into a trivial incident that after all had been—
well, trivial. "Besides which *ladies*—" he emphasized the
word "—do not carry a pistol in their purses."

"I wouldn't have to pester you if you'd teach me," Neala
retorted, ignoring his dictum. "What happens if you're hurt,
and unable to protect me?"

"What happens if you end up shooting me instead of the
killer, in your hurry to retrieve my gun, or the one concealed
in your purse?"

Neala emitted an unladylike sniff. "I'll have you know my grandfather taught me how to use a sword when I was all of ten years old." She flashed him an insouciant grin, the last of her uncertainty banished. "Of course, it was one of those wispy English swords instead of a stout Scottish claymore. He told me I wouldn't have been able to lift the one his great-granda carried."

"You and your grandfather were close, weren't you?"

The smile in her eyes faded. "Not for a long time. But when I was older…yes, we grew very close. You see, they named me after Grandfather because everyone believed my mother could never carry another child full term. Then Adrian was born, and Grandfather tried to force my parents to rename me, so Adrian would have the name of Neal."

Gray privately thought the old man heartless, but he'd learned the futility of making any negative reference, however oblique, to anyone Neala cared about. The woman was loyal, he'd grudgingly admitted. Loyal, fearless, and more stubborn than any Scots Highlander. She bore scant resemblance to her heritage with her froth of nutmeg-brown curls and innocent brown eyes, but despite his determination to remain distant, Gray found himself increasingly drawn to her undaunted spirit.

"Did you brandish a stick at your grandfather, threaten to behead him with the sword if he stole your name and gave it to your brother?"

"I was only four." Her shoulders lifted in a light shrug. "I'm afraid I made a poor showing of courage. I hid inside a cupboard. I thought if nobody could find me, they couldn't take away my name. Of course Father and Mother categorically refused, and everything turned out all right. Grandfather eventually apologized, but it was years before I quit being afraid that I was going to die, because of my name."

Gray stopped short on the path and turned to stare down at

her, outraged on a fundamental level he refused to examine. Instead he focused on the hint of a possibility. Was it possible she was targeted because she bore her grandfather's name? "What do you mean, you were afraid you were going to die?"

"Oh, I had a cousin—Grandfather's first grandchild—so of course Uncle Alexander and Aunt Matilda named him Neal. But he died when he was four—the same age I was when Adrian was born. I know now that I was being irrational, but…" She shrugged again. "Don't glare at me like that. I'm perfectly all right now. At any rate, I was afraid Grandfather was disappointed because I was a girl. I spent a lot of time with him, trying to prove myself. And like I told you, we became very close. I think that's why he gave me the crest badge. Our other two cousins died of typhus, back in the seventies, so that left only me and my brother."

She paused. "Adrian always insisted the clan crest ought to be his, as he would be the only male heir left after Grandfather and Father were gone."

"Understandable," Gray murmured, adding casually, "so your brother coveted the crest?"

"Well, yes. I suppose that's one way to put it." They walked a few paces in silence before she added in a wistful tone, "Adrian's not a bad person. He just, well, he *was* the only male heir, but he possessed neither the name nor our family's most precious heirloom. Somehow in his mind he grew to be resentful, mostly because of the name." She sighed. "I wish he hadn't run away."

"Mmm." Gray casually took her elbow and they resumed walking. So Adrian kicked up a fuss about the crest badge after all the other male relatives died, did he? And then conveniently disappeared after the death of his own parents. An ugly worm of suspicion squirmed its way into Gray's mind, one he knew he'd need to investigate further. But not, he determined, until Neala had learned to trust him completely.

"I'd like to see this famous heirloom," he said. "Is it here with you, or locked away somewhere?"

"I keep it with me. At some point, after the War of 1812, I believe, it was turned into a brooch. But it's heavy, and I haven't worn it here, except in the evenings when I need my cloak. I promised Grandfather— Oh, hello, Mr. Crocker!"

Gray stiffened into alertness as he watched the approach of a tallish man dressed in the simple shirt, trousers and over-apron of a groundskeeper. Pleasant-looking enough chap, though the sun had pinkened his fair skin the hue of a poppy.

"My, you may have escaped the hornet's nest last month, but your face!" Neala was exclaiming. "Did you forget your cap, Mr. Crocker?"

"I'm afraid so, Miss Shaw." He glanced at Gray. Something Gray recognized as incipient jealousy flickered behind a pair of light brown eyes. "How are you doing this fine morning?"

"I'm doing well, thank you very much. I haven't seen you much these past weeks, so you won't have met my friend Mr. Faulkner." As though the now beet-red groundsman were another guest, Neala introduced him to Gray; of the three of them, only Neala seemed unfazed by the strained atmosphere. "When we return to the hotel, I'll fetch some vinegar from the dispensary," she continued, fussing over the other man in a manner that instantly raised Gray's hackles.

Before he could stop the movement, he had taken hold of her hand and looped it through his arm, covering the hand with his own. "Leave the poor fellow alone," he ordered with a crocodile's smile. "He's old enough not to need mothering."

"Oh, everyone enjoys a bit of feminine coddling," Mr. Crocker refuted, though he did back up a step and refused to look at Gray. "You're very kind, Miss Shaw. But you don't need to fret about me. I'll be fine."

After shooting Gray a look of dislike, the groundskeeper departed.

"You were rude," Neala said, tugging on her hand. "And it was plain you hurt his feelings."

"You were much too familiar with the hired help." Gray tightened his hold of her hand. "Especially under the circumstances. You've had other conversations with Crocker, I take it?"

"And intend to have many more. I never took you for a snob, Mr. Faulkner. Just because he's a groundskeeper doesn't place him beneath my notice. Frankly, I'm more comfortable around him than I am most of the guests here."

"My rationale has nothing to do with social or economic status, *Miss Shaw.* My concern is that you know nothing about this man. What if he's the one who's trying to kill you, and he's adopted the guise of a lowly gardener in order to be near at hand every day, waiting for the opportunity?"

"The same thought occurred to me…but then I have that same thought over every man I encounter here." She shook her head. "What am I supposed to do? For the first week I stayed glued to Mrs. Wilkes, until I realized my cowardice might cost a dear friend her life. I couldn't stop thinking about my friend Abby, back at the Academy, and how she almost died when that boulder crashed down. So I started wandering on my own, waiting to see what would happen."

"It's a miracle you're still alive."

"Perhaps." For a few steps they walked in silence. Then her face brightened and her shoulders squared. "I like to think that I have the Lord's protection, and now, yours as well." Without warning she leaned to scoop up an acorn, then tossed it at Gray.

He snagged it out of the air without looking away from Neala, watched with a puff of masculine satisfaction as her eyes widened with admiration. Little minx. Trying to test him, was she?

"So…based upon your reaction to Mr. Crocker, am I to conclude that you're going to be rude to every man between sixteen and sixty who condescends to speak to me?"

"Only the ones I haven't investigated, and those I'm satisfied have no desire to kill you." She winced, the air of mischief fading. Good. He was beginning to wonder if her cavalier attitude was the product of a character flaw, rather than a deliberate effort to maintain her sanity while living the nightmare of her present circumstances.

Somehow he needed to discover a way to make her more suspicious of every person—except him.

The irony would keep Aunt Bella chuckling for a week.

"What did you find out about George Watlington?" Neala asked. "Before you arrived, Mrs. Wilkes was determined to marry me off to him."

"Fine by me, if you'd rather die of boredom instead of a sadistically arranged 'accident.'"

After a stilted moment, he impatiently tugged at his too-tightly knotted tie. "Sorry. But you asked." He kicked a pebble on the path with the toe of his boot and sent it flying into the grass. "Thus far I haven't discovered anything that incriminates—or absolves—every man here. George Watlington's nice enough, but he likes to gamble. Peter Vandermoot, another of your would-be suitors, came here to pick a gullible young lady such as yourself who wouldn't notice how many mistresses he keeps tucked away in several New York brownstones."

"What? He doesn't! He was so kind to me. Until you arrived, at any rate."

"They're all kind, you little innocent, because that's typically the fastest way to get what they want. An infatuated woman has little brain to speak of. Even less common sense."

Abruptly she yanked her hand free, stepped back and

gathered up her skirts. "Mr. Faulkner, I may be grateful for your protection, but I refuse to listen to any more of your disparaging remarks. Enjoy the rest of the walk by yourself. I'm going to return to the hotel and freshen up as you rudely suggested earlier, before we meet Mrs. Wilkes. Hopefully the murderer won't accomplish his deed between here and there."

Before Gray realized she actually meant to dart off without him, she'd set off across the lawn, skirts frothing about her heels. Alternately railing at himself and Neala, he followed more slowly, unwilling to garner more attention than they already had.

Knowing Mrs. Wilkes, it promised to be a long and painful luncheon.

Chapter Thirteen

Some years earlier, a race track had been built in a flat meadow across Howard's Creek, much to the dismay of the dignified Old South guests. But despite its lack of universal appeal, the races were well attended.

On this particular day several were scheduled for that afternoon. Neala, still smarting from Mr. Faulkner's regression to the persona she'd first met so many months earlier, informed him that she planned to attend the races. With or without him. The luncheon with Mrs. Wilkes had been an utter disaster, since her sponsor was completely smitten with the man who had succeeded in twisting Neala up like a skein of wet yarn. What a bother! Who cared that his pedigree rivaled a European aristocrat, or that his notoriety merely enhanced his desirability among elderly dames and eligible belles alike? Neala Shaw had neither the time nor the inclination to lose her heart over an ungodly man who plainly could not be trusted with it.

After the meal, Neala escaped to the sanctuary of her room until it was time to go to the races.

Of course, Mr. Faulkner had moved out of his Baltimore quarters and somehow contrived to be given the room next to hers. With only a wall between them, Neala's sanctuary no longer offered the same pretext of self-reliance. Never mind that she slept more securely at night, knowing Grayson Faulkner watched over her.

He was still a cynical man who switched moods as capriciously as a bee in a flower bed.

At a little before five, Neala hurriedly gathered her hair at the base of her neck, grabbed a shawl and sneaked down the hall as silently as she could. Grayson neither opened the door of his room as she passed, nor accosted her in the lobby. She was aware of the risk in attending the races without his protection, but at the moment she was more determined to prove a point. She had survived without Grayson Faulkner for two months, she had emerged unscathed from several attempts on her life, and ultimately she prayed she would continue to do so.

She was through being pummeled by his contrary personality—one moment the confident and charming companion, the next a hard, cryptic man whose attitude toward the gentler sex left Neala feeling frostbitten.

A party of young women who thus far had failed to snag at least one proposal from an eligible bachelor invited her to ride to the race track in a buggy they'd commandeered from the stables. Either too old, too young, or—as with Neala—without a name, extraordinary beauty or connections, the three other women made for lively and uncritical companions, far more so than most of the debutantes. With only a slight niggling of guilt, after asking one of the bellhops to inform Mr. Faulkner of her whereabouts, Neala climbed into the buggy.

By the time they arrived at the races, the crowd milled eight deep around the track. Chatting and flirting, her companions wormed their way through to a spot on the rail, Neala safely ensconced in the middle. For a few moments she enjoyed the spectacle, exchanging comments with the others while struggling to keep her balance in the enthusiastic crush of race goers. When someone trod upon her foot, she jerked back—and without warning memories of the Grand Ball swooped down, taunting her with how close she had been to death. How the murderer had talked to her. How he had even touched her.

She was alone.

No. She was safe, surrounded by other women and countless other harmless hotel guests. Nobody could hurt—

She was alone.

Alone.

Faces swam around her in a dizzying swirl. The air, thick with toilet water, pomade, dust and horses thickened until she could scarce take a breath. A buzzing sound intensified in her ears.

When a hand closed around her arm, Neala didn't think. She reacted, jerking backward into the rail while she rammed her elbow into a man's midriff.

"Oomph. That hurt! Miss Shaw, you promised never to be out of earshot. I ought to handcuff you to— Hey!" He managed to deflect her free hand before she smacked his jaw with it.

"Are you all right, Neala?"

"What's going on? Is that man accosting her?"

"No—that's her new beau!"

"Neala, you look dreadfully pale…"

Through the clamor of voices, Neala managed to grasp one blessed fact: the man holding her firmly, both hands now around her upper arms, was Grayson Faulkner. *Not* the murderer. She sagged, gasping in air, only realizing then how close she had come to swooning like a pea-brained idiot.

His voice murmured close to her ear, "All right now?"

She tried to speak, but nodding her head seemed simpler.

Around them the crowd's attention shifted as voices shouted

out that the race was about to begin. Pressed from all sides, Neala felt Grayson's arm wrap firmly about her waist. His commanding voice ordered people to give her room to breathe.

From the other end of the ring the starting pistol rang out. Neala struggled to focus on the clutch of horses thundering down the track, but fear dragged at her lungs and weakened her limbs. Beside her, someone burst into excited screams for horse number two; on the other side several people yelled for Burberry, horse number six. Everyone surged forward, straining to see. The protective arm sheltering her fell away.

The horses rounded the first bend, less than fifty feet from where Neala stood. Excitement finally swept her along in its momentum, dousing most of the panic. She leaned forward, caught up in the drama.

Something hard plowed into her back.

Neala lost her balance and fell against the rail with such force the thin wood splintered.

With the sound of galloping hooves and screaming voices flooding her senses, she toppled onto her knees into the dirt track, directly in the path of the horses.

Gray didn't know how it happened, nor did he care. He only knew that clutching hands had yanked him away from Neala, and because of it she was about to be trampled to death. Diving headfirst onto the track, he rolled over her, wrapping her in his arms. A cacophony of screaming and shouting, thudding hooves and choking dust swirled around them. He felt several blows, but only peripherally. Somehow he managed to roll them back underneath the fence, into the grass, where dozens of hands appeared to help.

"Get back, give us room!" he ordered, then spoiled the effect by coughing until his eyes watered.

"Is she dead?"

"I never saw anything like it in my life…"

"What a magnificently brave gesture…"

"Blamed foolish if you ask me. Both of 'em should be dead…"

The roaring in his head stabilized, then vanished altogether. With more force than politeness Gray shoved aside the hands attempting to pat him down, to pull Neala away from his death grip. "Fetch Dr. Dabney," he snapped next. "Now!"

Carefully he lifted himself off her limp body. Advice, exclamations of horror and excitement whirled in the air, coating like dust. Gray scarcely noticed. Frantically he searched for blood, for splintered bones. She was unconscious, but her breathing was steady, and even as he finally allowed himself a shuddering sigh of relief she stirred, eyelids fluttering. A garbled moan whispered between dirt-caked lips. "Can I get some water, a cloth?" he asked, without looking away from Neala.

Seconds later he was handed a large napkin and a collapsible metal cup filled with water. "Thanks. Easy does it," Gray spoke to Neala as he carefully dabbed her mouth and face. "Don't move, Ne—Miss Shaw," he corrected himself. *In a public venue protect her reputation as well as her life…* "Just be still, now, and let me make sure nothing is broken."

"I say, is he getting fresh with her?"

• "Shouldn't you wait for the physician?"

"Is there any blood?"

"Neala! Neala?"

A young woman pushed her way through the crowd and dropped to her knees beside them. Because he recognized her as one of Neala's friends, Gray didn't order her to leave.

"Oh, sir, is she all right?" she asked, stretching her hand to fleetingly brush trembling fingers against Neala's.

"I think so. Here—let me shift her around, examine her head. If there's no evidence of cranial injury, how about if we lay her head in your lap?"

"Oh, certainly!"

His own fingers none too steady, Gray probed Neala's scalp, dislodging pins until his hands filled with a mass of tangled, dust-coated curls. A dusky bruise smeared her forehead, but he thought that particular blow occurred when she hit either the railing, or the ground; he'd seen the damage a horse's hoof could inflict, and he thanked whatever gods were listening that Neala mercifully had been spared. Gently he probed her shoulders and collarbones, felt her stir, then stiffen.

"What...you *doing?*" she mumbled. Her eyelids finally lifted, and a pair of smudged brown eyes dazedly searched his face. "Grayson...did you know there's blood...on your lip? I have a hankie..." Her arm actually twitched as she made as though to search for it, and she didn't seem to notice her lapse into familiarity.

Gray needed to remove her from the crowd, as soon as he collected the strength. For the moment, he captured her hand, held it. "Never mind my blood. We need to find out how badly you're injured."

"Neala, dear Neala." Her friend brushed a lock of hair from Neala's face. "Can you see me? It's Dora. Do you know me?"

Gray watched the emotions streak through those defenseless eyes. He could read each one as easily as if he were inside her head—confusion, fear, dawning awareness...and embarrassment. "Dora. I'm so sorry. Someone pushed me. Are the horses all right?" She blinked a time or two, focused back on Gray. "Are you all right, Mr. Faulkner? Did they push you, too?"

"Neala, he saved your life," Dora exclaimed, undisguised adulation plain in her voice. "He threw himself right into the path of the horses to rescue you!"

Behind them Gray heard more feminine demands to be let through, that Neala was their friend. The crowd around them

was growing; doubtless a near-tragedy provided more entertainment than a humdrum horse race. Human beings were
ever a bloodthirsty lot.

The murderer was likely one of the onlookers, standing a
yard away from Neala, yet Gray wouldn't know it.

Rage pumped through his veins, flooding out the fear for
Neala that had sheeted him with ice. If the bounder chose to
lift a knife or even a gun to finish the job, at the moment Gray
doubted he'd even be able to draw his own weapon. Even if
he managed to, he couldn't very well fire into a crowd of
teeming hotel guests, whose only crime was morbid curiosity.

He hadn't felt so helpless—so impotent—since he'd
watched Marty die in his arms.

He didn't realize the crowd had drawn back and grown
quiet until he felt a light hand brush the fist he had pressed
against his thigh. He blinked, realizing he'd been searching
every face that surrounded them, and that doubtless his gaze
reflected the rage. With difficulty he dropped his head, inhaled
several more calming breaths, and focused back on Neala,
wrapping his fingers around her wrist. Beneath them, her pulse
thrummed a rapid tattoo.

"Mr. Faulkner," she whispered, her eyes dull with awareness, "he tried again, didn't he? The killer…he tried again."

"What are you talking about, Neala? Are you sure a hoof
didn't strike her head, Mr. Faulkner?"

"Did she say the chap tried to kill her?"

Like a flash fire voices rose afresh, speculating, question-
ing, demanding answers. Neala's other friends shoved their
way through, their questions peppering him like buckshot.

With a bitten-off oath Gray abruptly lifted Neala into his
arms and surged to his feet, forcing the onlookers to scramble
backward out of the way. "I'm taking her to the infirmary. The
doctor can meet us there." He pinned Dora with a look. "Don't

repeat a word of what you just heard. Do you understand? Not a word to your friends, or to anyone else."

"I—all right. But I don't understand. What—"

"There's nothing to understand. She's overwrought, frightened, only half-conscious. You'll cause incalculable harm to her reputation by repeating nonsensical words. Clear a path!" he shouted in a voice honed on subduing hard-bitten criminals.

Against him he could feel the warmth of Neala's slight weight, the tentative flexing of her hands on his shoulders, her breath in his ear. *She could have died, right in front of him. Just like Marty.*

"If you ever run off without me again, I'll let the killer have you."

She shuddered once, then seemed to shrink within herself, making Gray even more angry, this time with himself. Stupid, heartless cad.

"You've a right to be angry." The words drifted on a sigh between them. "But I'd appreciate it if you'd save the lecture for later. Otherwise I'm afraid I might enrage you more by weeping." He heard her swallow twice. "I'd really rather not. My nose always turns red and becomes stuffy. I detest stuffy noses."

He never would have expected to feel like smiling after a near-death experience, but the urge blindsided Gray like a punch to the solar plexus. In his entire life, he could not remember a time when the threat of feminine tears provoked the urge to laugh. Without exception, tears hardened his heart into what one mewling woman had called "a lump of lead, like the bullets you shoot from your gun."

Of course, never in his life had he met a woman like Neala Shaw.

"I'm not as angry with you as I am myself," he heard himself admit. "I should have guessed that, after this morning's walk, you'd finally do something to rebel against our sham courtship."

"Not completely." She pressed a hot cheek against his neck, and Gray had to strain to hear the rest. "Not like Adrian… He lied, about where he was going. I didn't lie." Gray felt a tear dampen his skin, slide down beneath his collar. "Told bellhop to tell you where I was going. So you'd know. You'd know…" Her voice broke.

"Yes," Gray said, "I knew. I found you, Neala. You're safe now."

She lifted her head. Tear-dark eyes blindly stared over his shoulder. The swelling bruise mocked his statement. "For how long?" she choked out. "How much longer will I be safe, G-Grayson?"

The answer to her question that popped into his mind unnerved him, so Gray didn't respond at all. Holding her close against his chest, he carried her the rest of the way to the hotel clinic in tomb-like silence.

Chapter Fourteen

Upon hearing about Neala's misadventure at the race track, Will Crocker debated over the advisability of risking a visit to her room. Rumors of her physical state flew thick and fast. She was mortally injured. She was only bruised. She'd broken bones.

Worst of all for Will was the uniform consensus that her suitor, Mr. Faulkner, had carried her away from the track. In his arms.

In the end he couldn't help himself. The following afternoon, after cleaning up as best he could, he hurried down to the head groundskeeper's quarters. Lloyd owned a cracked but full-length mirror, and he was generous about allowing other workers to borrow it whenever they had their half day off and wanted to spruce themselves up. Well, it wasn't Will's half day off, but he still wanted to look the best he could.

He studied his reflection glumly; compared to that arrogant Grayson Faulkner, Will more resembled a train-hopping hobo. Angrily he swiveled and left the room. Looks, he'd learned, could reflect how much money a man possessed, but looks could also camouflage. At the moment he was a lowly groundskeeper. But one day, that would change.

As he cut furtively behind trees and cottages to avoid questions from fellow workers, Will fixed a picture in his mind of Neala. People liked her—well, most people liked her. Some of those high-nosed debutantes—the "belles," they were called—treated her the way they treated Will, as though she were invisible. That was another connection between them, he reminded himself. With Neala, he never felt invisible. To Will's way of thinking, Neala was far more beautiful than any of the White Sulphur Springs belles. She smiled at him as if he were a real person. She'd turned the humiliating experience with the wasps into a shared secret between just the two of them. And she'd revealed a sliver of her mind that Will figured she hadn't shared with anyone else.

A newspaper reporter, of all things!

Though the very idea outraged his sense of what God intended a woman to be, Will didn't care. She was changing something inside of him, something that, if acted upon, would turn his entire life upside down.

If his mother knew what he was thinking—what he was doing—likely she'd throw one of her bad fits in an attempt to control him. Will smiled grimly. Oh, he understood her, right enough, understood from years of experience that the best tactic was to allow her to maintain the illusion that he was her meek, obedient son. She'd been dealt a loser hand, right enough, and he'd spent most of his life helping her atone for it. But this time things had changed.

This time he would have to be more firm about his own goals. As he approached the main hotel, Will decided that after his visit with Neala, he would write his mother. He wouldn't be there to calm the inevitable hysterics, but he also wouldn't have to defend himself from her fists, or flying crockery. Hopefully, by the time he was able to return home for a visit, she would listen to the details of what he planned to do.

As he slipped inside, he realized that he needed for his mother to understand something he scarcely comprehended himself. He also realized a groundskeeper's presence in these cool, largely deserted hallways constituted a significant risk, one he would not have been willing to take two months earlier. Fortunately he passed only two guests, who after mildly curious glances at him continued without comment on their way.

Sweat gathered in his armpits, the small of his back. With each step, a growing seed of doubt sprouted more leaves. Perhaps he shouldn't be exposing himself this way. Opening himself to more ridicule, or worse, condescension. What if Faulkner was there? Or the tyrannical widow?

Only the memory of Neala's friendly smile propelled his feet to the third floor, down the hall to her room. Sure enough, Faulkner was sitting on a chair just outside the door, his arms folded across his chest, the gun openly displayed at his side. A gun, at White Sulphur Springs! The management should do something other than fawn over the man, but Will knew they wouldn't because of the Faulkner name.

If a nobody like William Crocker strapped a gun to his waist, he'd be in jail before sunset. His mother was right about one thing. Life wasn't fair.

Will's jaw jutted; he walked right up to Faulkner. "I'm here to see Miss Shaw." He forced himself to sound courteous instead of demanding. "I heard about the mishap, at the track yesterday? Is she all right?"

"You're one of the groundsmen? Crocker, right? The one we spoke to briefly the other day."

"That's right. Will, Will Crocker."

Despite himself he shifted uneasily. There was something about the way those lake-blue eyes stared at him, as though they were peeling him like a grape and exposing his naked soul. Faulkner's right hand rested on the butt of the gun.

With the resolve cultivated over the years, Will maintained his air of polite calm. He also knew instinctively that, should he move in a way that Faulkner didn't care for, the barrel of that gun would likely be sticking in his face. Belatedly he remembered his cap, whipped it off, stood twisting it in his hands. "She's special, is Miss Shaw. Not like most of the others… She's been nice to me."

"I saw that."

The dry tone stung. "I'd like to speak to her," he repeated. "I won't stay long—I know it's unusual, but…" He stopped, words sticking in his throat. He'd as soon take a bullet than beg.

"Wait a moment. I'll see if she's awake," Faulkner announced unexpectedly. He opened the door, went inside and shut it in Will's face.

For a few shard-tipped seconds Will considered barging in. He had as much right as that uppity bruiser to pay Neala a visit. More, if truth be told.

Fortunately the door opened again almost immediately.

"Come in," Faulkner invited in that same irritating dry tone. "She's delighted you're here."

Will brushed by without even glancing up; Neala was ensconced in a lounger, with a light quilt covering her from the waist down. Several bouquets of flowers were scattered about, reminding him anew of her popularity, as well as his own cloddishness in not bringing her flowers himself, and him a groundsman.

Sunlight poured through a window behind the lounger, highlighting her pale face, a bruise on her forehead and a couple of scratches on her cheekbone. But she was alive. And her eyes were smiling at him. He ignored the widow seated in a rocking chair nearby even though her expression conveyed more plainly than words that lowly hired help deserved about as much welcome as a chamber pot that needed to be emptied.

"Thank you so much for stopping by, Mr. Crocker," Neala said, and Will focused his attention on the only person who was glad to see him.

"I don't mean to intrude," he began. The old woman made a noise deep in her throat, and Will felt a band of red climbing his cheeks.

"You could never intrude." Neala awkwardly gestured toward the room. "I know we're breaking all manner of propriety—"

"Absolutely," the widow interrupted testily. "Which is why I shall remain here, and visits with members of the opposite gender will be strictly limited to ten minutes."

Dressed in black, with a diamond stickpin flashing at her throat, she reminded Will of a buzzard circling in to feed on its carcass.

"Mrs. Wilkes, do stop intimidating every male who crosses the threshold." Neala smiled at Will. "Don't pay her any mind. She reacted the same way to several other gentlemen callers."

Will looked away.

"I beg your pardon," Neala said. "That remark didn't come out the way I intended."

"Another reason I plan to remain here," Mrs. Wilkes put in, laying aside a small embroidery hoop. "All this drama has muddled your mind as well as your mouth." She peered at Will over dainty spectacles. "Well, don't stand there gawking at her, Mr. Crocker. You've obviously come to inquire as to her health. Kindly do so before she commits another faux pas."

Will half turned to leave.

"Please, Mr. Crocker," Neala said. "Think what a favor you've accorded me, giving me someone else to talk to. Here— pull up a chair. Tell me if you've encountered any bees, or forgotten your cap again."

Gratefully Will started for the chair, but Faulkner abruptly materialized in the doorway, grabbed the chair and plonked it down a good three yards away from Neala. Then he went to the other side of the lounger to stand beside her, looking more than ever like a scowling bodyguard instead of a devoted escort.

An escort who apparently ignored, with the old widow's blessing, those ten-minute limitations on visiting.

Will would ponder the implications—later. "I've not forgotten my cap anymore," he said to Neala as he sat down. "But I did forget to bring you some of the black-eyed Susans I was pruning earlier."

When she gave him that shy, delighted smile, the one that made him feel more alive than he'd felt in years, Will wondered if his life could ever be the same, when the time came for him to leave White Sulphur Springs.

Chapter Fifteen

Four days after her nightmare day at the races, Neala gave in to Grayson's persistent bullying to accompany him for a walk about the grounds. The fact that she was still afraid chafed both spirit and mind, because she had never considered herself a spineless person afraid of her own shadow. As a devout believer, she was assured that God Himself watched over her, protected her, strengthened her.

Yet ever since the head-ringing had ceased, and she had worked the stiffness out of her knocked-about muscles, Neala was afraid to be alone. And she was more confused than ever. Why would God allow such dreadful calamities, when for all her life she had tried so hard to be a good person and a faithful follower?

Mrs. Wilkes produced a pragmatic maid, hired to remain in Neala's room overnights; Neala was too grateful to protest any more intrusions upon her privacy. An Ulster Scot brimming with self-confidence, Deirdre McGee towered over Neala, more resembling a stevedore than a lady's maid. She certainly snored like a stevedore, but Neala surprisingly found a modicum of comfort from the noise. Surely no self-respecting assassin would risk tangling with an Amazon whose snores fair shook the bed.

Truth be told, Deirdre was almost as tall as Grayson. Grayson himself pronounced Deirdre an acceptable night watchwoman, he called her with a grin.

"At least she saves me from camping outside your door every night. I'm told Mrs. Wilkes is relieved."

Neala tried to emulate his matter-of-fact attitude. But the realization that he had been prepared to sleep outside her door jangled her nerves almost as much as her fear of another murder attempt. She didn't understand Grayson at all. Every time she remembered regaining consciousness, felt his strength surrounding and protecting her, her stomach flip-flopped like a beached trout. Cravenly she admitted to herself that one of the reasons she didn't want to go for a walk was because she would be alone with Grayson.

"Here. There's a south wind blowing." Deirdre handed Neala her plain straw hat, to which she had nimbly fastened a spray of silk flowers. "This 'twill keep that sheep's head o' hair from curling about your face. And mind you don't come back with a crop of freckles."

"You're worse than Mrs. Wilkes," Neala complained with a small smile. "Sometimes I'm tempted to shear my head like a sheep."

"Himself wouldn't be liking that a' tall."

A light blush heated Neala's cheeks. With the passing of every hour her feelings toward Grayson seemed to shift and alter like windblown desert sand. When his manner was aloof, almost abrasive, Neala simply erected her shield of friendly tolerance toward an irritable puppy. But when he looked at her in a certain way, when the cold blue of his eyes deepened and seemed to pour over her like water from a lovely sun-warmed lake, her heart squeezed until it was difficult to breathe, and her palms turned all clammy. Because she simply did not feel the time was appropriate for entertaining such feelings, Neala found it easier to provoke Grayson than to risk having him catch her gazing at him with calf's eyes.

Which was why for the past twenty-four hours she had resisted going for a walk. If Grayson were forced to come to her rescue again, Neala wasn't sure she could control those jangled feelings clamoring inside for release.

"Himself doesn't have any say in what I choose to do with my hair," she told Deirdre firmly as she pinned the hat equally firmly in place.

"Ah-mm," Deirdre responded. "Keep telling yourself that, lassie."

A knock sounded. Reflexively Neala froze, then sidled over behind her bed, her gaze fixed on the door. Shaking her head, Deirdre lumbered over, yelled through the panel to ask the knocker's identity, and opened it with a resigned flick of a gaze toward Neala so that Grayson could enter.

"Miss Shaw still shies at every noise, Mr. Faulkner."

Gray dropped his homburg on the writing table and strolled across to Neala. "She's cause enough," he said. When he reached her, in a surprise move he lifted her hands, carried them to his mouth, and dropped a light kiss on the back of each one. "But that's going to change." He tugged her gently around the bed, then led her across the room. "Starting right now." He returned his hat to his head while never releasing his firm grip on Neala's forearm. "The first outing is always the hardest," he murmured. "Trust me, Neala. I won't let him close enough to even think about harming you."

"Aye, you do that," Deirdre added. "Bring her back with a bloom to her cheeks. I'll be seeing you tonight, miss. Ten o'clock, without fail." Shutting the door, she handed Grayson the key, then walked past them down the hall, her heavy skirts practically wide enough to brush both sides of the walls.

"Her father was a dockworker from Derry," Neala said, watching her dignified passage. Words spilled forth as she battled a stubborn case of the flutters. "And she told me her mother was the only daughter of a Scottish minister who was killed in the siege. They emigrated to Pennsylvania. Deirdre has six brothers. Six! Apparently she grew up on stories of battles rather than baking. By the time she was fourteen she could arm wrestle—and win—half the boys who worked in the steel mill where her father worked."

"Where on earth did Mrs. Wilkes dig her up?"

"She knows everything about everyone. I believe Deirdre was a nanny for some acquaintance of Mr. Carnegie, and Mrs. Wilkes met her here last year when that family came down for the season. They're letting me borrow her right now."

Grayson chuckled, the low deep-in-his-chest laugh that tripped Neala's heart up and set it to pattering. "Between you and Mrs. Wilkes, every guest here is wrapped around your little fingers."

"Everyone except the man who wants to kill me."

Beneath her fingers she felt the muscles in his arm flex. "Let's talk, all right? While we walk?"

Anything was easier to bear than having the heart flutters over a man who didn't like females, especially cowardly ones. "All right. Will you be able to talk and keep watch?"

"I reckon I'll manage," he drawled. Then, more seriously, he said, "We've both read through everything in that trunk over the past several days, and I think it's time to take the next step."

"Next step?"

For a moment or two he didn't respond. Neala opened her mouth to inquire again, then closed it when Grayson resumed talking.

"I've had people looking for your brother," he said.

"Adrian?" The world tilted; the breeze stilled. "Did they find him? Is he… Is he—?"

His hand covered her fingers, and Neala realized she'd been practically clawing his arm.

"Last fall, his name was on the passenger list of a schooner whose destination was Charleston. My contacts haven't picked up any further information. But he was alive a year ago, Neala."

Her breath expelled in a long sigh. "Thank you. You don't have to keep looking for him, Grayson. But I appreciate your efforts."

"I don't know why you care. I've heard and seen no evidence of familial responsibility on your behalf. In fact, more than once I've considered the possibility that—" He stopped. "Never mind. Let's talk about your grandfather, hmm? I've come up with a plan."

Stung by his uncomfortably accurate summation of her brother, Neala grappled with hurt for a moment before she decided to simply be grateful that at least Adrian could still be alive. She pinned a smile on her face. "What's your plan?"

"Since the best we can determine all the deaths are limited to your paternal grandfather's side of the family, I'm thinking we need to investigate Neal Shaw more closely. So—" he glanced down at her, then hugged her arm to his side "—I'm leaving for North Carolina day after tomorrow," Grayson announced quietly. "And you're coming with me."

"I see." Neala chewed over his words for a few moments. "That sounds like a good plan to me. Deirdre shouldn't…" She plowed doggedly ahead. "What I mean is, it's unfair to expect Deirdre to be my faithful watchdog during the day as well as all night. I'm sorry I'm not brave enough."

"Don't be ridiculous. I'm relieved." He glanced down. "You

may not have noticed, but basically I didn't give you a choice in the matter of coming or no."

"Oh." The tightness crushing her middle loosened a bit. "That's true. You didn't ask, you ordered." Yet instead of feeling resentment over his high-handedness, a long-absent sense of freedom trickled through her. Freedom—and security, because she would be with Grayson.

She sifted through possibilities, her enthusiasm growing. "Do you know, I should have thought of going to North Carolina myself, last spring. We knew Grandfather settled in Wilmington, but never the address where he lived. I doubt there's anyone still alive who knew him. I mean, it has been fifty years."

"That's why it's known as detective work. Here's your chance to do some investigating like your favorite heroine, Nellie Bly."

"You're absolutely right. And I shall do so even when you laugh at me, like you're about to do." They exchanged smiles, but Neala's faded swiftly. "How do we slip away from here without alerting the murderer?" she asked, her voice quavering a bit on the last word.

Gray stopped suddenly, and before Neala could draw a breath he'd pulled her off the path beneath the boughs of a monstrous hemlock.

"Shh." He wrapped her in an embarrassingly close embrace, dropping his head until his lips brushed her ear. "I think someone might be following us. I need for you to relax, put your arms around me as though we're about to share a kiss. Can you do that for me, Neala?"

Share a kiss? "Um…of course. Are we?"

He'd turned his head slightly, his gaze scanning the rows of cottages off to their right, then the trees lining Howard's Creek, where they were headed. "Hmm? Are we what?"

"Nothing." Neala plunked her forearms against the soft lawn shirt and casual jacket he had worn that day. His necktie, she noted, matched to perfection his deep blue eyes. "Is this acceptable?"

"Only if you're about to shove me away." He returned his attention to her, searched her face a long uncomfortable moment. Something flickered within the blue gaze, something silvery and ominous that backed up the breath in Neala's lungs. "Here," he murmured, "like this." He drew her arms up and placed them on his shoulders. "No, don't stiffen up. Relax, Neala. I promise, this won't hurt."

"I think you're taking undue advantage of me, Mr. Faulkner," Neala muttered against his shirtfront. "There's nobody following us at all."

Grayson went still. Then, very softly, he said, "If I'd wanted to take undue advantage of you, Miss Shaw, I could have done so on many other occasions than this one. Furthermore—" his hand burrowed between them to cup her chin "—if there's advantage being taken here, more likely it's all on your side."

"M-my side?"

"Mm-mm." His other arm shifted to embrace her waist, and the hand holding her chin slowly slid up to a couple of wayward curls dangling in front of her ear. "I think it might be this hair you love to hate." His fingers lifted the curls, which wrapped around them in hairy chains. "I can't seem to stop wanting to do this. I've never felt hair so soft, yet so strong it defies every attempt at control."

His voice deepened, and Neala's knees decided to buckle. "Mr. Faulkner…Grayson. I don't think this is—"

"Shh." His head dipped and he cut off her protest with a light but electrifying kiss. "You think too much, love. This is the Old White. We're surrounded by eligible bachelors and available belles who contrive to steal a kiss or two at every opportunity." He kissed her again, another teasing brush that singed every nerve along Neala's spineless spine.

"Fine," she managed to say, and hauled herself out of his arms. The effort felt as though she were trying to wrest herself free of a vat of molasses. "We can kiss, then. But you may *not* call me terms of endearment. They're lies, and I won't have it." Breathless, she struggled to control the annoying trembling, and was forced to bite her lip as well as lock her knees.

"Most women," Grayson mused to the branches above their heads, "enjoy my, ah, terms of endearment."

"I'm surprised you even know any," Neala sputtered, "seeing as how you don't regard women very highly. Unless you're taking advantage, that is."

"Little cynic. You surprise me, Neala." He grinned wickedly, and Neala to her utter stupefaction found herself grinning back. "I was frankly halfway steeling myself for either a slap or a swoon."

"Stuff and nonsense," she retorted. "Your sisters read too many gothic novels. I grew up watching my friends turn flirting into an art, instead of reading about it. Pretending to evade a kiss is a time-honored device to allow a pursuing male to feel the matter is in his hands, when of course it's the—" She stopped, a blush hotter than the summer sun scalding her cheeks. She could not believe what had dribbled out of her wayward mouth, and almost yielded to the temptation to flee like the simpering damsels in gothic novels.

"I'm—"

"If you apologize, I'll kiss you again. And this time it won't be a mere touching of our lips."

Wide-eyed, Neala searched Grayson's face, tried to determine if the light in the back of his eyes was laughter or irritation. "I don't know what to do with you," she whispered, half to herself. "Nothing seems to be the way I thought. The way it's supposed to be. I don't understand you—I don't understand anything." Her voice wobbled. "Everyone in my family but my brother is dead, and I don't know why. Now the murderer wants to kill me. It's not right. It's not fair. And—and I can't even pray like I used to, can't hear God talking to me anymore."

The painful revelations burst forth, smearing the tranquil air with their corrosive sense of betrayal. "All my life I've trusted God. Ever since I was a child. I sat on Grandfather's knee, and I could recite all the Beatitudes to him when Adrian couldn't even manage the Twenty-Third Psalm. I only missed church once, because I had the measles. I've tried, for my entire life, to be good. To honor God because—" she gulped back a sob "—because I t-trusted Him."

"Neala…"

She flung up her hand, pressed her palm against his lips. "No! Don't say anything. This is all your fault, anyway. Yours, and Mrs. Wilkes, for harping on the illusion that you're courting me, until I don't know what's real and what's not. Well, for your information, Mr. Black-sheep-of-the-family Faulkner, I don't want to marry you. Right now, I wouldn't marry anybody even if I did want to because it wouldn't be fair. Do you understand me?"

"If you don't lower your voice, you'll be able to ask half a dozen or so interested guests if they understand. I confess I don't, but—"

"Flumagudgin. You don't understand. I don't understand."

Oh, the glorious freedom of tossing all restraints aside, prying open the locked box of her feelings and heaving them over the side and into the whirlwind. "Understanding is irrelevant. All that matters is that you promised to protect me, and to help me find out who is trying to kill me. Seducing me is *not* necessary. You can kiss me if you must—but only while we remain here at the Old White." She lifted her chin. "After we leave, you will not take advantage due to propinquity."

"I've never responded well to ultimatums," Grayson answered in such a mild tone Neala's passionate tirade abruptly collapsed. "I don't want to marry you, either, so we can snip that particular thorn and be done with it."

He took a step closer, but his hands were clasped behind his back so Neala was unalarmed.

"As for the rest, seems to me you're placing a bit more blame on God for all your troubles than is probably fair. From the little I recollect, God's not the one responsible for all your woes. Mankind's the culprit, love—sorry. *Neala.*" He arched an eyebrow. "I may still call you Neala, right? You've not objected to that familiarity, nor have you shown any reservations about calling me by my Christian name."

Was there a trap buried somewhere within the smooth-tongued sentences? Neala didn't know. She did know, however, that she was drained, and bewildered, by her outrageous behavior. "I much prefer my Christian name over terms of affection," she said tiredly, "and since I've been calling you Grayson for weeks, it would be hypocritical to object now."

"Fine. Now, as I was saying, God isn't killing off the members of your family. The responsibility for that falls squarely on the deranged but nonetheless human individual inflicting the mayhem. He's the one to whom you ought to direct all this wrath and hurt." He lifted a hand and Neala automatically tensed, but he only brushed a windblown lock of hair off his forehead. "As for divine protection, I have to say in my experience—which I'm sure you'll concede is far broader than your own—that there is no such thing. God's in His heaven, I suppose, but I've witnessed precious few examples of proof that He intervenes in human affairs."

Diverted, Neala studied him for a moment. "Do you really

believe that?" she finally asked. "How can you? Of course God intervenes—" She stopped.

For almost eighteen months she had been pleading with the Lord to help her understand, to give her peace. Patience. Perseverance. And thus far she was limping along blindly, sliding into despair instead of peace. Resignation instead of patience. And in another second she might throw her hands up and ask Grayson to stake her like a sacrificial goat, just so she could get her murder over with.

What kind of Christian did that make her?

"I'd be seven kinds of fool to believe anything other than what I said," Grayson retorted, his voice short. "You're far better off depending on your own resources, using the mind God gave you, and strengthening whatever skills are necessary to survive. When you left Sumner you came here, didn't you? Not because God told you to, but because you thought this would be a safe place."

"Sumner?"

"Sorry." He shrugged. "The Isabella Chilton Academy for Single Females. When I was a boy, the place was a family estate, known throughout the South as Sumner. I still think of it that way. At any rate, you left because you made the decision to do so. Now that you've been discovered, another course of action is called for on our parts. Ours, not God's. When we leave here for—"

He clamped his lips together. "Never mind," he muttered next, and before Neala had time to blink twice he'd casually whipped out an arm and tugged her back against his chest. In movements too swift to block he deftly removed hat pins until he lifted off her hat and dropped it to the grass. "I think I need another kiss," he whispered against her mouth, and followed words with action.

Only this was no brief, almost teasing kiss. This time he

lingered, drawing Neala into a blinding cocoon where shooting stars burst into Catherine wheels behind her tightly closed eyes and the ground beneath her feet seemed to dissolve.

When he finally released her, he pressed her cheek against his chest and rested his against the top of her head. His arms held her close. Beneath her ear she could hear the thunderous beating of his heart, feel his rapid breathing stir her hair. "Neala Shaw," he eventually murmured, then heaved a long sigh. "Since I don't see the Almighty sending along any other reinforcements, I will protect you to the best of my ability. But I can't help but wonder…" he finally set her back, his hands clasping her upper arms, thumbs moving in restless circles that did little to calm Neala's own runaway pulse "…who's going to protect me from you?"

"What do you mean?" It was a fatuous question at best, but there was no help for it. Her mind was naught but the remnants of sparks from those Catherine wheels. "Are you… Do you mean the murderer might harm you, to get to me? If so, I release you. I don't want anyone else hurt because of me. Please, Grayson. I couldn't bear it."

"All right. Don't worry about it, Neala, it's all right. I can take care of myself." He squeezed her arms, smiled at her, a strangely bemused smile. "Believe me, I've been in far more dangerous circumstances."

"Oh. Well, then…" She couldn't seem to stop gazing up into his face, couldn't stop a tickly smile of her own. "I'll try not to worry about your safety, but I will warn you that I find your notion of God dreadfully hilter-skilter. Furthermore, just because I'm muddleheaded right now doesn't mean I'm wrong. On our trip to North—"

"Shh." Instantly his palm covered her mouth. His smile disappeared. After tugging her back into his arms, he lowered his head so that his lips brushed her ear. "Neala…you deserve to know," came a husky murmur that tripped her breath anew, "the first time I kissed you was deliberate. You see, somebody really is following us, and I needed ah…a plausible maneuver, to confirm what my instincts were telling me."

"Very clever," Neala murmured, then cleared her throat. "Who was it?"

"Couldn't tell." He shrugged. "I do know today's not the first time, however."

"Oh." A shiver that had nothing to do with being kissed under the trees danced along her veins. "But you kissed me again. Why did you—I mean, it wasn't necessary…"

He lifted his head, muttered something beneath his breath Neala decided she was better off not knowing, then cupped her face in his hands. "Someone should have taught you prudence years ago. Looks like I'm stuck with the job." His teeth flashed in a quick smile.

"It's not a joking matter."

"How do you know I was joking?" He pressed his thumbs against her lips. "Shh. We'll discuss it later. Right now, I need you to listen. Until we're on the train—and then only if I tell you—don't mention our plans out loud. Not where we're going, not when we're going. Nothing. Don't tell anyone, particularly Mrs. Wilkes."

"Deirdre?" Neala queried hazily. Grayson had rendered her incapable of concentration. His eyes were bluer than a blue jay's feather, and his hands…oh, but they were warm, warmer than—

"I've already told Deirdre. We need to maintain a point of contact here, and I can't think of anyone safer. That woman could outsilence a tombstone if the situation merited it." Finally he released her, stepping back and casually adjusting his cuffs. "But absolutely nobody else can know. Not your friends, not the maid, or the bellhops. Nobody but Deirdre."

"I understand," Neala said, and swallowed hard. He sounded as though he genuinely admired Deirdre McGee. "I understand, Grayson. I won't tell anyone other than Deirdre, or talk about it."

All at once she felt exposed, stripped to her drawers, vulnerable and frightened and ashamed. He had kissed her only as a diversion; now he lectured her as though she were six years old. Obviously she was an inferior bolt of cloth compared to her nightly bodyguard. Yet not only had she allowed his kisses—she had reciprocated, which certainly couldn't speak well for her character.

Even more unsettling than her questionable decorum, however, was her wavering faith. No longer was she blithely confident of God's protection. Instead, somehow over the past few weeks she had willingly entrusted her life to Grayson Faulkner, and she was terribly afraid that she had just handed him her heart as well.

Chapter Sixteen

Wilmington, North Carolina
September 1890

The sultry, cloying month of August grudgingly gave way to September. In North Carolina, however, the fry-an-egg-on-stone temperatures refused to acknowledge summer's passing. Gray lounged on the warped front porch of Uriah Coolidge's boardinghouse, where he and Neala had spent a fruitless ten days searching for people who remembered Neal Shaw, of Strathspey, Scotland, and the address where he had lived here in Wilmington, North Carolina.

Dressed casually in uncollared shirt and light flannel trousers, Gray nursed a tepid lemonade while he waited for Neala to return from her visit with the octogenarian grandmother of a woman who for some reason refused to allow a man in her rambling old house. Neala had promised to try and discover the answer to at least that mystery.

Gray leaned his head back against the wicker rocking chair and contemplated the peeling paint on the porch ceiling.

Uriah's wife had run the boardinghouse with the punctilious-
ness of a martinet, according to the older residents. Meals
were plain but plentiful, floors swept, whitewash applied
spring and fall. After she passed, Uriah hired a decent cook,
but he let things go some, though when he took a notion he
was a dab carpenter, and a pure genius with flowers. Gray liked
the man, but more than once found himself marveling that
Uriah still grieved the passing of his wife, even after four
years. Most marriages, as far as Gray could tell, consisted
either of long-suffering tolerance, passionless friendship, or—
he slumped down in the rocker with a reminiscent smile—in
the case of his youngest sister, a mind-numbing succession of
battles as fierce as any fought in the War.

   Then there was Aunt Bella and Uncle Everett. Sighing, he
straightened in the chair and set it to rocking. Their marriage
defied both convention and all Gray's preconceptions; the
wealthy eldest son and heir of one of the South's most prestigious families had married, of all things, a governess. They
used to laugh at the timeworn cliché of it, Gray remembered.
Yet over the two decades of their union they forged a legacy
that withstood every societal spear, every bit of anecdotal
wisdom that had prophesied a doomed relationship.

   Everett and Isabella Chilton contradicted every scrap of
reality Gray had accepted as truth since he was old enough to
wonder why his mother and father never shared a bed.

   Aunt Bella insisted the reason for their abiding relationship
was Jesus. "He's the glue, the reason a man and a woman cling
together and transform two ordinary, ornery individuals into
a couple. A united entity that paradoxically strengthens their
individuality while cementing their couple-ness as well."

   The notion that one could only have a successful marriage
if one were a devout believer annoyed Gray.

   During his travels over the past decade, he'd met a lot of

married folks who did not consider themselves Christian. It was inconceivable that none of them would be allowed to enjoy a life of connubial bliss simply because they did not consider Christ as the head of the household.

He might tackle Neala with the subject. Certainly she possessed more knowledge of Scripture than a rebellious backslider like Gray. He appreciated the fact that she didn't force her faith on anyone, including him. On the other hand, she never tried to hide its importance in her life. Come to think of it, he decided he found her steadfast faith in God almost as annoying as his aunt's. And yet, somewhere deep inside, a part of himself he'd considered long dead seemed to be quickening, prickles of pain in a frostbitten limb. Aunt Bella and Neala had suffered devastating losses, yet both of them faced life with far more optimism than Gray. Sure as he was sitting on Uriah Coolidge's front porch, Gray knew they would credit that optimism to their faith in God.

Abruptly uncomfortable with the train of thought, Gray stirred in his seat, gulped another swallow of lemonade, tried to steer his mind onto another subject. How was he supposed to ask her anything, when she'd absented herself for—he yanked out his pocket watch and glared at the time—two hours? She'd been gone two hours, and it was high time for her to return.

All right, she'd warned him that she enjoyed visiting, expressly ordered him not to "sit on the porch waiting for me all by yourself. Talk to somebody. You've been a detective. Do some detecting."

The smile slowly returned over the memory of her ferociously serious face as she delivered the lecture, just before she left, while a soft wind blew tousled brown curls all about her cheeks and forehead until she'd smashed them beneath her hat. Gray heard her mutter some preposterous expression. Then she'd laughed, waved a hand and set sail down the walk, unaware that he'd watched her until she turned the corner three blocks away.

With a long, cleansing breath, Gray allowed himself the luxury of thinking about nothing but Neala. With each passing day he was growing more accustomed to the strange, still uncomfortable emotions she aroused, even when she wasn't in the room.

She was frightened, yet refused to dissolve into uselessness, or endless bouts of weeping. When she did cry, it was brief, honest, and without apology. Gray found it most unsettling that Neala's occasional emotional lapses did not automatically raise his hackles.

She was homeless, for all intents and purposes orphaned and indigent. Yet she befriended everyone she met, without guile or greed. For some reason, she seemed to simply like people. In the eyes of the world she was helpless, at Gray's mercy, shunned by polite society because she was traveling unchaperoned with a man.

Except by their second night at the boardinghouse, every resident including Uriah was enchanted, and had promised to do what they could to aid her search for her grandfather.

His mother would have ostracized her; despite her overt matchmaking Frances Wilkes would snatch her bald-headed, as Gray's old mammy used to say, and send her off to a convent or something. Then she'd come after Gray with her knitting needles. Aunt Bella… He slugged down the rest of the lemonade and slammed the glass on top of the wicker side table. Aunt Bella would understand, he told himself staunchly. She would understand, because she knew his heart, and Neala's.

The thought of Neala's heart unraveled something inside, something he feared he would never figure out how to wind back together. Because whenever she looked at him with those guileless brown eyes he could see…he could see…

Abruptly he stood, and stomped down off the porch into the blistering sun.

Infuriating female. Where had she taken herself off to? Just because he had determined they were safe here, that their midnight exodus from the Old White had been successful, didn't mean Gray was willing to allow her more freedom than he felt was wise. Yes, he'd agreed she could pay a visit on her own. But he also remembered how he'd watched her marching down the road, and how he'd barely throttled the urge to chase her down. That she was willing to undertake the task without him testified more to her courage than to Gray's confidence in her safety.

He flipped open his watch again. Should have been back an hour ago. How long could it take to ask an old woman if she remembered one Neal Shaw, and what she remembered?

For several moments he paced the hard-packed earth in front of the boardinghouse. Then, with a frustrated oath he set off down the street. If his heart was beating faster, it was due to the heat, not because he was worried; the feelings roiling around his gut were annoyance, not fear for her safety.

But he was responsible for her, blast it.

He never should have agreed to let her go by herself, never should have let the big-eyed waif with her stubborn chin and determined expression talk him out of his responsibility. If something happened to her, if he'd slipped up somehow and the murderer had found out where she was, he didn't know how he'd survive it.

For the first time in years, Gray found himself wanting to believe everything that Neala claimed about God. Like his aunt, she believed the Almighty kept a divine finger on the pulse of every creature, including nondescript birds nobody else cared about or even noticed. To Gray's way of thinking, that either made God a sadistic busybody or, as Neala insisted, an all-loving caretaker, Who was as concerned about Gray as He was Neala.

But if God cared, if God were omnipotent and omniscient, His lack of interference in Neala's plight made no sense. And Neala's faith was faltering because of it.

Gray realized with another unnerving jolt that he didn't want Neala's faith in God to be misplaced.

When he heard her voice, calling his name, and saw her waving her arm, he quickly thrust the uncomfortable thoughts aside. But he couldn't ignore the urge to thank God for her safe return as he lengthened his stride to meet her.

She was smiling; he could see the smile yet he could also see her eyes, and their expression quickened his pulse. "What is it?" He reached her and clasped her hand. "Neala? What is it?"

"I found out," she said breathlessly. "I found out where he lived, Grayson! But I learned more than the address."

Her voice rose, and without thinking twice Gray took her other hand and tugged her close. "Tell me."

"Grayson, Grandfather eloped! He and Grandmother met at their boardinghouse, fell in love, and they eloped!"

White Sulphur Springs, West Virginia

She was gone. For two days, Will trudged through the hours, halfheartedly performing mindless tasks. In between he wandered the grounds, hoping for even a glimpse of Neala.

By the third morning he was forced to accept the truth that she was gone.

Why had she left without telling him goodbye? Rationally he accepted that his feelings toward her were one-sided, futile. But he could not quell the longing any more than he could squash the bitterness twining upward through his insides, like the infernal poison ivy with which the groundskeepers waged a ceaseless war.

On a dreary morning early in September, Will packed up his meager possessions and set off for home. Momma had been writing him twice a week, asking when he would return, demanding information he did not want to share. He dreaded their reunion, and despised himself for it. Something inside him had changed over the past several months at the Old White, something fundamental. Life-altering. His lifelong goals remained the same, but from now on there would be significant modifications in how he achieved them.

Rutter, Virginia

It was late, almost ten at night, when Will reached the lane leading to their house. Crickets chirruped without pause in the stultifying darkness, and somewhere a whip-poor-will called its mate in a mindless repetition that grated his nerves. As a child, he'd been constantly tormented by a couple of snot-nosed brats who lived next door to his grandmother. They used to threaten to whip him, taunting him that God sent a bird demanding that they "whip poor Will."

Grimly Will thrust the memory aside. The future would be different, he vowed with every step down the lane. Different, and brighter.

"William? Is that you?"

His mother appeared in the doorway of the house, the single lantern she held outlining her spare form beneath a shapeless sack dress.

"It's me, Momma!"

When he reached her he dropped his battered suitcase and wrapped her in a cautious hug. "It's good to be home," he said, and released her before she could stiffen.

"It's so good to have you back. I've waited so long, William. I was frightened that you were never coming home. I was afraid that you'd changed your mind, that you were going to betray me like everyone else."

Will casually grabbed his suitcase and stepped inside. "You know better than that. I love you, Momma—I could never betray you. We're in this together, remember?" Slowly his gaze swept the room. "Momma," he finally said, "you knew I was going to be home this evening. Why didn't you clean? I remember how you used to always want me to come home to a—"

"I told you I was afraid you weren't coming!" She crossed her arms across her flat bosom, glared at Will with reproachful eyes. "What use was there to clean? What use is there to do anything, if you're just going to give up? That's what you've come home to tell me, isn't it? That you're giving up our dream?"

Wearily he set about picking up the untidy little room. "I'm never giving up on our dream," he promised her as he collected old mail and scattered newspapers, stacking them in a neat pile. "In fact, I've made a decision, one that will finally bring the dream within our grasp. I want to share with you what I've decided. But not—" he held her gaze until the defiance faded from her expression "—until you promise that you'll start taking better care of yourself when I'm not here."

"I try, William. It's just taking so long. I'm not a young woman any longer, and look at you. Half your life is gone and still we live in a miserable hovel. We've let your grandmother down. And all I hear are promises, promises that never come to pass." Her bottom lip quivered.

Sighing, Will walked over to her. The lantern light was unflattering, giving her the sullen appearance of a hard-bitten cracker. Her lace collar was faded and grungy, ripped in two places. When he realized he was comparing his mother with Neala Shaw, Will had to close his eyes.

"Momma, we're closer now than we've been in over twenty years. I promise to tell you all about it in the morning, after I've had a decent night's sleep."

"Never mind that *I'll* never be able to sleep, wondering what's going on inside your head. I know you, William. There's something changed about you, something I'm not sure I like."

Her voice was rising as she worked herself into one of her tantrums. This time, fortified with what he'd decided over the last weeks, Will refused to be swayed, regardless of the outcome. "Momma, I'm going to bed," he repeated firmly. "I'm exhausted, and I need time to think. You can either go to bed as well, or you can stay out here."

"Don't you treat me like a child! I'm your mother, and I deserve respect. You don't understand—"

"I understand perfectly," he interrupted. The power sweeping through him was heady, like the occasional glass of champagne at the Old White he used to sneak on weekends. He should have stood up to his mother years ago, instead of trying to appease or apologize or simply allow her to manipulate him. *I've had enough, Momma.* "Now you must understand me. All my life I've done whatever you asked, applied myself to the goal of reclaiming what is rightfully mine—a goal *you* determined for me. The goal remains. Only the means of attaining it will change."

He paused, waited. His mother did not respond.

"That's all I plan to say on the matter until morning." Ignoring the hectic color splotching her face, Will leaned down and pressed a kiss against her quivering cheek. "Good night, Momma."

"For you, perhaps. I doubt I'll ever have another good night, thanks to my selfish son." She clamped Will's arm in a frenzied grip. "Don't you walk away from me! If you do, I promise you'll be sorry."

As gently as he could Will pried her fingers away, then held her hand so she couldn't lash out. "Threats won't work anymore, Momma. I've changed. You might as well start accepting this, because I'm not going to change back. And it's all because of her." He grimaced, steeling himself.

"All because…" she hissed, head tilted, muscles in her throat quivering like a rattlesnake's tail. "Who are you talking about, William? Tell me, tell me this instant."

Stoically Will surveyed the woman who was his mother, the woman he had idolized, struggled to please, and after forty years finally managed to free himself from. Whatever her reaction, he may as well endure it now than wait until morning.

"Neala Shaw," he stated, and watched all the color leach from her face, leaving her as pale and haggard-looking as a corpse. "I met her, talked with her. She's not at all like those White Sulphur Springs belles. She's not like any woman I've ever known. And that means, Momma, that I'm changing our plans."

He half expected her to lunge for him, to scream invectives, to strike out—all reactions he'd grown used to over the years. This time, however, she surprised him. Worse, unnerved him.

"I'll see you both in perdition first," she said, lips barely moving.

Then she walked around him as though he were invisible, went inside her bedroom and shut the door.

A chill skittered through Will's body. As though he were invisible. For a long time he stood, teetering on the edge of a black, bottomless pit because a snide little voice inside his head warned him that his mother had just renounced him. And he was fading, fading into the darkness, indistinguishable and overlooked, as he had been his entire life.

Neala, he thought, repeating her name in a litany. Somehow he would have to find her again, before it was too late for them all.

Chapter Seventeen

Wilmington, North Carolina

" . . . and it was the town scandal for years," Neala finished, bewilderment spilling over as she shared the story.

Because the afternoon remained unpleasantly warm, Grayson had insisted on renting a hack to drive to the street where, almost sixty years earlier, Neal Shaw had met and fallen in love with Annie Bremmer. Neala scarcely noticed their surroundings; immersed in the past, she let the words flow while her mind grappled for understanding. Insight.

"But I don't understand why it was a scandal," she confided. Again. "There's nothing wrong in what they did. I asked Mrs. Percy if she could try to recall anything else that would explain." She sighed, absently twirling a lock of hair around her finger. "She wasn't very helpful. All she remembered, she kept telling me over and over, was that it was a scandal."

She peered sideways, into Grayson's face. "You have that look again."

"What look would that be?"

"The one like you just swallowed a bite of cake I baked for you, but it tastes like…like coal dust, and you don't want to tell me."

"Mmm. Very colorful," was the unhelpful response. "Neala, I can think of one or two salient causes for a scandal. They lived in the same boardinghouse, which would make it very easy to yield to temptation, and then—"

"Grandfather would *never* have behaved in such an ungentlemanly manner. It wasn't sordid. They fell in love. It's the most romantic story I've ever heard."

"I thought you didn't read gothic novels," Grayson inserted.

His teasing jab worked. Neala swatted his arm. "This is not a novel. This is my family's history. We have to find out what happened. If it really was a scandal, or just gossipmongering that over the years took on a life of its own. That happens, you know."

"Neala, after all this time, second- or third-generation hearsay is the most we can hope for. We'll do the best we can, but you need to prepare yourself for disappointment."

"I'm prepared. But I can also hope for a—a Godly serendipity." Determinedly she lightened her voice, thrusting aside Grayson's pragmatism, and her own qualms. "At least I'm riding in a buggy down the street where they met, and fell in love." More enthusiastically, she finished, "We can park the buggy, take a stroll, just like they must have done."

Despite the bleak, even sordid possibilities swimming beneath the surface, for the first time since Mother and Father were killed, and Adrian deserted her, anticipation buoyed Neala's heart. At last, she was doing more than running away, hiding like a coward while helplessly waiting to be murdered.

"I think this is the street," Grayson said, deftly turning the horse onto a broad tree-lined avenue flanked with elms. He slanted a look toward Neala. "You all right?"

"Perfectly. Well...I, ah, I don't know." She shifted on the seat. Inside her gloves, the palms of her hands had dampened; her fingers chilled. "I thought I was—in fact I couldn't wait for this moment. Now, I feel a bit anxious. Like you reminded me, this could very well turn out to be nothing but another dead end."

"Then we'll just move along to the next clue," Grayson calmly replied. "That's the way it works."

"Of course. You would know, wouldn't you?" She gave him a quick smile. "But I still wish it would work faster."

"Mmm. I remember feeling that way once, until the band of outlaws I was chasing with a U.S. marshal decided to ambush us. Things happened so fast I suffered nightmares for a year."

"You did?"

He nodded. "I did. The marshal was shot in the back. I took one in the shoulder, and for about a half hour I was convinced my time was up."

Neala turned on the seat so she could watch him. He sat there, relaxed and competent, loosely holding the reins and talking, though his eyes were never still, constantly searching out their surroundings, a habit, he'd told her, that had saved his hide more than once. Neala still struggled to reconcile the image of that man with the unruffled one sitting beside her now, a man who seemed both a kind friend, yet an enigmatic stranger. Then there was the urbane gentleman at White Sulphur Springs, who fit among the more exalted guests as to the manor born.

She supposed he *was* born to wealth, seeing as how the Faulkners could stand shoulder to shoulder with the Vanderbilts, Carnegies and Hunts. Not for the first time, Neala wondered why Grayson had separated himself from his family. Miss Isabella refused to divulge any personal information other than the fact that he had endured a difficult childhood. Mrs. Wilkes, on the other hand, peppered Neala with his connections, his striking looks, his wealth, and that she was only too happy to overlook his notoriety if a marriage between Neala and Grayson could be arranged.

That thought triggered a now familiar sensation of stumbling over a log and falling, not to the ground, but into a bottomless abyss.

"You're staring at me. Why?"

Neala quickly averted her gaze but she knew Grayson had spied the hectic blush because he reached across and lightly stroked his finger down one hot cheek. Since they'd left the Old White he hadn't kissed her, or even embraced her. But he certainly seemed to, well, touch her frequently. Never in any manner that would arouse her ire, or that could be labeled disrespectful.

Just enough to keep her middle a-twitter, as Grandmother used to say.

"Such a blush. Now you've aroused my curiosity."

"I was wondering what happened to make your childhood so awful you renounced your family," Neala blurted out, unsurprised when his face hardened into that of the man she'd first met, the one whose heart seemed encased in an iron vault.

"Who's been your informant," he asked without inflection, "my aunt or Mrs. Wilkes?"

"Neither of them," Neala replied. "Miss Isabella mentioned in passing once that you'd had a difficult childhood, and have spent most of your adult life out west, that's all. Mrs. Wilkes glossed over all your peccadilloes because she was determined that I land you for my husband."

"Ah. Well, we've both determined that that particular fate is not likely to occur between us. Like I've told you before, I plan to shun the institution of marriage until I've drawn my last breath."

"I'm quite aware of your feelings on the subject," Neala returned with stilted dignity. "As you should be aware of mine, which preclude not only marriage at this time, but marriage to you at any time."

"Now that we have that settled—" he turned to face her and for a tingling second Neala forgot to breathe "—I'd still like to know what you were thinking to bring a blush to your cheeks that near burned my finger." He returned his attention to the road, then added coolly, "If it was speculation about my childhood, since the curiosity is about to eat you alive, I'll satisfy it—to a degree."

"Fine. Whatever you're comfortable sharing, Mr. Faulkner."

For a moment the only sound between them was the steady clip-clop of the horse's hooves and the faint crunching of the buggy wheels in the packed-dirt street. Then, they both turned to glare at each other, the glares melting into rueful smiles.

"Sorry," they both said together, which prompted laughter, and the atmosphere lightened into the comfortable camaraderie of the past several weeks.

"I'm touchy on the subject of my childhood," Grayson admitted. "But since you're entrusting your life to my care these days, I suppose it's only fair to trust you with my own. In a manner of speaking."

"I didn't mean to pry." Neala hesitated, then laid her hand on his forearm. "You needn't tell me anything, Grayson. I trust you, regardless of whatever happened that turned you so sour in your views toward women. I…um…appreciate you moderating your attitude while you're protecting me."

"It has been an effort."

She balled her fingers and punched the muscular forearm. "And here I was actually thinking about how you unsettle my insides, and that sometimes it's difficult to bre— Oh!" Swiftly she turned away, staring sightlessly at the passing houses. "I can't believe I said that," she mumbled in a small voice.

"Neither can I."

Suddenly he pulled the buggy to the side of the road, stopping underneath the sloping branches of a hundred-year-old elm. "You, Neala Shaw, are by far the most complicated, convoluted woman I've ever known. Certainly the most…indiscreet. I don't know what I'm going to do with you."

As long as he didn't kiss her again she was prepared for just about anything. Neala clamped her bottom lip between her teeth to make sure she didn't speak the thought aloud. "Hopefully you're going to keep me alive," she offered eventually. "And perhaps help me discover who hates my family enough to kill everyone in it."

For some reason, verbalizing the last sentence out loud, on a quiet, well-mannered street in a lovely Southern town on a somnolent late-summer afternoon, ignited the fuse on all the roiling emotion Neala had managed through sheer will to tamp down some place deep out of sight. Without warning icicles frosted her spine. The humid air thickened until she couldn't seem to breathe; a sensation of unreality whirled her into a dizzying vortex where visions of all the members of her dead family pressed closer and closer. "Grayson…" she barely whispered. "Grayson, everyone's dead. They're all dead but me. He wants to kill me. Someone wants to kill me and I've done nothing wrong…"

"Easy, love. You're all right."

Somehow his hand was on the back of her neck, pressing her head down, down. She wanted to fight the pressure but the dizziness was making her nauseous and weak. Vaguely she heard his voice, speaking words she didn't understand except for the tone. She'd never heard him speak so gently. She tried to tell him, but what emerged sounded more like a gasping croak and she gave up. *I give up, Lord. I'd rather go ahead and die than suffer this unbearable waiting.*

"No, you don't want to die. Besides, I'm not going to let you."

"Is your wife unwell, sir?"

"Just overcome by the heat a bit."

"Would you like to bring her inside? We live right here."

"Do come in," a feminine voice urged.

Her soft Southern drawl sounded like Mother. Fresh pain squeezed Neala in a vice but the whirling vortex had slowed. She tried to sit up, mortified to her bones, but Grayson's hand firmly held her.

"Let's wait a bit, love," he said. "I don't want to risk your passing out on me."

"Oh, do bring her inside, out of this dreadful heat. Dolly, could you fetch us some smelling salts, please?"

"Yes, ma'am."

"I'm all right," Neala whispered. "Please, Grayson…I'm all right."

"Of course you are." He finally allowed her to sit up, but his hand cupped her chin and she was subjected to an intense scrutiny that made her close her eyes. "If you're sure it wouldn't be too much of an imposition," she heard him say, "I think perhaps we'll accept your kind offer."

"She looks so pale. Do you need my husband to help you carry her?"

"Thank you, no. I can manage."

She had never been so humiliated in her life, but Neala simply couldn't find the energy to protest. It was as though everything that had happened in the past eighteen months had ambushed her, like those outlaws who had ambushed Grayson. "So sorry," she mumbled without opening her eyes. "Don't understand…"

"You've been carrying a load that would have crumbled a lot of men, certainly every woman I've ever known." Before she quite knew how he'd managed it Grayson was on the street, on her side of the buggy, and lifting her into his arms. "Frankly, I've been waiting for something like this to happen."

He'd been waiting for her to swoon—well, almost swoon, like some silly widgeon. Did that mean he now viewed her with the same sneering contempt with which he viewed all women? The prospect distressed Neala more profoundly than she liked, especially when she felt her eyes sting.

"I'll see to your horse," the man's voice said. "Evie, can you hold the door for them?"

"Yes, dearest," the woman whose voice sounded so like her mother's responded.

"Hold on," Grayson murmured in her ear as he began following the woman called Evie.

"You broke your promise." Desperately Neala swallowed, squeezed her eyelids tightly together. "You called me 'love.' I told you not to use terms of endearment."

"So you did. Sorry, love."

If she'd possessed the strength she would have punched him again. Since she didn't, Neala gave in and relaxed against him like a sack of potatoes. Just for a little while….

Chapter Eighteen

Moments later, Neala was ensconced on what was regrettably known as a fainting couch. The woman, a plump but pretty lady who looked to be in her late fifties, hovered over her with smelling salts, which Neala refused with sufficient firmness for Gray to wave them away. He was crouched beside her on the floor, his face inches from hers. The concern Neala read there reassured her, and within moments she was able to sit upright and apologize for making a spectacle of herself. The couple introduced themselves as Alton and Evie Young. Mr. Young discreetly retired to the other side of the parlor to spare Neala further embarrassment.

"We were out for a drive, exploring where my grandfather lived when he came over from Scotland," Neala explained. At Gray's gentle insistence she took another swallow of the blackberry tea Mrs. Young's maid, Dolly, had provided. "There used to be a boardinghouse on this street. He met my grandmother there."

"How delightful." Mrs. Young beamed. "Well, I can tell you that at one time there were several boardinghouses along here, one of them just two doors down. That one burned down, I'm afraid."

"Burned down?" Neala echoed blankly. "Oh." Swallowing hard, she stared down into the dark swirling tea, but her mind had gone as blank as a fresh sheet of foolscap.

"What about the other boardinghouses? The one we're looking for would have been used in that capacity back in the 1830s," Grayson continued. "We haven't been able to find much else out about it, other than the name of the street, and that—" he hesitated, glancing at Neala, and whatever he saw in her eyes must have provided enough impetus to forge ahead "—that a large magnolia tree grew near the front porch."

And Grandfather used to snip petals off the flowers and sneak them into Grandmother's room. Until the day she died, Grandmother loved the scent of magnolia above all other flowers. Trying with little success not to tremble, Neala handed the cooling tea to the Youngs' maid, who after a quick troubled look at her, took the cup and saucer and whisked from the room.

"Goodness to gracious," Mrs. Young suddenly exclaimed. "Your grandparents must have lived two doors down, then, in the house that burned. I remember that magnolia. Our family's lived on this street since before the conflict with the British in 1812. My mother told us about that boardinghouse, way back when I was a girl. As I recall it wasn't too long after the fire that the Sandersons bought the lot and built their home there."

They'd found the place after all, only to find that it had burned. Only two houses down. She was sitting less than a hundred yards from where her grandparents had lived. Dizziness set the room to spiraling until Neala realized she was holding her breath; Grayson's hand covered hers, soothing with reassuring strokes, and after a moment the dizziness receded. Without fanfare Grayson shifted to sit on the couch beside her.

"Do you remember anything else your mother told you?" he asked Mrs. Young.

"Not much, I'm afraid. You all never would have discovered anything by driving up and down the street. Only reason I'm sure of the place is your mentioning the magnolia tree. It was the largest magnolia on this street in its day. But the fire damaged it, and the Sandersons eventually had to have it cut down, oh, going on 'bout thirty years now. Mr. Young and I used to love sitting on the porch when that tree was in bloom, smelling the sweet scent." Her eyes misted. "I reckon we're near about the only folks who still remember. Lots of families had to leave back in the seventies, don't you know. Times were real bad then. Quite sad, really."

"Someone torched the place, I believe you told me?" Mr. Young queried, as though to keep his wife from rambling. "The fire was not an accident."

"Yes, dear. Didn't I say so? The lady who ran the boardinghouse died, along with several residents. Oh—surely your grandparents weren't—no." She fanned herself with a hankie she tugged from her sleeve. "How silly of me. You wouldn't be here in our parlor now if your grandparents had perished, would you, honey?"

"No, ma'am," Neala replied faintly. Instead her grandparents had lived to produce children and grandchildren so they could be hunted down, one by one, exterminated like vermin. She didn't realize she was digging her nails into Grayson's hand until he pried her fingers open, then laced his through them, all the time keeping an attentive gaze upon Mrs. Young.

"My mother was only a child," the lady chattered away, "but she said the neighbors talked about it for years."

"I imagine they would," Grayson returned amiably while his thumb burrowed beneath their intertwined fingers to stroke Neala's palm in mesmerizing circles. His calm strength and vitality seeped into her bones like an unguent. "Did they ever discover the perpetrators?"

"There were a lot of rumors, but nobody was ever charged," Mrs. Young said. "Here, dear, you're looking flushed now. Should I have Dolly fetch a cool cloth? It's no wonder, learning that your dear grandparents almost perished in a fire."

"No, thank you. I'm fine. Truly." Or she was as fine as was possible considering she was sitting beside a man who was not her husband, soaking up his tender attentions while listening to stories of fires and deaths and waiting on tenterhooks to learn something about her grandparents.

"What were the rumors?" Grayson prodded after glancing down at Neala. A corner of his mouth twitched.

"Well, I don't rightly recollect all of them." Mrs. Young folded her handkerchief and made an elaborate production of stuffing it back in her sleeve. "Something about someone left a candle burning. Or that one of the gentlemen was purported to be a heavy pipe smoker, and fell asleep in his bed."

"The rumor she doesn't want to tell you fed the gossip mill for years," Alton Young put in dryly. "The one where a woman dressed all in white, or a ghost, if you want to venture into the supernatural, heaved a lighted torch through one of the windows, then disappeared, never to be seen again."

"A woman?" Neala frowned, struggled to collect the scattered pieces of information in her still-scattered brain. While she sorted through her thoughts she finally slid her hand free of Grayson's, under the pretext of smoothing down the pleats in her rumpled shirtwaist. "Why would a woman do such a thing?"

"Women commit countless crimes for a number of reasons," Grayson said.

Neala doubted if the Youngs heard the nuance of cynicism coloring the words.

"Did you tell me your grandfather's surname?" Mrs. Young asked. "I don't recall."

"Shaw." Neala spoke through stiff lips. "Neal Shaw."

"Wait. Everything is coming back to me," Mrs. Young announced excitedly. "Oh, my soul and body!"

"What? What is it?" Neala pressed a fist to her midriff. "Did you know—did your mother know—my grandfather?"

"Not as well as she knew the woman with whom he eloped. Her name, as I recall, was Miss Brind…Breem…Bremmer! That's it! Miss Bremmer."

Neala smothered a cry. Mrs. Young stood, her face plainly revealing distress. Mr. Young walked across and put his arm around his wife's shoulders. "It was a long time ago. Just tell them what your mother told you. They deserve to know."

Nervously Mrs. Young twisted her hands. "Miss Bremmer—she was your grandmother?"

Mouth dry, Neala nodded.

"Yes, well, she was a teacher—Mother was one of her pupils. She thought the elopement very romantic, of course, though she told me she cried for days because she loved Miss Bremmer."

"Her name was Annie," Neala whispered. "Annie Bremmer."

"Ah." She shook her head. "Well, now, what I haven't told you, since I've just now remembered, is the reason for the elopement." Apricot color tinged her plump cheeks.

A giant snake wrapped Neala in its coils and squeezed. Grayson could not be right. She didn't want to believe that her grandparents—

"It's not what you're thinking," Mrs. Young hastily interrupted. "Leastways, Mother never mentioned…um…*those* sort of rumors. However, I'm terribly sorry to be the one to inform you, Mrs. Faulkner— What is it, honey? Here, drink some more tea. Oh, dear. Dolly took it away. I'll ring for more."

"No need." Mr. Young stepped forward. "Here, Mrs. Faulkner. A glass of mineral water." He handed her a crystal goblet.

Anything to divert the phrase Mrs. Faulkner *from clanging in her ears like a fire-alarm bell.* Neala grabbed the glass and took a quick swallow, which of course set her to coughing again. Eyes streaming, she glared up at Grayson, who had the effrontery to smile at her. And shrug.

"I beg your pardon," she told Mrs. Young. "You were saying?"

"Well, I do hope this doesn't upset you further, but I have to tell you that your grandfather and grandmother ran away on the very day your grandfather was to have married another woman."

Oh, no. No. This was even worse than the usual reason couples were forced to marry in haste. "Another woman?" she eventually murmured. "Grandfather…jilted some other woman? On their *wedding* day?"

"I'm afraid so. And seeing as how it was Judge Rutledge's only daughter, you can imagine how the scandal was difficult to live down. The Judge ended up paying a sharecropper to marry Letitia, I believe was the daughter's name, and sent them off to somewhere in another state to live."

After leaving the Youngs, for several blocks Neala and Grayson drove in silence. Above them the sun burned through the late-afternoon haze, while the steady clip-clop of the horse's hooves beat in rhythm with Neala's overflowing heart. She wanted to fling out her arms and embrace the moment with an excitement as glowing as the sunset. Words abruptly bubbled up in a froth of emotion.

"I've been so disheartened, and my faith was even wavering," she exclaimed to Grayson. "And yes, I'm disappointed by Grandfather's behavior. And I feel dreadful for poor Miss Rutledge. Why do you suppose her parents forced her to marry someone else?" She shook her head. "Never mind, I think I understand. My parents were most concerned about my future, especially after I turned down my second proposal."

"You've refused two offers of marriage?"

"Yes. Oh, never mind all that. It's not important. I just hope Miss Rutledge developed an affection for her husband." And she mentally winged a thank-you heavenward to her own parents, for not forcing her into an arranged marriage. "I know my grandparents loved each other very much, or they never would have eloped in the first place. When Grandmother died, Grandfather refused to leave her grave for two days. So you see, he never meant to hurt Miss Rutledge, he just loved my grandmother too much to not take her for his wife."

She stopped, thoughts crowding her mind faster than her tongue could translate them into words. "I just realized…we have a name, Grayson! When I least expected it, God gives us a clue. Miss Rutledge."

"Might be we just happened to be in the right place at the right time."

"Stuff and nonsense. The timing was right because the Lord arranged it. He knew when we'd be passing that part of the street, so He arranged for the Youngs to be there."

"I suppose He also arranged for you to pass out in the buggy?"

Provoked with him, Neala blew out an exasperated breath. "In the first place, I did *not* faint. In the second, it wouldn't matter to me if I had. Otherwise the Youngs would have passed by, like two ships in the night, and we never would have learned what we did."

Beside her Grayson muttered something beneath his breath. "If God really wanted to help," he observed impatiently, "He would have provided the state and city where the jilted bride and her poor dupe of a husband were exiled to. Along with the name of the dupe."

"Oh, stop being so cynical. You, Grayson Faulkner, can scoff all you like. But what happened today was not chance or happenstance or coincidence. And someday you're going to find yourself in a place where you'll admit that God cares about us, that He watches over us, that He loves us. And you'll be thanking Him for it."

"And someday, Neala Shaw, you're going to realize that humans are not puppets dancing to God's tune. If He wanted puppets, He wouldn't have created humans with free will. Most of the time," he added with a bite to his voice, "humans choose their own tune, not God's. You believe He cares for you. But I've learned that kind of faith doesn't mean He's going to protect you from all harm. More than likely, He'll stand by and let the murderer have his way with you the same as he did the rest of your family."

For the rest of the journey, they sat side by side in a silence that now seemed as wide and deep as the ocean.

Chapter Nineteen

White Sulphur Springs, West Virginia

For a week he scrounged for information, waited and smoldered. She'd escaped. Again. The failure was insupportable, something that ate into him like a canker, ruined his sleep, and sent him prowling the grounds of the hotel resort until the moon waned in the sky.

After days of subtle investigation, he was still unable to ascertain the whereabouts of either Neala Shaw or that interfering Grayson Faulkner. He wasn't a man. He was a predator, swooping in for the kill, claiming a woman he had no right to. Regrettably, neither the old widow nor the giant of a woman hired to sleep in Neala's room offered any useful information. He'd charmed the widow one evening at dinner and, on another afternoon, under the guise of hiring her as a nanny had plied the Irish skirt with questions.

The sense of hurt, even betrayal, fomented and bubbled. Over the last eighteen months he had come to regard Neala as his own. He alone was responsible for her life—and for her death. Like a secretive shadow he had stalked her, watched her, learned her personality with all its fascinating idiosyncrasies. When she allowed Faulkner to dupe her, she had betrayed the man who knew her the most intimately. *Him.* Watching her seduction at the hands of that profligate filled him with indescribable hurt.

As September slipped into October, hurt escalated to rage. Neala was going to pay for her defection. She had chosen to allow Faulkner to spirit her away. Therefore something would have to be done to bring her back, something he would not relish, nor be able to enjoy. Neala would pay for that as well.

He'd made it a practice to avoid doing away with bystanders. It defaced the nobility of his mission. Now he was forced to break his rules, to kill an innocent bystander, because nothing less would be able to lure Neala away from her seducer, and return her to White Sulphur Springs.

Once he settled on his decision, he focused his attention upon the victim: Mrs. Frances Wilkes.

For three days he observed her every move, all her daily habits and rituals, and concluded that the task was too risky to accomplish in broad daylight. He could arrange it, of course, and the challenge appealed to his pride. But he simply didn't want to take the time testing his craft and cunning on someone who amounted to nothing more than a pawn.

A simple suffocation in her bed would have to suffice. He was sorry for the indignity of it, but his purpose must take precedent.

Two nights later, with a sliver of a moon shrouded in clouds, he changed from the neat English woolen jacket and striped trousers he'd worn for dinner and the concert on the lawn into what he referred to euphemistically as his night clothes: every item from soft-soled shoes to the wig was black. He waited until all sights and sounds of other guests faded, and the only sounds to be heard were the interminable chirping of insects and a light southerly breeze that aided his cause by pushing more clouds over the moon.

Once more he had made himself invisible.

At a little past two in the morning, he crept through deserted lobbies, down long corridors until he arrived at the widow's suite of rooms. He'd thought about entering through the window, but that would have been too simple, outraging his sense of professionalism.

When he reached her door, he paused, readying himself for the task, forcing rage to life. It curled upward through his body until it propelled him through the door and across the parlor to a sumptuously arranged bedroom incongruous with the almost Spartan bedrooms of other guests. These quarters reeked of wealth and prestige. He didn't even hesitate as he selected one of the embroidered pillows gracing a chair near the bed.

For a long moment he stood over her, watching the rise and fall of her chest beneath the bedcovers, listening to the soft snores that occasionally passed her lips. Then, fueling the rage to swamp out any insidious remnants of regret or conscience, he leaned over and pressed the pillow over the widow's face.

Wilmington, North Carolina

The telegram arrived before breakfast. Gray read it through twice, crumpled the piece of yellow paper and savagely hurled it across his bedroom. With helpless fury seething around him, he stalked from his room, slammed the door and strode outside, the openmouthed stares of several early-morning residents following in his wake.

What would this do to Neala? For months she had kept her spirits high, refusing to succumb to despair, except for that one brief episode in the buggy, before the Youngs came along.

Even the couple's happenstance arrival she regarded as divinely inspired.

So what kind of God helped one person, about the same time as another one was being slaughtered like a sacrificial goat? As clearly as if the murderer instead of Deirdre had sent the telegram, Gray knew the motive for Frances Wilkes's murder, and he had no doubt of its effectiveness.

His vow to protect Neala was about to be tested in a lake of burning fire.

Eventually the rage burned itself into manageable flames, and Gray retraced his steps to the boardinghouse.

Neala waited on the front porch. She was sitting, alert and unsmiling, in the same wicker rocking chair where Gray had waited for her a week earlier.

"Mr. Coolidge told me a telegram arrived for you," she said as he walked up the steps. "Is something wrong in your family? Do you need to leave? I'll be all right, and can—"

"How about if you hear what the telegram says before you plan what we're going to do?" He sat down beside her on the edge of a glider and propped his elbows on his knees. How best to break the news? Tease her into relaxing? Just tell her and get it over with?

"Grayson, I can tell something has happened, as can the residents who witnessed your departure from the house. What is it? Just tell me and you'll feel better for it."

She looked so sweetly earnest that for a moment Gray found all he could do was to look at her, absorb her goodness and her pluck. There was something different about Neala Shaw, something he couldn't quite put a finger on. Whatever it was, she stuck in his brain like flypaper, even when she wasn't around. Perhaps it was her innocence, but he didn't think so. Innocence for the most part in a female was either calculated or boringly predictable, two descriptions that could not be attributed to the woman sitting beside him.

Her courage? She was carrying a frightful burden, yet still she could scrape together the resilience to meet each day with a smile.

What would this news do to her?

"Grayson…"

Sighing, he worried his hair with his hands, then lifted his head and faced her. "Neala—" he reached and folded her fingers within his "—the telegram was from Deirdre."

"Deirdre? Why would she send— No. No. Don't tell me, I don't want to hear this, Grayson." She tugged at her hands though her gaze was fixed upon his and it implored him to say anything but the knowledge already filling her eyes.

So he told her as fast as he could, to get the deed done. "Mrs. Wilkes is dead. She died in her sleep, but we both know this likely wasn't due to natural causes."

All the color leached from her complexion, and the hands Gray held might as well have belonged to a corpse.

"My fault," she whispered through lips that scarcely moved. "This is my fault. He's telling me this will keep happening if I disappear so he can't find me."

"Yes."

For an interminable moment she seemed to stare through him. Then she sat up straight, gently but firmly separating herself from Gray. "I'm going back to the Old White," she said. "And I'm going alone. I don't want you anywhere near me. I want you to go back to the Academy and make sure Miss Isabella and all the students are safe."

"I don't think so." It took a monumental effort to keep his voice calm and matter-of-fact, even more of an effort to rope-tie the fear. "From this moment on, Neala, you will not leave my sight. As for my aunt and the school, I'll make arrangements for their protection. I have a lot of connections, and a lot of friends who'd be only too happy to spend a few weeks squiring a group of young ladies around."

"Thank you for that. It's difficult enough, remembering what happened to my friend Abigail." She stopped, swallowed several times while she stared up at the peeling-paint ceiling. "I can't think about Mrs. Wilkes right now. I just can't, or I won't be able to function." Her lips trembled and she wound her fingers together. "And I can't allow you to continue protecting me. I…can't."

The embers of rage reignited. Gray stared down at his knees for a protracted moment. "If you think for one second I'll stand by while you whistle yourself back to White Sulphur Springs on your own—which we both know is precisely what the murderer wants you to do—then let me disabuse you of that notion."

"I know you're far too honorable to send me into the mouth of the lion. That's why I'm not giving you the option." She licked her lips. "I renounce your protection."

With a stifled growl he leaned forward, clamping his hands on the arms of the rocker and effectively trapping Neala. "You're stuck with me, Neala Shaw. I gave my word to protect you, and that's precisely what I'm going to do. Even if I have to marry you to accomplish it."

The words punched out, a one-two blow that left him reeling, because they couldn't be stuffed back down his throat. Furious with himself, with Neala, with the untenable circumstances, Gray abruptly straightened, swiveled on his heel and stomped to the end of the porch. A cardinal chittered from the branches of a dogwood. The bold red color reminded him too much of blood; with a stifled sound he snatched up a dirt-covered spade lying on the railing and hurled it at the bird, who flitted off to parts unknown with a contemptuous chirp.

Just like the infernal madman who traversed the country with impunity, seeking out Neala Shaw. Until and unless Gray could catch him, neither he nor Neala would ever know another moment's peace.

He heard a floorboard creak and turned around, bracing himself.

"I know you didn't mean it," Neala said. She stood a scant yard away, freckles accentuated in her too-pale face, her brown eyes wretched. The effervescent mass of curls was strangled at the base of her neck within the clasp of an enameled clip. "Don't worry, Grayson. You haven't frightened or offended me. I appreciate the gesture, but it's impossible." Above the simple white shirtwaist, the pulse in her throat fluttered like butterfly wings.

Irrationally piqued by her stilted refusal, Gray leaned back against the porch railing and folded his arms across his chest. "Because neither of us wants to marry the other? Under the circumstances, I don't think our wants matter. Unless you're willing to allow me to remain with you every hour of the day without the legality of marriage, I don't see much of a choice for either of us."

For an interminable span of time Neala stood without responding, staring at him as though she could somehow force him to dematerialize, or worse, imprint her will upon his. *Not a chance, sweetheart.* He'd learned before he was out of short pants how to circumvent women and their torturous schemes.

"Marriage is sacred," she finally whispered. "Ordained by God. I can't marry a man who trusts neither God nor the nature of a loving relationship between husband and wife."

"I'll concede the point," Gray said. "On the other hand, marriage is also a legally binding contract between two parties that more often than not is arranged for reasons other than God and undying love." He stepped closer, his voice hardening. "It's

time for you to face some unpalatable truths about the world,
Neala. People seldom cooperate with your idealized notions
of how they should act. Life doesn't work like that. Most
people are greedy, selfish and immoral. They act out of self-
interest, not altruism or nobility."

"In that case," Neala whipped out, "you should have no
trouble doing what I asked. Leave me. Go pursue your own
godless life. Regardless of what you think of me, I don't want
another death on *my* conscience."

"Neither do I!" Grayson shouted back. He snatched Neala
into a fierce embrace. "I don't want your death on *my* conscience." Much like his earlier impetuous declaration, words
spewed forth from someplace so deeply buried he hadn't
known it existed. "Regardless of what you think of me, I'm not
a misogynistic heathen who doesn't care a fig for anyone but
myself. I spent a miserable childhood with a mother who
refused to let me grow up, who smothered me with overpro-
tectiveness until I ran away so I could learn what it meant to
be a man."

"I didn't mean—"

"And I vowed," he swept on, "that I would show my
mother—my entire family—that I could not only take care of
myself, I could take care of others." He glared at her, indifferent to the moisture stinging his eyelids. "I wanted to *help
people!* I wanted to protect the innocent, pursue justice! I
wanted to prove I could stand on my own!"

With an oath, he shoved Neala away from him. "So don't
stand there in your pristine righteousness and call me a godless
heathen, when all I'm trying to do is to save your life!"

Breathing hard, he clamped his mouth shut until his jaw
throbbed. He couldn't believe what he'd just done—manhan-
dled her, shouted at her, doubtless terrified her out of her wits.
He was no better than the conscienceless fiend trying to kill her.

Then Neala spoke. "I'm sorry, Grayson," she said, her words contrite. "You're right. What I said to you was cruel, and untrue. Will you forgive me?"

Forgive *her?*

Gray blinked. "You're not making sense. I'm the one who should beg for forgiveness. I had no right to shout at you." His throat felt as though a vicious genie had dumped a shaker full of hot sand down his gullet. "To grab you."

"Oh, that's nothing." She waved away his execrable display of temper as though he'd done nothing but spit in public. "You should hear my brother. He used to screech like a steaming kettle when he didn't get his way. Father, now, he was mild tempered, but Grandfather would bellow when he was angered. Grandmother once told him he sounded like a wounded moose, which of course only made him holler louder."

Tentatively she reached out a hand, and almost in a daze Gray clasped it in his. "You didn't hurt me, or scare me. I don't have a problem with spilled tempers," she promised him earnestly. "I just don't know what to do about…us." The words quavered as she tried a smile that barely tipped the corners of her trembling lips. "Grayson, I don't know what to do."

Very slowly, Gray drew her closer, until he could rest his forehead against the soft crown of her hair. "Neither do I, Neala," he finally confessed against the curls. "Neither do I."

Behind them someone cleared his throat. Gray's head whipped up as he automatically pulled Neala behind him.

"Oh. Mr. Young." Gray nodded to the older man, and ignored the heat he could feel spreading across his cheeks. As far as Alton Young knew, Gray and Neala were a happily married couple enjoying a spot of canoodling on the front porch.

"I'm on my way to work," Mr. Young said as he mounted

the porch steps. He tipped his bowler to Neala. "The streetcar passes a block down, so I told Mrs. Young I'd stop by on the way to bring you this." He held out a piece of folded paper. "Last night we got to talking, and she recollected that the daughter of one of her mother's friends keeps an ear to the ground, concerning all the goings-on in Wilmington society. Nothing would do but we had to pay a visit then and there. Thought your missus might be glad to know the name of the sharecropper fellow old Judge Rutledge married his daughter off to."

Gray took the paper, opened it up. "Hiram Buxton, married Letitia Rutledge, September 1832. Moved to Twin Oaks, North Carolina."

Neala turned around to beam at Mr. Young. "This is wonderful! Thank you so much, Mr. Young. Please tell Mrs. Young how grateful I am—we both are."

She was practically vibrating with excitement and before he even thought twice Gray wrapped a restraining arm around her shoulders. "As you can tell, this means a lot. But—" The noose tightened around his neck. He gave a mental shrug, and jumped. "My wife's obviously forgetting that the circumstances which necessitated Miss Rutledge's marriage to this man were doubtless painful rather than celebratory."

"Well, Mrs. Young wondered about that, but since this happened so long ago, and far as we know all these folks have gone on to their rewards, there didn't seem to be any harm in letting you know."

"Of course not," Gray said, but kept his thoughts to himself.

Courtesy of the wifely reference, Neala now stood like a cornstalk on a frigid winter day. Gray squeezed her shoulders once, then stepped forward to shake the older man's hand.

After Mr. Young tipped his hat and set back off down to the corner to catch the trolley, Gray glanced down at Neala. "Go ahead, rip a strip off my hide for referring to you as my wife," he said. "But be warned, I'm not in the best frame of mind for any more fireworks. Besides which, I think we have more important matters to discuss." He waved the paper in her face. "I'm thinking we need to pay a visit to Twin Oaks."

For a moment Neala regarded him in silence, head tilted to one side while her fingers absently played with a dangling curl. "I won't tear any strips," she said at last on a long sigh. "But one day I'll have to write the Youngs to explain. If I live long enough."

"What kind of talk is that, from my upbeat little Christian woman—oof!" He rubbed the ribs Neala had just elbowed. "All right. If you promise not to make any gloom-and-doom remarks, I promise to keep my, ah, endearments, under control."

Neala shrugged. "Grayson," she said next, the words dragging, "why would an eminently respected, prestigious judge marry his only daughter off to a sharecropper? She was the one who was jilted, after all."

"I've had a thought or two on that since Mrs. Young first shared the story yesterday. You might not like the tenor of them."

"They probably echo mine," she returned bleakly. "I just don't want to believe Grandfather was that irresponsible."

Gray could think of a few less flattering descriptions, but he figured Neala had enough to contend with. "The woman he married might not have been with child," he finished levelly, "but I'd bet my boots that the woman he left waiting at the altar was."

"I think so, too." She half lifted one hand, shook her head. "Grayson…that would mean I have another relative. An aunt, or an uncle—Letitia's child. If we can find them, I'd have family."

"Neala." He kept his voice gentle. "I'll find them for you.

But you need to accept that they might not want anything to do with you. After all, you represent everything they lost, because your grandfather chose to marry Annie Bremmer instead of Letitia Rutledge."

Up went her chin and back went the shoulders. "They might be the only family I have left. I'll just have to find a way to convince him or her that we *are* family. And together we may stumble over a clue that unearths the Shaw executioner."

Gray decided no answer was the smartest response. As he led Neala across the porch to the front door, it also occurred to him that right now might be an auspicious time for him to see if her notion of God was worth pursuing. His gut warned him that they would need any and all divine assistance that might be flung their way, over the next few days.

But at least the news about Letitia Rutledge had successfully diverted Neala from the death of Frances Wilkes, and returning to White Sulphur Springs on her own.

Chapter Twenty

October, 1890

On the long train trip back to White Sulphur Springs, Neala argued with her conscience, debated with her mind, and ignored her heart, in a vain attempt to convince herself that her actions were necessary. Even honorable. She could not face herself in the mirror every morning if she did not pay her respects to Mrs. Wilkes. What difference did personal safety or family history matter when compared with the monstrous act perpetrated against a woman whose association with Neala had cost her life?

Nor could she ever hope to re-stitch her tattered self-respect if something happened to the man with whom she'd stupidly fallen in love, because she wasn't brave enough to try and survive on her own. In the dark, stuffy coach car, she prayed. Prayed for courage. Prayed God would at last heed her prayers and protect her, because she possessed not a shred of an illusion that Grayson Faulkner would be doing so any longer.

Grayson.

Blindly Neala stared at her reflection in the train window. Beyond the greasy pane of glass an indifferent world slid past in darkness, while the rhythmic clickety-clack of the train wheels rushed toward a destination that would lead either to absolution—or her own death.

By now Grayson would know she was gone. Would he bother to read her letter, or would he rip it to shreds and consign Neala Shaw to the fate she deserved? Mrs. Oppenheimer, the aging spinster who had roomed next to her, had proven to be an artful accomplice. She'd told Grayson that Neala needed some time alone, that she planned to take supper in her room and would see Grayson in the morning. After the meal was over, Mrs. Oppenheimer would give him Neala's letter.

God forgive her for the lie. Because after choking down a few bites of her meal, Neala had set the tray aside, then slipped down the servant stairs, out the back door and into the hack Mrs. Oppenheimer had arranged to take Neala to the depot. Grayson was contentedly eating supper with the rest of the boarders, not knowing that yet another woman had betrayed him.

Throat tight, Neala leaned her head back against the antimacassar and closed her eyes. *Lord, what else was I to do?* She never could have convinced him to save his own life at the expense of her own. What decent man would? For all his notorious shenanigans and caustic attitudes, Neala had come to know him better, to see the goodness in him he could no longer see in himself. On the surface Grayson might be portrayed as the reckless, wayward youngest son, but Neala had watched him sit and chat with Mr. Coolidge for hours, though the landlord tended to repeat every other sentence until her eyes crossed. Over the course of these past few weeks, Grayson had also spent many idle hours playing dominoes with Mrs. Oppenheimer, and entertained an excessively shy schoolteacher with stories of the western frontier.

As for Neala herself… She swallowed hard several times, and tried to erase from her mind the memory of his tenderness. His kisses.

Though it may cost her her life, and the love of her life, Neala was willing to accept the consequences in order to save Grayson. Sadly, he would never see it that way. She stirred in her seat, clasping and unclasping her hands.

Lord, he'll blame himself. Not only would he never forgive her for leaving—if the killer succeeded this time—Grayson would never forgive himself for failing to protect her. Oh, but this was too much!

Neala knew he had begun to feel something for her other than tolerance and exasperation. Not love, certainly. But at least perhaps a sort of affection. She also knew her actions would likely forever harden his heart not only toward her, but toward all women, yet another burden to crush her. No longer would he play parlor games with lonely widows, nor draw out shy schoolteachers.

Never hold her again, never tease her or call her *love*.

But he would be alive.

Why did she have to fall in love with him?

Nothing but burdens. Her life for the past two years had reaped nothing but more boulders, tripping her up, crushing her, smashing her world into so many fragments she would never be able to put them all back together. And so far as she knew, this solitary journey might be one of her last nights on earth.

It wasn't right that she had to endure this alone, afraid, full of regret and—and—

In a jerky motion she sat up, startling the sleeping governess from South Carolina who shared the seat. Neala apologized, the woman grumbled something, turned and dozed back off seconds later. Neala felt as alone as she had the day Adrian disappeared from her life.

And she was angry at God.

There. The awful thought was laid bare in her mind, and she half steeled herself for a lightning bolt to strike her dead and save the murderer the trouble.

Bleakly she sat, desolate and lonely, wondering with every mile if she would ever know why she had never measured up enough for anyone. God claimed to love everybody, but He hadn't spared a thought for a nondescript woman whose name wasn't even her own.

She had wasted her entire life, struggling to either compensate for the void, or to fill it through her own actions. Neither was sufficient. Oh, her parents had loved her, yes, but mostly because compared to Adrian she'd never caused any trouble. Grandfather had finally come to love her, but he'd wanted her to be a boy.

She didn't want to think about Grandfather.

So…what about her brother? Adrian… Her hands fisted in her lap. Face it. He never really loved her at all. She'd been nothing but a convenience, someone to fetch and carry and bail him out of trouble.

As for the Isabella Chilton Academy, if she'd been there longer, perhaps the ties would have become strong enough to allow the affection Miss Isabella and the students had shown her to blossom into a deeper love, bonds that finally would have blessed her with a sense of her own worth.

Such speculations were futile, chasing the wind.

What would it matter if she did return? After four months she was naught but a memory in the tides of their lives, like a finger pulled from the ocean. Just as the waters flowed over and completely erased where her finger had been, so would memory of Neala What-*Was*-Her-Name fade from Miss Isabella's mind, Abby's, Liam's, Mr. Pepperell and Miss Crabbe—until even her existence would be forgotten.

She was doomed to dribble out her remaining days in isolation and despair. Drifting like a severed branch down the stream of life, without the comfort of knowing that at least one person cared whether she lived or perished.

If this was life, she no longer possessed the stamina to fight. Her faith was shattered, her courage wavering, and hope? Well, at the moment her only hope was to find out where Mrs. Wilkes was to be buried, and to be able to ask her forgiveness over her grave.

She supposed she could hope that the murderer would be swift.

Right now, death would be a relief.

The train pulled into the station at two o'clock on Thursday afternoon. All around her autumn colors poured like spilled paint over the earth in breathtaking hues of red and orange and gold. The air was crisp, unlike North Carolina, with an invigorating clarity that partially lifted Neala's spirits. Clutching her cracked leather valise, the only luggage she had brought along, she waited until she knew her legs would do their job, then lifted her chin and faced her future.

An hour later she was sitting in the manager's private office, sipping hot tea while he informed her of the circumstances surrounding Mrs. Wilkes's death.

"It was her maid's off day, or we would have discovered her sooner, perhaps before—" He coughed, then hurriedly continued. "At any rate, without her maid, and without you here, she wasn't missed until lunchtime, when she was to have met several other ladies in the dining room. They'd planned an outing to the Chalybeate Spring."

Without her here. The cup and saucer rattled as Neala carefully set them on a piecrust table next to the chair. "Does the physician think she suffered?" she asked.

"Likely not," Mr. Eakle tried to reassure her. "He thinks she suffered a massive heart attack in her sleep, and never woke. In some ways, you can consider it a blessing, since she would not have suffered."

"She was having more difficulty breathing," Neala recalled slowly, longing to believe Dr. Dabney's diagnosis. That in fact Mrs. Wilkes *had* expired from natural causes.

"Of course," Mr. Eakle continued, his gaze avoiding Neala's, "I feel I should warn you that the Vances' nanny put up a bit of a fuss. Apparently she had some connection with you?"

Neala managed a nod.

"Ah." Though plainly mystified, the manager did not pursue the matter. "Well, I frankly didn't pay her much attention. But since you were Mrs. Wilkes's protégée, and apparently Miss McGee was a companion of sorts?"

"That's as good a way to define it as any," Neala murmured.

"Ah. Yes, Miss McGee assured me, most strongly, that she planned to tell nobody but you and Mr. Faulkner, myself and Dr. Dabney. I've debated over these past few days, on the advisability of bringing the matter to your attention." He hesitated, then planted his forearms on his desk and leaned forward. "Miss Shaw, since you've explained Mr. Faulkner's absence I am more reluctant than ever to mention this. I fear this claim might cause you unnecessary distress."

"I'll be fine," Neala replied faintly. 'Twas a good thing she was seated, for the bones in her limbs were dissolving. The ceiling seemed to have descended so that its weight bore down upon her shoulders. "Tell me what Miss McGee said?" she eventually prompted, though she knew the nature of the answer. Had known it all along. Knowing, however, was not the same as confronting its reality face-to-face.

Mr. Eakle shook his head, shrugged. "She apparently thinks Mrs. Wilkes did not expire from natural causes. But since her only reason for making that claim is some sort of decorative pillow that was out of place, lying on the floor, I believe, nobody paid her hypothesis much credence."

"You're saying…" she drew in a trickle of air and let the words fall where they may "…that Miss McGee believes Mrs. Wilkes was…smothered in her sleep? Using a—a pillow?"

"There. I knew I shouldn't have told you, Miss Shaw. I can see the revelation, bizarre though it may be, has upset you. Please, sip some more of your tea. Shall I call Dr. Dabney?"

"No. I'm fine. Can I… I mean, where…ah… Mrs. Wilkes… Where is her—her body?"

"Oh, I say. That is…" He cleared his throat, his fingers nervously smoothing over his lapels. "At the depot," he said at last, flushing. "We telegraphed her nearest relative, a great-nephew, in Alabama. Apparently it was Mrs. Wilkes's desire to be buried in Charlottesville, with her first husband. Unfortunately, there won't be a train until the day after tomorrow."

He finally looked across at Neala. "It seemed more…discreet, to have the remains lie in state elsewhere than her rooms here in the hotel. I have a trusted chambermaid packing up her possessions." He cleared his throat again. "Candidly, I was hoping, since you've returned, if you might lend your assistance, being the closest to family Mrs. Wilkes has in the area?"

"Of course. I'll do anything I can to help." Neala stood, shored up her crumbling composure. "It's the least I can do." Seeing as how she'd left Mrs. Wilkes all on her own. Undefended. "I should never have left."

"Miss Shaw, there was nothing you could have done."

Mr. Eakle walked around the desk to briefly clasp her hand.

"Over these many years Mrs. Wilkes has cultivated many good friends here at the Old White, and certainly a fond loyalty among all of us on staff. Please do not distress yourself over your absence, and believe we are taking the best care of her as can be arranged."

"I have no doubt of that. The great-nephew—will he come here, or Charlottesville?"

"It is my understanding that he will travel directly to Charlottesville." The manager walked back around his desk, searched a stack of correspondence until he picked out a folded piece of paper. "Here is his letter." He held it out. "Read it, if you wish."

Neala took the letter, pretended to scan the lines and handed it back to Mr. Eakle. "She is—was—a very dear friend of my family."

"Mrs. Wilkes had shared that with me. She also told me about the deaths of your parents. You've not had an easy time of it, have you?" He hesitated. "Under the circumstances, I believe we could arrange for you to stay in your old room, free of charge." His hands fluttered through some papers. "I'll also provide a key to Mrs. Wilkes's suite. Thank you again for your assistance."

"I'm honored to help," Neala repeated mechanically. *The key to Mrs. Wilkes's suite.* Hurriedly she changed the subject, asking if Deirdre was still with the Vances.

Plainly relieved, Mr. Eakle's face cleared. "Why, yes. Though I believe they plan to leave within the week. Ah, you may recall that the season closes October 15?"

"I remember." Neala offered her hand, thanked Mr. Eakle, and wandered back out into the main lobby. Plenty of guests still strolled about, but the crowds and the liveliness had definitely slowed. After selecting a vacant chair in the middle of the reading room, she sank down to collect her thoughts. She longed to seek Deirdre out, if only for the comfort of her presence. But she didn't, because that would put Deirdre at risk. She also knew she should go straight to Mrs. Wilkes's rooms, but at the moment the prospect was too daunting.

What to do, what to do? She could go for a walk, wander over the footbridge and along Howard's Creek, allow the soft sound of the water to soothe her soul. *He leadeth me beside still waters, He restoreth my soul.* Ha! Defiantly, Neala closed her mind to further tidbits of Scripture. She was in no mood for empty words and false hopes.

Restive, Neala smoothed her skirts, then rose and marched from the lobby out onto the piazza, down to the path that led back to the depot. She would cajole the station agent into allowing her to pay her respects to Mrs. Wilkes, then she would walk by the creek and enjoy the fall colors.

Come and get me, she challenged the despicable man who had promised to take her life. *If you're still here, come and get me.*

Neala possessed few illusions about her capacity to defend herself, though she planned to try. Not for the first time since she'd boarded the train, she lifted her hand, cupping the clan crest brooch she had pinned to her traveling cloak. The colored-glass chips gleamed within the hammered pewter, reminding her that regardless of her isolation, she was a Shaw, and Shaws did not flinch from the valley of the shadow of death.

Nor did Shaws blench at responsibility.

When she reached the depot, the station agent was immersed in passengers, but the kindly colored attendant approached to ask if he could be of assistance. Upon hearing her request, he led her across to the baggage room, unlocked the door, and ushered her into a small storage room in the back.

"They put her here so's not to disturb the guests," he said

with a wry smile. "Reckon some folks don't see that she ain't here noways. Just a shell inside that box." Wise chocolate eyes studied Neala. "Don't you fret none, miss. I've knowed Miz Wilkes since afore you was born. She's up there with the Lord, sure as you and me be standing here. And she's directing His affairs, I expect, same as she did down here. Don't be sad."

He left her then, and Neala slowly approached the plain wooden coffin resting upon huge blocks of ice. Tentatively she laid her hand on the lid, and tears slowly splashed down her cheeks. "I'm sorry," she whispered in a choked voice. "So sorry. I miss you, and I hope you didn't suffer." *Perhaps I'll see you soon, along with Mother and Father.*

Neala no longer expected to feel the Lord's presence, surrounding and sustaining her. She no longer enjoyed the protection of the man she had grown to love, or the Goliath of a woman who kept the nightmares away or the indomitable sponsor determined to marry her off.

"Half your desire is fulfilled," Neala told Mrs. Wilkes then, and swiped away tears falling more freely now, soaking her face, but she didn't care. There was nobody to see her, nobody to chide, ridicule…or comfort. Like Grayson had in the buggy, holding her close, supporting her. Caring for her as nobody in her entire life had ever cared for her. "I fell in love with him," she finished, her voice breaking. "I fell in love, and so I left him."

The words hung in the close, dank air.

When the spate of grief passed, Neala lifted her hands, and slowly unpinned the clan crest. "I don't deserve to wear this right now." Dullness filmed her heart. Feeling nothing beyond the numbness that had invaded her limbs, she gently laid the clan crest on top of the coffin. Her actions did not seem illogical or irrational, but inevitable.

Stolidly she pressed a kiss to her palm, then placed her hand over the crest for the last time. "Goodbye," she whispered, to both of them.

Then she set her face and her feet toward Howard's Creek. It was a little past four in the afternoon.

Chapter Twenty-One

Slanting sunbeams gilded the clear water of Howard's Creek. A pair of mallards floated near some cattails. As Neala pensively enjoyed the ducks, a delicate white crane swooped down into the shallows. How lovely, she reflected, to be a bird, confident of your territory, contented with your lot in life.

Of course, if she were a bird, doubtless some hunter would bag her before breakfast.

Sighing, she continued strolling by the creek, her walking boots almost disappearing in the sun-warmed grasses. Every noise, however innocuous, wedged the breath in her throat and sent chills racing down her spine—the breeze rustling through the tree branches, the two guests strolling by, the startled groundhog who flattened the grass in his rush to flee from her. She could not, could *not* endure the suspense another day.

If unaccosted and alive by dusk, she would request a boxed supper, which she would consume on the bluff above the creek, within the darkest grove of trees she could find. During the day the collection of winding paths was a favorite destination for courting couples, but after dark the place was deserted, so the murderer faced little risk of exposure. Neala would consume her last supper, then wander the paths, which all bore names—Lover's Walk, Courtship Maze, Hesitancy, Rejection. Now there was the perfect path for Neala. She would consume her last meal there—no. In an even more fitting gesture, she would stake herself out at the end of the path dubbed Lover's Leap. The murderer could accomplish the deed by tossing her off the high bluff that overlooked Howard's Creek.

Would anyone appreciate the irony?

When a man stepped out from behind a clump of sumac and jutting boulders she jumped like a scalded frog. Then she recognized him, and her thundering pulse steadied. "Goodness, but you startled me!" She scraped up a smile. "It's Mr. Lipscomb, isn't it?"

"For the moment, anyway." He stood in front of her, a half smile showing beneath the trim mustache and full beard.

Though they'd encountered him infrequently, both Neala and Mrs. Wilkes had been favorably inclined toward the dapper gentleman, who always exchanged pleasantries but never intruded. Neala felt a soft spot for him because he sported a head of curly black hair as unmanageable-looking as her own.

"I…um…I'm taking a walk, before supper. It's a lovely afternoon, isn't it?" She willed the prickles coursing over her skin to subside and her mind to pretend everything was normal. She was merely a guest, out for a stroll along the creek.

"Yes." He sighed, his hand reaching inside the Norfolk jacket he wore. "And I hope it turns out to be a lovely evening."

He withdrew a folded-up handkerchief and a small stoppered bottle, his gaze never leaving Neala's as he opened the bottle and tipped the contents into the handkerchief. "This will be much easier for us both if you don't struggle. I don't want to hurt you, Neala."

Neala blinked. All pretense of normalcy evaporated as the

truth settled into her. *Mr. Lipscomb?* It was as much relief as surprise. "So, it's you," she murmured. "I had no idea."

"I know. At first, I never intended for you to know." He took a step toward her. "We'll talk later. Too much risk here, out in the open."

Of course. He should have waited an hour. She studied the soaking handkerchief, from which emanated an unpleasantly sweet odor. "Is that some poison, then? You're going to suffocate me with it, like you did Mrs. Wilkes?"

His eyes flickered. "No," he told her in a soft voice that instilled a bizarre sort of comfort, "this is only to render you unconscious. I really am sorry about Mrs. Wilkes. But you've only yourself to blame. You shouldn't have run away, especially not with that man." A chilling shadow chased across his countenance. "At any rate, I didn't have time to hunt you down again."

"Why?"

He shook his head. "I'll explain later. I'm glad you're not trying to run, Neala. I'd like to think it's because you believe me when I tell you that I've decided not to kill you after all."

The quiet statement plunged her more deeply within the mists of a surreal world, where anything could be said, everything exposed without terror because she was only reading a story. Nothing would actually happen. Lurid melodrama was not wreaked upon ordinary people like Neala Shaw.

"Good girl," Mr. Lipscomb said. He lifted the handkerchief. "Let me do this, and when you wake up, we'll talk."

Panic belatedly jolted her into action. Neala swept her arm up, knocking his hand away. "No!"

She leaped backward, then turned to run.

He caught her in less than half a dozen strides, clamping one strong arm about her middle while the other pressed the handkerchief over her mouth and nose. "Don't," he whispered in her ear. "Just breathe, and let go. I'm not going to kill you unless you leave me no choice…"

The words followed the darkness coiling around her like a monstrous snake, squeezing her into oblivion.

Once, when he'd been a raw eastern tenderfoot dumb enough to try and hide his inexperience, Gray stupidly accepted a dare to ride a wild mustang the other wranglers had whipped into a frenzy. The horse not only tossed him on his backside, but stomped the stuffing out of him before the wranglers dragged him free.

The pain from the bruises and cracked ribs was nothing compared to the pain he was fighting from Neala's betrayal.

The time he'd been shot, terrified he was about to die? A mere hiccup of discomfort, compared to the excruciating awareness that not only did she not trust him, despite the fact that he had shown her more respect, more gentleness—more of himself—than any other woman except his aunt…she could very likely already be dead.

No. She was not dead. He wouldn't think it, he refused to believe it, banished the possibility from his mind.

Anger, that's the ticket. He was angry with Neala for pulling such a thoughtless and dangerous stunt. In fact, when he found her, Gray chewed over the satisfaction of inflicting her with the worst of his undiluted temper.

As for the stoic German crone who aided and abetted her escape, lying to Gray with the expertise of a professional huckster, well, he was satisfied she'd think more than twice the next time she came between a man and his woman.

The phrase ricocheted around the stagecoach in which Gray was riding. It was four o'clock in the morning, the western sky as black as his thoughts, and he was sore from eighteen hours of travel in some of the most uncomfortable conveyances ever devised by man. He was grateful for the few hours of sleep he'd managed atop a pile of mailbags in the baggage car of a north-bound freight train he'd hopped outside of Sanford.

The stage wheels bounced into a rut, throwing him side-ways. Groaning, Gray jammed himself against the corner, crossed his arms and tried, mostly in vain, to stop thinking about Neala.

When Neala woke, for a befuddled moment she didn't know where she was. Blinking, she realized her mouth was very dry and that she felt vaguely queasy. She realized she was lying down, in a bed. But something wasn't right. Was she sick?

Stirring, she tried to sit up, but the effort intensified a sensa-tion of vertigo and she lay back, closing her eyes as foggy and unpleasant memories pummeled her. So she wasn't dead yet, then…

"Neala? Wake up. Please wake up so we can talk. I've been waiting all night."

The voice was familiar, but she couldn't place it immedi-ately so she reluctantly obeyed the plea to open her eyes. A man's face swam into view. "Mr. Crocker?" she whispered, mystified. "I— Did you find me? He didn't kill me. It's…Mr.…Lipscomb…" Her head throbbed, her mouth wouldn't work properly, and the only thought that didn't float away was that she was still alive.

She tried to smile for Mr. Crocker. "Saved me," she whis-pered. "You…saved my life."

The groundskeeper's eyes clouded, and he ducked his head. "I did," he eventually admitted in a low voice. "But you'll have to help me, to keep you alive."

"Help?"

The bed sagged when Mr. Crocker sat down beside her. A

flutter of disquiet whispered through Neala, but she couldn't shift away, much less vocalize a protest.

"Neala." He lifted a hand to smooth hair from her forehead, and Neala flinched. Mr. Crocker's face fell. "Try not to be scared," he said. "I'll take care of you."

"Where is Mr. Lipscomb?"

A half smile flickered as Mr. Crocker rose, walked away, returning momentarily with a canvas sack. "Meet Mr. Lipscomb," he said, his voice deepening, altering intonation so that he sounded exactly like the debonair gentleman from Kentucky.

Neala watched slack-jawed as he tugged a tousled black wig from the sack and casually fitted it over his balding pate. Next he produced a fake beard and mustache, transforming within the blink of an eye to Mr. Lipscomb, dressed in the garb of a lowly groundskeeper.

The deceit triggered the beginnings of outrage, deep inside. "Why?" She fought for lucidity; her body refused to cooperate. At the moment she could only lie there like a useless heap of rags, courtesy of the man standing above her.

A man she thought she knew. An unassuming, congenial gentleman who had turned out to be neither unassuming nor a gentleman.

Grayson hadn't trusted him from the first time they'd met.

Grayson, another man she thought she had known. And she'd been wrong about him, as well. "Sorry," she whispered, as desolation chilled her halfhearted attempt to regain consciousness and fight.

If she'd trusted Grayson more, she wouldn't be having to fight all alone.

"Neala! You must wake up!"

Startled, Neala blinked, tried to focus on Mr. Crocker. "You…lied to me."

"I told you, it was necessary." His hand closed over her upper arm, and he administered a light shake. "Don't go back to sleep. I need to explain, I want you to understand me, Neala."

She understood all right. She understood he was a scheming, deceitful… Her thoughts floated away. Eyelids drooping, she listened in a half doze while he talked.

"…and mostly because I needed to be able to follow your movements without risking exposure. Worked beautifully, didn't it?" As though embarrassed, he briefly turned his head and cleared his throat. "Over this past year, every time you managed to escape made me furious—yet relieved. Because the more I watched you, the more I realized you represent everything I've ever wanted. You're not like all the other women I've known. You noticed me, even when I was just Will Crocker, a lowly groundsman, instead of a wealthy gentleman. That's why I decided to warn you, the night of the ball. It seemed fitting somehow. Fair."

He rubbed his hands together. "Then I thought of something even better."

Chapter Twenty-Two

The stage pulled into White Sulphur Springs a little past seven o'clock Friday morning. Within another hour Gray ascertained that as of the previous afternoon Neala Shaw was still alive, and that he could find Deirdre McGee with the Vance family. After securing a room, where he cleaned himself into respectability if not affability, Gray made his way outside to the grounds behind the main hotel, where he found Deirdre reading a book while a group of children played croquet. When she caught sight of him, she laid her book aside and stood.

"Mr. Faulkner. I've been hoping you would come." She studied him, tapping one long finger against the corner of her mouth. After a moment the aura of censure dissipated. "I…see. So you were not after abandoning her to the wolves, as it were. She's a mind of her own, that girl."

"Lack of a mind, I'd say. At the moment I'm sorely tempted to abandon her to those wolves." They both sat down on the bench. "Actually, the little fool abandoned *me*. Left in the middle of the night." He reined in the runaway emotion. Deirdre's face revealed far too much sympathy. "Have you talked with her?"

"She refuses to have aught to do with me either. Sent a note yesterday, when she arrived, informing me that she'll not risk anyone else she cares about so I was not even to acknowledge her, should we cross paths. I would imagine the reason for her abandonment of you to be the same."

"If she cared a plugged nickel about me, she wouldn't have crept off in the middle of the night." Never mind what Deirdre assumed, or what Neala said in the letter she'd written to him. Actions, to Gray's way of thinking, most certainly did speak louder than a handful of tear-splotched words asking his forgiveness, urging him to forget about her.

"The lass would not be thinking clearly, what with the death of Mrs. Wilkes," Deirdre pointed out, her brogue thickening. She flicked Gray an apologetic smile. "Begging your pardon, Mr. Faulkner, but I was fond of the lady, don't you know. She was a grand dame, and didn't deserve to die, not like that."

"Nobody does. Even Neala, who's all but staked herself out for the fiend. Have you seen her at all, even from a distance?"

Deirdre shook her head. "But then, I've been at my duties to the children there, keeping them out of trouble and helping the Vances pack." She paused, added quietly, "I'll be leaving with them day after tomorrow. If Neala won't have me with her, there's naught I can do."

"It's all right." He failed to keep the bitterness out of his tone. "God knows there might be little I can do myself."

"Did you know how she fretted about your views of God?"

Gray made a derisive sound. "Her views aren't much better, to my way of thinking. Right now she's probably deluded herself into believing that all she needs is God's protection. That when she confronts this madman she'll convince him of the error of his ways, talk him into turning himself in, then take meals to him in prison."

"Wouldn't surprise me," Deirdre replied. "She's a stout heart, Mr. Faulkner, and a way about her that draws people."

"She's a foolish heart, and her naïveté about people is about to get her killed."

"Then I expect you better be off about your duty, hadn't you?"

And with that Deirdre picked up her book, called to the children, and left Gray standing in fulminating silence.

When Neala next awoke, the room was dark save for the flickering flame in an oil lantern on top of a bureau standing against the far wall. She had no idea of time, whether it was day or night, or how long her captivity had lasted. She supposed she ought to be afraid, but she felt nothing, not even gratitude that she was still alive, much less a compunction to pray for divine intervention.

God was not a loving heavenly Father, just a distant, austere Presence, dispensing judgment and justice at His whim, doling out tidbits of comfort when He so desired, never mind the needs of His suffering children. Yes, He was the Author of life. But He never lifted a finger to protect the innocent from senseless slaughter.

A shiver tapped with frost-tipped fingernails down the back of her spine. She should plot an escape, not lie here wallowing in a stupor of drugged self-pity. But Mr. Lipscomb—no, not Mr. Lipscomb. Will Crocker, the groundsman who she'd thought was her friend—Will Crocker, the villainous wretch, would hunt her down again.

For a while Neala idly watched the lantern flame, while she tried to drum up some outrage. Vaguely ashamed of the apathy, she finally rolled onto her side and managed to sit up. Cascades of curls drifted across her face, spilled over her shoulders and down her back. Neala didn't care. The room seemed to expand

and shrink around her; blinking her eyes several times did not dispel the fuzziness. Chloroform made for an excellent jailer.

At the moment, if she attempted a grandiose dash for the door, she'd collapse on the plank floorboards like an under-baked soufflé.

So where was Will?

Disinclined for anything beyond a cup of hot tea, Neala cleared her throat again. "Will? Hello? Are you here?"

Her abductor materialized in the doorway. Blearily Neala watched him cross to her, dressed in the dapper attire of Mr. Lipscomb.

"It's about time," he said, his head tilted to one side while he examined her with a thoroughness that roused her from some of the stupor.

His neatly pressed suit and spotted silk necktie made her feel more disheveled, even sordid. She gathered the mass of hair and, ignoring Will's presence, tried to plait the strands into a braid; neither her hair nor her fingers cooperated. Fine. She would ignore her hair as well. Neala lifted her chin. "I'm very thirsty. Is there anything to drink?"

"Of course. I had some refreshments delivered." A corner of his mustached mouth twitched. "Mr. Lipscomb is a particular, private individual, who faithfully orders the same tray every Friday morning. The bellhop who delivers it is quite friendly, because I tip him very well. Nobody suspects a thing, Neala. I told you, I'm very good at what I do."

At last a ripple of anger sloshed over the apathy. "It's not something to brag about." If her legs hadn't still felt noodly and the room weaving about, Neala would have been tempted to cannon into Will with the express intent of knocking him flat on the floor. "I liked you better as a groundsman."

"I know. That's why you're not dead."

Leaving her slack-jawed and silent, he returned moments

later with tepid lemonade and a plate of soggy sandwiches. No utensils she might have used for a weapon were included with the meal. Nor would he allow her to eat at the table in the other room. Like an invalid—or the condemned prisoner—she was forced to eat sitting up in the bed. But Will did produce the mother-of-pearl hair clip she'd been wearing when he abducted her, handing it to her without comment.

Humiliated, Neala scraped the mess of curls together at the base of her neck, fastened the clip, then turned to the tray. Her stomach churned but she choked down the food. It was difficult, holding on to anger when one was weak from hunger and trepidation.

If only she had listened to Grayson.

If only. Was there any other phrase in the land that could equal that one, for proclaiming the agony of abandonment by everything and everyone you loved? Including God?

When she finished eating, Will removed the tray and set it on the floor, then pulled a straight-back chair next to the bed and sat down. "You're awake, and I've fed you. Now we're going to talk." He leaned forward. "I used to wonder why they named you after him," he observed almost dreamily. "All through the years, I wondered. I'm glad my mother was wrong. You're nothing like him."

Impatience abruptly tightened his face and the dreaminess vanished. The light brown eyes turned opaque, like muddy water. "Before I share the rest of my plans, tell me where you've hidden the crest badge. It's mine, you know. I've been searching for it all my life." Without looking away from Neala he scooped up the glass of her half-finished lemonade and downed it in a single gulp. Against the dark contrast of false beard and mustache his lips appeared almost red, shiny from the liquid.

Anger stirred inside Neala like a bucket of hissing snakes.

She shimmied backward on the bed until her spine pressed against the iron rungs on the headboard. "Will Crocker, you may have successfully abducted me. But you most certainly do not have me." If only she possessed the strength to dump the bucket of snakes over his head. "Nor do you have *my* family's crest badge."

Wait. The badge. His comment about her being named after Grandfather. Why would he care about the badge, or her name, unless… No. Oh, no. Dry-mouthed, Neala sensed what was coming, and resisted with every drop of sluggish blood in her body. In a futile and childish reaction she squeezed her eyes shut.

Instead of reacting with more anger she heard Will laugh. "You can't run or hide anymore, Neala. It's like God's will. You can't escape it. Or me. *I'm* God's Will." Another laugh grated her ears, this one full of bitterness.

Reluctantly Neala opened her eyes, drew up her knees, and clasped them with clammy hands while she waited for the man in front of her to finish destroying her life.

"Grandmother and Momma used to tell me that, you know. Tell me over and over that I was God's Will. And I never understood, it was the same as the neighbor boys who thrashed me. I hated them, hated my name. Hated *you.* I never understood—until I slipped into your room one day, when you were out with your seducer." He spewed the word as though spitting out a vile potion. "I held the crest badge in my hands and realized they were right all along. The crest badge was meant to belong to me, just as you are meant to belong to me. To *me.*"

Time ticked into immobility, like a clock winding down, as Will ceased the verbal onslaught. A welter of emotions swirled around the air between them, sucking the breath from Neala's lungs. As the silence stretched, crushing knowledge settled irrevocably inside her heart.

"Your grandmother was Letitia Rutledge," she said dully. "The woman my grandfather jilted."

"He ruined her. *Humiliated and ruined her.* Her, and my mother."

Before Neala could blink his hands were around her throat, thumbs pressing against her windpipe. "She was forced to marry a country bumpkin because she was carrying Neal Shaw's child. A sharecropper. A nobody who treated her like she was a slave."

A dark flush stained his cheeks. "I'm Neal Shaw's firstborn male progeny. You have no right—for half a century nobody's had the right to the name, to the family heirloom—but me. Not that pompous Alexander Shaw, or his two whelps. Not your stuffy, insignificant father or your coward of a brother. My name should be William *Shaw,* and my mother should be living in that mansion on Grace Avenue in Richmond. *I* should be wearing the clan crest. Not you."

With each word, his fingers squeezed her throat more tightly. "I'm finally taking the name that should have been mine forty years ago. Now—" he lowered his face until they were inches apart "—tell me what you've done with the crest badge."

"I was told that Miss Shaw was staying in this room. She checked in yesterday afternoon," Gray queried the maid who was loading up mop and buckets and soiled linens outside Neala's room. "What do you mean, you haven't seen her?"

She finally glanced up from behind the large push cart holding all her supplies. "Well, she ain't been 'round. I put away her things, like, but I don't know nothin' else."

Gray dismissed the sullen maid, then shut the door and spent several moments thoroughly searching the room. In her impulsive flight from North Carolina, Neala had scarcely packed enough to fill the single case now tucked away in the chiffonier. He found nothing of value in his search, not even a slip of paper in her handwriting, or a handkerchief carelessly left on the counterpane. Setting his jaw, Gray headed for Mrs. Wilkes's suite of rooms on the first floor.

The parlor was meticulously clean—and jarringly silent. When he reached the widow's bedroom he paused, staring at the bed while his chest tightened and impotent rage swam through his veins.

There was something despicable about murdering an elderly woman in her sleep, something lacking in the villain's moral fiber that rendered him more monster than human being. Such a person did not deserve to live.

If he'd harmed Neala, if she was—

With a muttered oath he swiveled on his boot and stalked out, slamming the door behind him. The Old White covered forty acres, with cottages and service buildings scattered everywhere. Gray planned to search every inch of the grounds, every one of the buildings.

By noon he learned that after Neala arrived the previous day she had walked back across to the depot. For the few moments it took Gray to walk there himself he nursed the illusion that she'd been smart enough to board the first train passing through. That faint hope was snuffed out the moment he talked to Hank, the old porter, who kindly led him to the storage room where Mrs. Wilkes's coffin lay on huge blocks of ice. Grimly Gray set about searching every dusty corner until he determined that at least Neala had not been murdered and stuffed behind the stacks of steamer trunks and crates.

Finally he approached the coffin—and discovered her prized crest badge lying on top.

She'd been here. At some point in the last twenty-four

hours, Neala had been inside this room. And for some reason, she had left her most valued possession behind. A clue, in hopes Gray would discover it? Or, knowing Neala as he did, more likely she'd left the crest in a gesture of renunciation, and perhaps atonement, since she blamed herself for Mrs. Wilkes's death.

A puff of empathy dusted over Gray. *My fault.* He remembered the words she'd spoken, that she believed with all of her anguished heart to be true. *This is all my fault.*

"In a pig's eye," Gray declared now, empathy rapidly displaced by frustration—and fear.

He scooped up the crest, studied it in the dim light, surprised by its weight and, upon closer examination, its monetary value. Obviously Neala knew next to nothing about gemstones; she'd declared the crest to be mostly of sentimental value. She seldom wore it, explaining to Gray that it was far too heavy for spring and summer costumes, and her light woolen shawl. On the few occasions she'd needed her heavy cloak, Gray had idly noted the badge pinned to her shoulder, but his attention had been focused on Neala, not an unremarkable cloak or a cumbersome Scottish memento of only sentimental value.

Perhaps he should have remembered the first rule of investigation: notice everything.

Well, he was noticing now. Two deep red rubies, probably Burmese, winked at him from the metal strap and buckle that circled a hand holding a dagger. Three smaller emeralds of equally fine quality were embedded in the dagger's shaft, while a narrow rope of cornflower-blue sapphire chips formed the base of the hand.

Neala's sentimental crest badge, with its motley collection of what she'd assumed was colored glass, would fetch a hefty fortune, particularly if the gemstones were pried free and sold off.

For several moments Gray stood silently, almost absently caressing the badge's contours. Eventually he noticed the lettering engraved along the top half of the metal strap and buckle, no doubt added back in the thirties or forties, when Queen Victoria's fondness for Scotland invaded England with far more success than her northern neighbor ever enjoyed politically. The light was too dim to read the words. Gray walked behind the coffin, shoving aside some trunks in order to reach the storage room's solitary window. He turned so the light fell directly upon the crest.

"Fide et fortitudine." He read the Latin phrase aloud. Fidelity and fortitude—no. If he recalled his Latin, the correct translation would be *by* fidelity and fortitude.

Chest tight, Gray returned to the coffin. After a somber moment's reflection, he removed his hat. According to Hank, Mrs. Wilkes would depart the Old White for the last time on a four o'clock freight train, bound for Charlottesville, Virginia. One hand resting on the coffin, the other holding Neala's clan crest, Gray spared a brief moment to bid Mrs. Wilkes farewell. "I'll find the man who did this," he promised her aloud. "And I'll find Neala. Rest in peace, Mrs. Wilkes."

Somebody ought to be able to rest in peace.

He left the storage room and motioned to Hank. "I need for you to hold on to this until I return," he told the porter, and handed him the badge. "It belongs to Miss Shaw. I'd hate for it to be misplaced, or lost."

They shared a look of wordless communication.

"Don't you worry, suh," Hank said as he withdrew a large paisley handkerchief and deftly wrapped the crest badge inside its folds. Then he tucked everything inside the inner pocket of his uniform. "I'll keep it safe, whiles you fetch Miss Shaw. I reckon it be your job, keeping her safe."

His job. As Gray made his way back to the hotel, he faced

squarely that keeping Neala safe was no longer merely a job. *By fidelity and fortitude.* "Hold on, love," he whispered. "Hold on to your faith, and your fortitude, for both of us."

Chapter Twenty-Three

Breathing hard, Will stared down at the woman he held captive, whose creamy complexion was now mottled with red and bruised-purple splotches because he was choking her. His fingers were wrapped around that soft, slender throat not in a caress—but to kill.

With a strangled groan he yanked his hands away and stepped backward, two steps, then three, his gaze transfixed upon her face. The darkness had consumed him, causing him to almost kill Neala despite his resolve to achieve his lifelong goals, not through her death—but through marriage.

She gasped, then coughed, tears leaking from the corners of her eyes as her body spasmed back to life.

"It's too easy," Will murmured, trancelike, his gaze falling to his hands. "Too easy to take someone's life." Finally he blinked, focusing on Neala once more. "I don't like who I am, don't like what my mother and grandmother turned me into."

He swiveled, walking unsteadily to the other side of the room. For several long moments he stood without moving, until the bloodlust finally subsided. The darkness receded, and he regained the sense of self, the man he longed to be.

Silently he fetched more lemonade, then held her so she could swallow, closing his eyes to savor the feel of her soft hair, the shape of her head. When she pushed his hand away, he set the glass aside and sat back down, watching her. Waiting.

After a long moment, she sighed. One trembling hand lifted to cover her eyes, then dropped back onto the bed. "What Grandfather did to your grandmother was…a grievous sin," she whispered, her voice papery thin. "I—I can't blame you for being angry. For feeling betrayed."

Her understanding gutted Will. He had expected fear, even hysteria. Perhaps anger, given the spark of temper he'd briefly witnessed. But not this—this softness, this compassion, toward the person who had threatened her. He didn't know how to react, what to say. How to explain the longing he had tried to strangle out of his entire life, like he had almost strangled Neala.

"I have something to ask you," he eventually confessed. "I don't care what Grandmother and Momma told me about your grandfather, because I—"

"Our grandfather," Neala interrupted softly. "Mr. Crocker— Will. We share the same grandfather. We're…family."

The word pricked him on the raw, all the more because her declaration ruined the moment of his own. "We're no more 'family' than a flock of wild geese flying south for the winter. But when we marry, *then* we'll be family."

"Marry?" she spluttered. "Marry…you?" Now temper licked through the words, banishing all trace of the compassion. "I can't believe you'd have the—the audacity to suggest such a thing. It's monstrous, sickening. This prattle about marriage is a form of torture, isn't it? Like pretending you've changed your mind about killing me."

Relief at the outburst spread inside Will. Long inured to his mother's emotional outbursts, he found anger and contempt more palatable than displays of softness or compassion. "I knew it would take time to convince you." Calmer now, he quietly padded across the room and opened the top drawer of the bureau. "Time, unfortunately, is not something we have a lot of." After retrieving what he wanted, he returned to Neala. "Defy me if you must. But you won't be the only one to suffer the consequences."

"What is that supposed to mean?" She pressed her fingers against her temples as though holding a headache at bay, then laid her hand over her bruised throat. "I can't believe I actually felt sorry for you. You've treated our family—*your* family, not just my family—like a flock of wild geese! Shooting us down, one by one, because your grandmother and your mother poisoned your heart. Our grandfather was wrong, but your grandmother was, too. She had no right to inflict her lack of forgiveness on you, and your mother. They ruined your life, and now you've ruined an entire family—what could have been *your* family."

"You don't know what you're talking about. I've only done what had to be done. And will continue to do so." Slowly he tugged at his tie, loosening its constricting folds. She used words, trapped him with them the way he set up snares for rabbits. Momma had warned him, but he hadn't wanted to listen.

"Why didn't you write Grandfather?" Neala persisted, swiping her dampened eyes in a gesture reminiscent enough of his mother to prick his own temper. "Why didn't your *grandmother* write him? He would have accepted her child as his own. Yes, it might have been awkward, but if he had known, he would—"

"He did know."

The assertion fell between them like sulfuric coals, filling the air with their stench. Neala blinked once, twice, shook her head in denial. With a hiss of rage Will whipped off the tie, balling it in his fist. "My grandmother showed me the letter she wrote, demanding that he take responsibility for her and his baby—my mother. And do you know what your grandfather wrote back? *Do you?*"

Dropping the tie, he reached forward and grabbed her shoulders, shook her. Hard. "Answer me!"

It was as though his anger fueled Neala's. "I don't know!" she yelled back. "You let go of me, Will Crocker! Remove your hands this instant!"

Will released her abruptly and took two backward steps, but Neala was too incensed to notice. Oh, but she was weary of the role of peacemaker.

Of being nice.

"I will not be treated as your kicking post another minute! Not one more minute! Do you hear me? Whatever Grandfather said or didn't say, whatever he did or didn't do, *is not my fault.* What's more, I don't care what he wrote your grandmother! You don't like the name you have, but at least it's yours. You didn't have someone trying to take it away from you because you were only a girl. You didn't have a brother who resented you his entire life when he should have— Oh, why am I bothering?"

She glowered at him, funneling a lifetime of resentment into the bubbling core of her first temper tantrum. "You don't care. Nobody cares. It's a good thing Adrian at least disappeared somewhere even you couldn't find, isn't it? Otherwise he would have been one more goose in your gunnysack."

"Your brother's a cur," Will muttered sullenly. "He wasn't worth my time tracking him down."

"Ha! He's just better at covering his trail than I was. Maybe at least he found some happiness somewhere." Furiously she swiped her dripping nose and unwanted tears with her sleeve.

She was a prisoner, wasn't she? Doomed prisoners didn't bother with gentility. "I had dreams, like my brother. Like you." The words tumbled free, gathering fresh momentum. "I entertained longings for the future. I had hopes. But not anymore. You…destroyed every one of them. You should have been my cousin," she finished, pain thickening the statement. "It's a shame you're not a very good marksman. I wouldn't be here now, waiting for you to finish your—your life's mission, making all of Neal Shaw's legitimate children pay because he made the mistake of falling in love with someone else."

For a humming moment, Will stood there, staring down. "I never realized it, but you have a shrew inside of you, just like my mother. I don't like it, Neala."

So nothing good blew in on the storms of an unleashed temper, not even satisfaction. Nor did Neala much care for the debris littering her heart in the backwash, especially when that terrifying opaqueness once again darkened her captor's eyes, giving them a reptilian chill that boded nothing promising for her future.

"I do have to leave for a little while now," Will announced suddenly. "I can't trust you, of course." He reached behind his back, then produced a pair of metal handcuffs. "These will keep you from trying to escape. I'll try to fix it so you can sleep."

Stupid of her to have expected otherwise. Dully she assessed her options—door, window, physical attack—and discarded them all. Will remained stronger, quicker, and certainly more ruthless. She needed to make the effort however, and shoved herself forward on the bed.

Then Will was beside her. The room tipped into a slow swirl as he looped the chain on the handcuffs through one of the bed rungs, then handcuffed her wrists together. "If you want to stay alive, keep quiet."

Next he removed a snow-white linen handkerchief. "This will help," he said as he gagged her mouth with it. His hand closed over her forearm, just above the cuffs, in a fleeting caress that chilled her to the bone. "To avoid further discomfort, keep still."

The door shut behind him. Neala was alone with a bitterness that splashed her soul like acid heedlessly spilled on unprotected skin.

By two o'clock, Gray reached the conclusion that nobody had encountered Neala on any of the paths leading from the depot back to the main hotel. Or if she had, regrettably nobody he talked to had witnessed such a meeting.

By four o'clock, he discovered that the groundskeeper Neala had befriended had given notice and quit the previous week.

"Did he give a reason?" Gray inquired of the head groundsman.

"Nay." The gaunt Irishman shrugged, then spat a wad of tobacco. "But would no' surprise me if 'twere the woman. He was sweet on one of the lasses—not a belle, mind you. The lad knew his place, right enough, when it came to mingling with belles and blue bloods. But seems she left, and he grieved, something fierce, I recollect. Never knew her name. Will always kept to himself, like."

"Any ideas where he may have gone?"

"No, sir. Like I said, Will kept to himself. Nice enough, never a moment's trouble. Did his job in fine fashion, don't you know."

The suspicion crawling through Gray's mind settled coldly in his gut. "His name was Will?"

"Aye."

"Will—what was his last name?" he asked, wanting to be sure.

"That would be Crocker."

"Did he supply you with any references when he was hired?"

"Wouldn't be knowing that. You'd have to check with Mr. Eakle, the hotel manager."

"Do you know what Will did on his off days?"

The other man winked. "Now why would I be knowing what the man was up to on his own time?" He pushed the brim of his flat cap up on his forehead, his ruddy countenance sobering as he studied Gray. "Sorry to be so little help, lad. But the truth is, I never saw him when he weren't workin'."

Gray thanked him, tipped the man a quarter and left him to his business. A headache thudded at the base of his skull; the back of his spine itched like blazes. Why hadn't he taken Crocker more seriously? That day, the day Crocker paid a visit to Neala after she'd almost been killed at the racetrack—the signs were unmistakable—and Gray had ignored them. At the time he'd been more annoyed with the groundskeeper's effrontery than suspicious, despite the fact that Crocker's infatuation with Neala blazed forth plain as a wall-eyed pike. Gray might have wanted to toss him out the window, but he could hardly blame the poor fellow when he'd been struggling with the same uncomfortable emotions himself.

Now he cursed himself for not paying closer attention. Infatuation rendered men's brains the consistency of mud.

But unrequited infatuation could also turn to hatred. No doubt Crocker had accepted as truth Gray and Neala's sham courtship, since Gray had gone to great lengths to convince every guest and every employee of the Old White that verisimilitude equated with truth.

But for Neala the sham courtship had swiftly become fact. She was neither experienced enough, jaded enough, nor manipulative enough, to be able to hide her feelings from him.

Briefly he closed his eyes, struggling against an avalanche of self-condemnation. *He* was experienced enough, jaded enough, and manipulative enough, to ensure the affections of a young woman whose arsenal of female arrows remained sheathed.

Neala hadn't smothered him with pleas or expectations, had placed no demands upon him. In fact, the contrary woman had renounced his protection altogether, and run away. While he might tell himself that her actions spoke louder than what he'd seen in those expressive brown eyes, he knew he was deceiving nobody but himself.

As for his own feelings…

Hoist on your own petard, aren't you, pal? Yessiree, despite himself Gray had succumbed to his own fabrication.

Though he despised himself, he at least could be man enough to admit that his heart was irrevocably lost to the only woman on earth who hadn't demanded it. Which made the "esteemed" Grayson Faulkner with all his wealth and family connections, all his hard-won skills and fierce independence, the equal of an inconsequential groundskeeper. If God was really up there, all-seeing and all-knowing, no doubt He considered that Gray deserved every one of the boulders avalanching his way.

What if Will Crocker couldn't accept the seeming loss of Neala's heart to another man? Instead of getting himself roaring drunk, or looking for another pretty face to pursue, what if he'd determined to seek revenge on the woman who had rebuffed him?

His brains were turning rotten. Tales of rejected lovers had fueled the gossip grist mill here at the Old White for decades. And to Gray's knowledge, not a single discarded male ever took a nosedive off Lover's Leap. Outside of a few illegal duels, none of them had resorted to murder, either, particularly the murder of an innocent friend of the erstwhile sweetheart.

Like countless other guests from European princes to genteel Southern paupers, Will Crocker had merely slunk off to lick his wounds. This was Greenbrier's White Sulphur Springs, not some two-bit hotel over a saloon, or vaudeville on Coney Island with its exaggerated villains, heroines and heroes.

Yet over the years Gray's idealism, sanded down through brutal reality, had been forced to accept that most acts of murder were crimes of passion as opposed to the cold premeditation with which the Shaw family had been stalked and subsequently slaughtered.

God knew he'd witnessed one of those inexplicable crimes of passion himself.

Which meant *Crocker* might be responsible for Mrs. Wilkes's death, and Neala's disappearance from the hotel. Will Crocker, lowly groundsman. Not the elusive, cold-blooded bounder who'd been dispatching members of the Shaw family.

Gray was probably tracking not one, but two killers.

Too much. Such a likelihood was too much for a man to handle.

For the past twenty-four hours he'd fought his way through a foreboding cloud of uncertainty. Now the cloud chilled, whirled around him in a sucking vortex until it swallowed him up completely. He could scarcely breathe. Mind spinning, he collapsed onto one of the many benches scattered about the grounds. Dropping his head, he propped his forearms on his knees and stared unseeingly at the grass between his boots. Two ants trudged their way between the blades. With a quick move, Gray could grind those ants into oblivion with his heel.

A sensation of profound inadequacy seized hold, suffocating in its intensity. Right now he felt as powerless as those ants looking up at his descending boot heel. He didn't know which way to turn, how to proceed. Neala might already be dead—

and all of Gray's experience and touted capabilities had proved worthless. Like Marty. Just like Marty. Even if he telegraphed for reinforcements, odds were they'd arrive too late. So like a mindless chump, he sat on a bench and did nothing.

As though in a dream, Aunt Isabella's voice drifted across his mind, sorrowfully reproaching him for his hard heart, his unwillingness to allow God to be a part of his life. To guide his path, offer counsel and direction. "Why would I want to?" he groused aloud. What had God ever done for him, to foster the kind of faith his aunt—even Neala—professed?

Where had God been throughout his stifled childhood, or his painful journey to adulthood? When Marty's life was snuffed out, like Mrs. Wilkes's, for no reason? *No reason.* Black despair savaged his insides.

A faint but insistent voice deep inside his mind pointed out that his life without God certainly hadn't provided the faculties he needed to survive this present darkness.

With a guttural groan he surged to his feet. He absolutely did *not* want to hear that voice. But in vain Gray struggled to erase from his mind the vision of Aunt Bella with her knowing eyes, or the sound of Neala's confident assertion that God would protect her.

All right. *All right. If You keep her alive, I promise to give You a try.*

The vow squeezed through his denial. Once the thought entered his mind, however, Gray realized he couldn't ignore the tantalizing possibility that faith in God might actually help him. He felt numb, weightless, yet his knees threatened to buckle beneath the unbearable strain of not knowing. But what could it hurt, to see if Neala's and Aunt Bella's views of God possessed any merit?

Almost unconsciously he resumed walking, his footsteps taking him along toward Howard's Creek. She loved walking by the creek. Used to babble much like the water, about how peaceful it was, about the ducks and geese and mockingbirds and swallows and every other species of fowl she felt compelled to point out to Gray; about the smell of wild grasses and damp earth and some floral fragrance neither of them could identify. Every time they ventured forth for a stroll, Neala insisted upon a walk along the creek.

Awareness punched through Gray with the sharp crack of a rifle shot. *She would have come here to walk, after she saw the coffin.* To heal, to soothe the pain. Gray knew it as though Neala were standing here explaining her feelings.

Charged with fresh strength, he retraced his steps until he reached the bridge that led back to the hotel. Then, stropping his senses to razor-edge concentration, he methodically commenced a search of every square inch of turf. He didn't know what he was looking for, but he did know that if Neala had left any trace, no matter how infinitesimal, he would find it.

Chapter Twenty-Four

Late-afternoon sunlight cast a luminescent glow over the earth, turning the still water of Howard's Creek to a shimmery silver-gold. Oblivious to the beauty of his surroundings, Gray scoured every inch of the ground along the creek bank.

Thirty minutes later, he spied a lady's glove lying in the long meadow grass, next to a large outcropping of boulders and towering sumac. Disbelief all but knocked him backward into the creek. It was Neala's glove. Dizzy with the relief—and some unidentifiable emotion he couldn't describe—Gray held the scrap of soft leather against his face, inhaling the faintest tang of the vanilla lotion she liked. When his fingers traced over the indentation where a button was missing, he almost broke down. Three days earlier Neala had grumbled about having to find a haberdasher to purchase another button, and how she detested needlework.

"I'm too impatient," she'd admitted. "This is the third button I've lost. I never sew them on tightly enough."

It could have been any glove, but it wasn't. It was Neala's. What he wouldn't give for a good tracking dog… Instead, Gray tucked the glove inside his breast pocket, over his heart.

Then he examined every inch of the ground surrounding the spot where he'd found it.

Behind the boulders, pressed deep into the dirt, he found two footprints. Shoes, not boots, roughly size elevens. Weight on the right foot concentrated on the heel, which was more worn on the left side. Little disturbance in the earth around the prints. So, he'd been lying in wait, had he? Probably followed her, then cut around through the trees until he discovered this isolated spot.

He wouldn't have had much time beforehand to prepare, which told Gray the man was not only determined, but daring. But who was it? Will Crocker, or someone as yet unknown and unidentified?

Sheathing his mind from the fear, Gray poured sixteen years of experience into the task of backtracking the trail of those two footprints. They led across the meadow, past the bathhouse and onto the path leading to the spring. Gray ignored the curious stares of several strolling guests, ignored the deepening gold cast to the light, ignored the pressure building inside his chest. He would search nose to the ground if necessary, to filter through the hundreds of smeared prints marking the packed-dirt walkways, until he found a print that matched the ones by Howard's Creek.

All right, he knew he was crazy to even try. Knew the odds against him were laughable, they were so immense.

But he'd found Neala's glove.

An hour later, eyes straining in the purpling shadows of dusk, back muscles on fire, he tripped over a tree root a little ways past the Georgia Row cottages, and went down on his knees. Winded, fighting exhaustion, for a moment he didn't move; the urge to give in, to just roll over and let life crush him, gnawed his vitals like a cornered rat. He lifted a hand to swipe at his eyes, blinked several times to regain his focus.

Twelve inches from his knee, a size-eleven footprint, with the weight listing to the right side and the left heel more worn down, waited for his inspection. A light wind stirred the tree branches above him, and a dying sunbeam highlighted the print.

For a pulsating second that stretched heavenward, Gray stared unblinkingly. A single boot print might offer little in the way of conclusive direction, or even the identity of the wearer. But for Gray, the sight of it came close enough to answered prayer to lift him off his knees and to his feet.

Whoever made this print had to be either a guest, or an employee.

Gray set off at a run for the main hotel. The register would supply names. And hopefully Mr. Eakle, or one of the other hotel employees, would supply the knowledge.

Unless she'd been murdered and hastily disposed of—a possibility Gray refused to accept—the murderer would not risk exposure by using the cottages as part of his abduction scheme. Most likely he'd been on foot. There had been no sign either of hooves or buggy wheels near the path by Howard's Creek. Regardless of whether Neala had accompanied him quietly, or as—he flinched from the thought—an unconscious bundle, her abductor couldn't travel very far, most likely within a one- to three-mile radius. Whether this footprint had been made before or after he snatched Neala, its presence indicated that in all likelihood the man—and Neala—were still within reach.

Somewhere within that one- to three-mile radius, he would find Neala.

And she wouldn't be dead. *She was not* dead.

God? If You're really up there, and You care, please don't let Neala be dead.

Fuming, Will locked the door to the second chamber with a vicious rattle, so that Neala would hear. Her tirade had made him late; as Mr. Lipscomb, he always took a stroll about the grounds in the late afternoons, but he could see through the window that the sky was streaked with deepening shades of rust-colored orange. The pole lamps scattered over the grounds had been lit, and the square nickel alarm clock on the mantel was relentlessly ticking toward six. He hurried across to his valise, which he'd left open on top of the library table in the corner of the room, and snatched up a fresh white collar and cuffs from the neat stacks of Mr. Lipscomb's clothes.

Then he realized he'd left his necktie in the room with Neala.

Kill her off now, and be done with it. She's never going to agree to your plan, and if she does it's a lie. She'll flee at the first opportunity. A guttural sound escaped and he paced the room, crushing the collar and cuffs while he struggled to silence the inner taunts, tried to formulate a plan when every moment brought his mother one step closer to discovering his lair.

To calm himself, he fetched the gold pocket watch and vest chain he'd treated himself to and fastened it in place. The cigars. He mustn't forget the cigars that Lipscomb smoked during his evening stroll. Only two remained in the cigar box. Well, he wouldn't be needing the affectation after tomorrow anyway, he reminded himself. Too bad. He'd developed a fondness for the taste of tobacco, and decided that he might cultivate the habit when he became William Shaw, gentleman and proud owner of a centuries-old heirloom unlike any other.

An image of Neala, lying bound and gagged on the rumpled bed, slowed his movements as he tucked the cigars inside the flap pockets of his jacket. The words she'd hurled at him rang in his ears. With a muffled curse, he smoothed the collar, then yanked it in place around his neck. It was wrinkled, but once he put on the coat nobody would notice, especially this late in the day.

The clock dinged six.

He fumbled with the button on the stupid collar. Stupid laundress had applied too much starch again. And the stupid button was too small for a man's fingers.

A firm knock sounded on the outside door. Rattled, Will dropped the collar, his gaze riveted to the door. Another knock, this one more forceful, made him jump.

"Just a moment," he called.

He retrieved the collar, but he'd never get it and the cuffs fastened in time so he tossed everything back into the valise, then feverishly checked his appearance in the oval mirror over the parlor fireplace.

He looked acceptable, despite that unfortunate scuffle with Neala. The fastidious, somewhat prissy gentleman of means from Kentucky. No resemblance whatsoever to Will Crocker, even without cuffs and collar, or necktie. Wig, mustache and beard remained in place, and above his vest the blue pinstripe shirt sported only a few wrinkles. The gold watch and chain polished the look nicely. He looked the very picture of a gentleman enjoying a peaceful afternoon in his private rooms.

After a last calming breath, he started back across the room—and remembered the valise. Lipscomb was supposed to remain until the last day. His valise would certainly not be on display, nor packed to the brim. "One moment," he called again, frantically closing the case and dropping it in the farthest corner, well beyond the light from the bulb hanging from the ceiling.

Drawing a deep breath, he fixed a smile on his face, and opened the door. Grayson Faulkner stood on the porch. The dying sun rimmed his silhouette in livid hues of orange, yet cast the rest of his body into the shadows of approaching night.

Will blinked, then collected himself. He was the honorable Geoffrey Lipscomb, and he had nothing to hide. "Hello… Faulkner, isn't it? We met a time or two."

"Yes." His gaze swept Will in a comprehensive survey, then moved to the room behind. "I understand you're remaining here until the last day?"

Will nodded. "I enjoy the fall colors. How about yourself? Planning to finish out the season as well?" He paused, investing what he felt was an appropriate amount of inquiry in his tone. Confidence poured over him in a welcome flood tide. "Is there something I can do for you?" It was a temptation not to laugh aloud in his face.

"I'm speaking to all the remaining guests," Faulkner said. "Trying to find information about Miss Shaw. Neala Shaw."

"Ah, yes. The young woman who accompanied you on several occasions, when we met on the grounds earlier this summer. Seemed a charming lady."

The other man obviously had no idea that the woman he sought was a dozen paces away. The novelty of it swelled inside Will. For a sliver of a second he was tempted to share his accomplishment, longed to feel the satisfaction of someone complimenting him on his mind, on a job well done.

"That's right." Faulkner's expression had turned to stone. "Miss Shaw. Have you seen her lately?"

Will professed confusion. "Why, no. Why do you ask? A lovers' quarrel?"

Their gazes met, and for some reason a chill danced between Will's shoulder blades. His palms began to sweat but he maintained eye contact, keeping his expression politely curious.

"Not a quarrel," Faulkner said. "There's a strong possibility something may have happened to her." He paused. "And if it has, I plan to see that the person or persons responsible pay. Dearly."

"Do you mean to tell me…some sort of foul play? Surely not, Mr. Faulkner. Things like that don't happen here at the Old

White. Why, that's tantamount to sacrilege. Surely the young lady has departed, and chose not to inform you. Perhaps her feelings did not mirror yours."

Too much, he warned himself. Too much. And yet, the temptation crested, sweeping Will into the backwash. Casually he tugged out the watch, flipped its lid open. "I say, I'm about to order up a late tea. Would you care to join me?"

For a deliciously frightening second he thought Faulkner would take him up on the offer. Then the other man shook his head.

"Thanks, I'll pass. I'm checking every cottage on the grounds. Every one," he repeated, eyes bluer than the late-afternoon October sky boring into Will. "I won't rest until I've found Miss Shaw."

"Well, I wish you success, and pray the young lady is well. It's a trifle late, but after tea I plan to take my usual afternoon perambulation about the grounds, before going to supper. I'll keep an eye open for Miss Shaw."

"Thanks." After a last lingering look, Faulkner swiveled on his heel and left.

Will shut the door, and clamped a hand over his mouth to stifle the wild laughter.

Forty minutes later, Gray completed his circuit of all remaining occupied cottages; he returned to the main hotel, where Superintendent Eakle assured him that every room in the main hotel had also been searched. No sign of Neala Shaw had been reported, outside of her belongings in her old room.

Restless, Gray returned to his own room, where he spent several moments writing out his thoughts, grappling with something—a feeling, a hunch. Perhaps it was foreboding, or fear. But something nagged his mind, vexatious as a chigger bite.

One by one he listed the remaining guests. Several, he decided, justified further scrutiny. The mantel clock chimed half past the hour; his stomach growled, reminding him he hadn't eaten much in the past thirty-six hours.

Something else to lay at Neala's feet, when he found her.

His skin felt as though it were on fire. In a surge of motion Gray stood, flung aside tablet and chewed-up pencil, strapped holster and gun in place, stuffed arms in his jacket and fled the room. He may as well go feed his belly. He wasn't about to while away two hours feeding the fear.

Halfway across the lobby Deirdre McGee hailed him. "Glad to catch up with you, Mr. Faulkner," she said. "I just met a woman. I'm thinking you need to meet her as well. She claims to be Will Crocker's ma."

"His *mother?*"

"Aye. My reaction as well. But that's what she says. I happened to be at the front desk, fetching the last of the mail for the Vances. Jimmy hands me the mail, then introduces us after telling Mrs. Crocker I might have some information as to her son's whereabouts."

"And why would Jimmy think that, Deirdre?"

She pulled a face. "I've not said a word, Mr. Faulkner, so don't be flaying me with those eyes of yours. But 'twas no secret that guests thought I was lady's maid to Miss Shaw, nor that poor Will carried a torch for her. Most of the staff heard of it, the day she was almost trampled at the racetrack."

"I know." He inclined his head in a tacit apology before shifting his attention to the thin, washed-out-looking woman standing with arms defensively crossed, in the corner of the lobby. Her gown was neatly pressed, but the style was a good fifteen years out of fashion, as was the hat on her head. She certainly looked more like a mother than a jealous woman who had chased her lover down. But why was she here at the Old White?

He didn't know if Will Crocker's mother's appearance was coincidence, or divine providence. But he couldn't help but remember Neala's words, the day they'd met the Youngs, and learned about Letitia Rutledge.

"Someday," she'd told him with the facile confidence that used to provoke him beyond measure, "you're going to find yourself in a place where you'll not only admit that God watches over us, you'll be thanking Him for it."

Gray set his jaw. "You told me Crocker left two weeks ago. What did Mrs. Crocker have to say to you?"

"She's that concerned about her son, she says. Claims he went home spouting plans about a woman he planned to marry, then disappeared. She's looking for him."

"What?" A passing bellboy stopped dead in his tracks, eyes rounded as he gawked at Gray. Gray lashed himself back under control. "Crocker told his mother he was going to *marry* Neala?"

"Aye, and if you hope to learn anything else, you'd best plaster a friendlier look on your face, laddie."

Jaw twitching, Gray tried to relax his taut neck and shoulders. "I didn't plan to roast her alive." Heat prickled the back of his neck.

"I'll introduce you," Deirdre murmured, and administered a light pat that almost dislocated his shoulder. "She's a mother, distressed over her son, same as you're distressed over Neala. You'll do fine, Mr. Faulkner. Myself, I'll not be able to stay but a moment. The Vances are expecting me." She tugged a slip of folded paper out of her pocket, hesitated before thrusting it out for Gray. "We leave in the morning. This is the address where I'll be. Would you mind, if you find Neala—"

"I will find her."

The corner of Deirdre's mouth flickered. "Aye," she murmured. "You will. Would you let me know?"

Gray took the slip of paper. Then, dragging his gaze away from the slight form of Mrs. Crocker, he looked across into the kind face of a woman who, much like Aunt Bella, saw far more than most other people. "I'll let you know," he promised. Then he brushed a kiss against her cheek that colored up lovely as a summer tea rose. "Thanks, Deirdre. You're a rare one, for a woman."

"Aye, that's what they all say." Charmingly flustered, she gestured across the lobby. "She's waiting."

"Then let's not keep her waiting any longer."

All right, God, Gray thought as Mrs. Crocker rose, staring at them with hope and fear blazing from her eyes, *let's see what You have to offer.*

Chapter Twenty-Five

"This is the gentleman I was telling you about, Mr. Grayson Faulkner." Deirdre introduced him with an encouraging smile to Mrs. Crocker. "If anyone can help you find your son, he can. Now I must be off, but rest easy. It will be all right," she promised. "Mr. Faulkner will make it so. 'Tis in his nature, don't you know, to take care of people."

Before Gray could growl a retort, she'd whispered goodbye, strolling with her immense dignity down the long hallway.

"Mr. Faulkner." Beneath an old-fashioned black bonnet, feverish bright eyes latched onto Gray. "You know my son William?"

"I've met him, yes." Would have been less awkward if Deirdre had remained another few moments. He scraped up a smile that hopefully mirrored Deirdre's. "He was one of the groundskeepers here. Did you know that?"

"Of course. I wouldn't be here otherwise, now would I? My boy wrote me every week, until—until—" Two spots of color smeared her bony, wrinkled face.

"Until what, Mrs. Crocker?"

"Until this young woman—Miss Shaw's her name—turned

his head," she declared. "William's shy, not one to chase the ladies. I brought him up to respect women. When he told me about her, I was very concerned."

Gray ran a hand around the back of his tense neck. "Why don't we sit down, Mrs. Crocker?" He gestured to a cluster of chairs off to the side, beyond the glare of the incandescent electric lights installed several years earlier. "Tell me when you last saw your son."

For a tension-spiked moment he was afraid Mrs. Crocker might bolt on him. Thin body poised for flight, fingers strangling the handles of her worn carpetbag, she stared at the waxed floorboards for a long time before speaking again. "You the law?"

He lifted an eyebrow at the tone. "I have been," he admitted. "But at the moment, no, I'm not the law. Why? Has your son committed a crime?"

Mrs. Crocker's head reared back. "My son is a decent, God-fearing man, not a criminal. He has lived a good and obedient life—until now. Until her. That woman. Neala Shaw. She's the one who's filled his head with nonsense, she's the one who caused him to turn into a stranger to his own mother."

A dull pickax hacking away at the base of his skull would have been more tolerable than listening to this tripe. "Why do you say that?"

"I know what I know. He ain't no skirt-chaser." With her mousey hair scraped in a severe bun and her narrow, wrinkled face, she could have been anywhere from sixty years and up, yet she talked as though her son were fourteen instead of a man pushing at least two-score years.

An uncomfortable tightness constricted Gray's throat. Grimly he quelled a spark of empathy toward Will. "You claim Miss Shaw caused some kind of rift to occur between you and your son? I find that hard to believe. Have you met her, Mrs. Crocker?"

A quick negative jerk of the head was the answer. Then she said, "You know her, Mr.…What did you say the name was?"

"Faulkner. And yes, I do know Miss Shaw."

Something akin to despair seemed to flatten out the sharp angles of her face, leaving her looking old and sunken. "You don't believe me. She's worked her evil on you as well. I can see it plain on your face."

Control thin as a thumbtack, Gray planted his hands on his knees. "Mrs. Crocker, I don't know much about your son, and I don't know what he told you, but I do know Miss Shaw. She is not the woman you have described. She in fact enjoys a sterling reputation here at the Old White, among staff as well as guests."

Stubborn memories mutinied against his resolve not to think about Neala. Everyone who met her responded to her sunny, generous personality—himself included. Even the sour housemaid's face lit up when Neala wished her a bonny day in an exaggerated Scottish burr.

Raw pain savaged his insides.

"Are you calling my son a liar?"

Pain and poignant memories evaporated. "I'm not calling him anything of the sort, Mrs. Crocker. I'm merely enlightening you. People who have met Miss Shaw do not share your opinion of her. Without exception they find her a charming young woman."

Mrs. Crocker suddenly emitted a strangled sob, and covered her face with her hands. "I'm sorry, so sorry," she sniffled, tears thickening the words. "It's just…I've been so worried. It's been over a month since he was home. I ain't been able to find my way here… I'm afraid something's happened to him. Something bad."

Gray fought the automatic urge to snarl, then bolt for the hills, far away from yet another distraught mother who thought all she had to do was turn on the tears and every male within hearing distance would buckle at the knees. But if he yielded to impulse, he would lose possibly his only lead to Will's whereabouts. To Neala's. So he waited in stony silence while Mrs. Crocker spilled out a largely unintelligible litany of fears, woes, worries and desperation about her missing son.

A trickle of memory meandered into his mind, then flowed faster until images and phrases drowned out the sound of Mrs. Crocker. Neala had wept in his presence, without apology or shame. And Gray remembered suddenly how he'd felt when she sobbed her heart out against his shoulder, how the comfort he'd ungrudgingly offered had produced a grateful smile. Even now the memories kindled a need to provide that comfort again.

Somehow Neala's forthright bouts of tears had cleansed them both, fostered intimacy instead of hindering it.

There was protectiveness as well, he realized. Protectiveness, and for the first time in years, contentment. She demanded nothing, which paradoxically released him to offer more of himself than he'd been willing to share with any other woman. Perhaps…just perhaps that was all most women wanted when tears flowed. Comfort. Arms that offered a protective bulwark, if only for a few moments, from whatever produced the tears. Not control, not guilt. Determination settled inside Gray, and he found himself relaxing back in the chair while he waited for Mrs. Crocker's lamentations to run their course. For Neala, he could be patient. He could even be…prayerful.

Eventually Will's mother sat back, sighed, and stiffly dug inside her disreputable-looking carpetbag, dragging out a crumpled, none-too-clean-looking man's handkerchief. She dabbed her eyes, her temples, and even wiped her nose, then twined her hands together in her lap. A spur of reluctant pity flickered within Gray. But despite the pity, he couldn't afford to drop his guard toward a woman whose son may or may not have murdered Mrs. Wilkes. Fifteen years left calluses as well as caution.

On the other hand, he hadn't bolted for the hills, much less snarled.

Because of Neala. Neala…who would probably inform him that his transformation was God's doing, not her own. Since he'd prayed more in the past twenty-four hours than he had since he was a small boy, Gray wasn't in a position to argue over her naive faith in God, especially considering the timely arrival of the woman sitting across from him.

"I beg your pardon," Mrs. Crocker finally said. "William gets very impatient with me when I weep."

"I'm afraid I, too, am guilty of such an insensitivity," Gray admitted gruffly.

"Well, Mr. Faulkner." Abruptly she rose to her feet, forcing Gray to hurriedly follow suit. "Sitting here won't find my son. That rather large young woman assured me that you would assist me." Noisily she cleared her throat, dabbed her mouth with the handkerchief. "But I'm sure you're much too busy for the likes of me. I can find my own way to his quarters."

"He's not there," Gray told her quietly. "I checked myself, earlier today."

"But he might be there now," Mrs. Crocker insisted. "You don't know my William like I do. He can be…secretive." Her eyes moistened anew. "That's one of the reasons I'm so worried."

"Why is that?" Despite his rising sense of urgency, Gray casually took her arm in a gesture of support. Its weightless fragility surprised him. "Tell me about it, while we both go and check his quarters again, hmm."

"Mr. Faulkner?" Jimmy called from behind the desk as they started across the front hallway.

Gray glanced down at Mrs. Crocker. "One moment." He gave her elbow a light squeeze, then hurried back over to the desk clerk.

"Here's the list you asked for, of the names of all guests who are first-timers this year. I'm going off duty, but I thought you might want this before tomorrow."

"I do. Thanks, Jimmy." He tipped the grateful young man a half dollar, turned to leave, then retraced his steps. "Jimmy, do you happen to know which of these guests arrived after Miss Shaw, this past June?"

"Let me see." He studied the list Gray handed back to him for a moment. "To the best of my recollection, that would be these folks here. The Stamfords, Burlingtons…Mrs. VanPeter, Mr. Lipscomb…and Mr. Lyle." He looked at Gray. "The Stamfords and Mr. Lipscomb are the only guests who haven't left yet. Does that help?"

"You've no idea, Jimmy."

Pulse pounding, Gray strode across to Mrs. Crocker. Keep calm, stay polite but firm. "Mrs. Crocker, something urgent has come up that demands my immediate attention. I need you to remain here, for just a little while, all right?"

"No. I refuse to be left behind like a stray puppy." She gripped her carpetbag and glared up at Gray. "It's William, isn't it? You're lying to me, you're—"

The supernatural calm enfolding Gray cracked. "I'm not lying to you! Mrs. Crocker, this has nothing to do with your son. Understand? Nothing."

He wasn't surprised when her shoulders hunched, because he was practically shouting at her. She hugged the carpetbag to her as though to buffer herself from his words.

All right, he *was* shouting. He felt like a man tied between two freight trains steaming off in opposite directions. It was imperative that he investigate this lead immediately; yet Mrs. Crocker offered his best prospect for finding Will. He couldn't afford to alienate her. Pinching the bridge of his nose, Gray sucked in a single calming breath and managed with an effort to moderate his tone.

"I want to find your son every bit as much as you do," he began. "But there's something I must see to immediately. Something vital that has nothing to do with your son. Would you wait here for me?" The urgency stomped his chest now with hobnailed boots, but Gray scraped up a coaxing smile. "Please? You've not eaten since you arrived, have you? How about if I arrange for you to be escorted to the dining room? They serve supper until eight. You choose whatever you like to eat, enjoy a good meal. I'll be back before you're finished—" he gestured to a bellboy, who snapped to attention at once "—and…um…and I'll have dessert with you. Then together we'll find your son."

"I don't…" Her throat muscles worked convulsively, her gaze darting between the ebony-faced bellboy and Gray. Then, with eerie suddenness, the wildness left her face. "Very well, Mr. Faulkner," she said. "Thank you. Your kindness…I appreciate it."

"I'll see you, soon I hope," he promised her as he slipped several bills to the bellboy.

"Yes, I expect you will," was the dull reply.

But Gray was already halfway to the door. The list had finally connected together the torn scraps of a picture that had nagged his brain for several hours. He marked the gathering darkness as he plunged down the steps to the grounds.

Lipscomb. Mr. Geoffrey Lipscomb, a man who claimed to be from Kentucky yet whose accent more resembled the distinct refined drawl of Tidewater Virginia or North Carolina, overlaid with the lightest dusting of a mountain twang. He could have recently moved to Kentucky, of course. But regardless of his home of origin, Lipscomb was not who, or what, he appeared to be.

He'd been perspiring heavily for a brisk fall afternoon. A man relaxing in the privacy of his room, with nothing on his mind save enjoying the fall foliage, should not have been sweating like a horse after a race.

Another image clicked into place: the wrists of his cuffless shirt. They'd been soiled. Not covered with dirt, not anything that would have immediately alerted Gray. But a man of means able to afford two rooms in cottages on Alabama Row, one who had made a point to present himself as a wealthy, dandified gentleman, would not wear soiled shirts no matter how casual the occasion.

And his hair. That outrageous head of curly black hair. Neala had remarked upon his hair every time they'd met Mr. Lipscomb, about how she empathized with anyone cursed with thick, curly hair. She'd wondered aloud how often he had to pay a visit to the barber, since whenever they met him, Mr. Lipscomb's hair almost brushed his collar.

When Gray talked to him this afternoon, the hair… What was it about his hair that chafed Gray now? As he sprinted across the grounds toward the cottages on Alabama Row, the blurred image suddenly sharpened in focus—Gray, standing on the porch; Lipscomb, lounging in the doorway. Sunset-tipped light had streamed around Gray directly onto the other man, illuminating his features with pitiless clarity.

The hair on the right side of Lipscomb's head had completely covered his ear. The hair on the left side, however, scarcely brushed the top of the earlobe.

Either the Old White's barber was going blind—or Master Lipscomb wore a toupee. More likely a wig, which would disguise not only the shape of his head and his real hair color, but would also completely change his appearance.

For the third time in twenty-four hours, Gray found himself praying.

Chapter Twenty-Six

Neala watched Will while he paced the floor beside the bed.

Ever since someone knocked on the door earlier, he'd been behaving strangely, either laughing—a guttural yet out-of-control sound that peppered Neala's skin with goose bumps—or pacing in that silent manner of a trapped wild animal.

All of a sudden he swiveled, crossed over to the bed. "We're leaving."

He reached toward her, hurriedly removed the gag, then fumbled the key into the handcuffs and released her wrists. The obscene clang of metal against metal jangled over the roaring in Neala's ears. "I'll give you a moment or two to make sure you can walk. Promise to be sensible, so I'll be able to keep you alive."

He tossed the threat at her in the same tone as one might order a breakfast tray.

Light-headed, her fingers numb and her limbs uncoordinated, Neala massaged her wrists and arms until the worst of the discomfort eased. The activity not only restored circulation, but gave her something other than abject self-pity on which to focus.

Slowly she maneuvered to the edge of the bed, shakily forcing herself to stand. When she was confident of her balance, she lifted her gaze to Will. "Let me go. My life is not your responsibility." It was difficult, forcing her tongue to form words when her jaw felt ossified, and her lips were dry as dust. "All you have to do to keep me alive is to let me go free."

"You will always be my responsibility."

Neala managed to choke back the hot denial. Distractedly she turned to straighten the bedcovers, fluff the pillow— anything to channel her antagonism into something noninflammatory.

"If we don't leave," Will continued, the words hoarse and low, "I might end up killing someone again."

Neala's hands stilled. She turned, for the first time openly searching his face. Droplets of perspiration dotted his forehead and temples. His Adam's apple bobbed convulsively as he swallowed hard, several times. His eyes... His eyes stared back at her, and they were black with fear.

"Will..." she whispered. "Who are you afraid is going to come through that door?"

Primitive rage flashed so swiftly she wouldn't have caught it had she not been watching every flicker of an eyelash. Then, as though redonning a mask, his expression reverted to the urbane Mr. Lipscomb, who seldom manifested emotion of any kind. "You're mistaken, Neala. I'm not at all afraid. I will, however, allow you to decide if you want the death of your former suitor on your conscience. Go ahead, try to escape. He cares nothing about you, remember? Show me that you care more for your own skin than his. Try to escape, Neala."

Her head reared back. "Grayson," she breathed. "That's the person who knocked at the door, isn't it?"

Will ignored her question, no doubt an answer itself.

Oh, but her heart fairly convulsed with fearful joy. Grayson had come for her after all. She hadn't expected him to, had given up any hope that she would ever see him, or anyone else on earth, again. She expected to die, and hours earlier had resigned herself to the inevitable. Yet Grayson had refused to give up on her. *She hadn't even told him she loved him.* Surely he realized his actions needlessly imperiled his own life. She had in fact done her best to ensure that he would not follow her.

But she wished she'd at least told him in the letter that she loved him.

A notion sparkled in a distant corner of her mind.

"You never looked at me like that," Will's abruptly petulant voice intruded, demanding her attention, snuffling the twinkling revelation. "Not once. Even when I explained..." His hands closed into fists. "I told you, I don't like what I've become. I want to put the past behind us. But I can't, not when I'm afraid you'll do something reckless." His gaze shifted toward the other room, then back to Neala. "Something stupid. Grayson Faulkner deserves killing for what he turned you into."

Keep him talking. Keep him distracted. Keep his mind... anywhere but on the possibility of killing Grayson. She shuffled one foot forward, stopped. "If we're leaving, I need my shoes."

As she had hoped, the non sequitur disconcerted Will. But instead of turning his back to her, he sidled to the other side of the bed, bent down, then tossed her traveling button-top boots into the middle of the bed. "You have two minutes."

Knees stiff, she retrieved the boots, and stumbled to the chair by the bed. "I'll tell you where to find the crest badge, if you promise not to harm Grayson," she tried next, keeping her gaze on the task of fastening buttons with fingers that still felt like uncooked sausage links.

Time stretched, quivered in air gone thick as Grandmother's sugarcane syrup.

"You think you can bribe me," Will finally said. All of a sudden the tips of his shoes bumped into hers. "You think you can bribe me?" he repeated, then snatched her to her feet. One hand shackled her wrist in a vicious grip. "You'll use your most precious possession—that's what you call it, isn't it?—you'll bargain with the legacy that should have been mine, to save the life of the man who ruined you?"

"Grayson didn't ruin me, Will. You did. As for the badge, what it symbolized to me doesn't exist anymore."

Red suffused Will's pallid countenance. But he didn't rail at her this time, merely hauled her across the room, indifferent to her uncoordinated scrambling. "Now I know why you won't marry me. I think I'll have to kill him after all."

Fear and fury geysered up in a heedless spray of words. "You'll never have the chance! I won't let you!"

She swung her free arm up and punched his jaw with her fist. The force of the blow knocked his head sideways and sent pain streaking up her arm. Will staggered, and the crushing hold on her wrist slackened. Neala tore herself free and ran for the door, fought with slippery fingers to turn the knob. Behind her, Will shouted a warning, cursing her as he leaped across the room. She felt clawlike fingers brush her shoulders and then the door opened and she flung herself forward, her gaze glued to the next door, and two seconds of freedom. With those two seconds, she could scream a warning.

She might have succeeded in her escape had her knee not buckled in the dash across the parlor. Staggering, she wavered, and by the time she regained her balance Will was there, blocking the outside door with his body. Breathing hard, he plastered his back against the panel. Watery light from the parlor lamp revealed a trickle of blood oozing from the corner of his mouth.

"Faulkner will be disposed of." He wiped the blood away with his hand, then reached inside his jacket. "But despite everything you've done, Neala, I still want to keep you alive." He withdrew his hand and flicked open the blade of a pocketknife. "Unless you hit me again."

Neala eyed the length of the blade, which could easily slice through a large potato, not to mention her throat. Resolve wavered. The prospect of imminent death lost its appeal when she was no longer handcuffed to a bed and drugged senseless, especially when Grayson was risking his own life to save hers.

"I won't hit you again, Will," she promised, joining him at the door. The odor of sweat and macassar oil rolled over her, making her head swim, but she forced herself to stand docilely, and waited for an opportunity.

Watching her, Will opened the door a few inches. The faint tang of pine trees and wood smoke wafted through the crack. Fresh air she hadn't breathed in over twenty-four hours dispelled some of the nausea and quickened her senses, filling Neala with yearning so intense she leaned forward.

Like a lightning bolt Will's hand flashed out, clamping her forearm in a punishing grip that seared all the way up her shoulder.

Neala struggled to twist free. "You're hurting my arm."

The fingers tightened. "Payment for my jaw, dear."

He shoved the door all the way open and dragged her out onto the porch. Twilight blurred the cottages to ghost-white structures, while the mountains loomed dark and forbidding all around them. Yet freedom spread like an unguent into Neala's skin, reviving senses and spirit. She wanted to lift her arms and embrace the night, but stifled the impulse, having learned that any movement on her part would precipitate swift, and painful, retaliation from Will. So she focused on a small bright star twinkling just above the mountains, savoring the resurrection of her lost faith. *Lead Grayson like Your star led the wise men, Lord...*

"Come on. We have to hurry," Will growled as he hauled her down the porch steps with a recklessness that made Neala tumble against his side. He wrapped her in a bone-crushing hug. "Be careful!"

"Then slow down! I can barely see," Neala retorted. "Do you want to risk my turning an ankle? What if I break it? I couldn't walk. You'd have to carry me, leave me—or kill me."

"Shh!" She felt the prick of steel against her throat. "Stop taunting me when I've told you I don't want to kill you." He moved the blade so it rested against the side of her neck. "But I can hurt you, Neala. And I'll do it where he can see, make him feel as helpless as he did when he watched his friend die."

So, he knew about Grayson's friend. The implications checked her recklessness even more than the knife at her throat. What else was going on inside a mind twisted from birth, whose sense of right and wrong Neala could scarcely comprehend?

Quiet enfolded them, a malevolent, waiting silence. Only a week earlier these grounds and cottages had teemed with life—guests strolling the lawn, riding horses and bicycles, enjoying board games or cards in the shade of the columned porches; children chasing hoops while their parents enjoyed a picnic lunch and the band tuned its instruments in the bandstand.

Now the Old White more resembled a cemetery.

Suddenly her gaze caught on a distant figure, moving fast across the lawn. Briefly one of the pole lamps lighting the pathways highlighted a silhouette—a man, who promptly disappeared into the shadows. A gasp escaped before Neala could swallow it back.

Beside her Will stiffened and muttered something unintelligible under his breath. He seized her elbow and dragged her after him as he set off in the opposite direction. "Keep up," he ordered, adding in a goaded undertone, "It's too soon. I'm not ready for this."

Another long row of gleaming white cottages materialized beneath the trees. Behind them, the twilight faded into night and darkness fell with the suddenness of a guillotine blade. Will didn't hesitate; with Neala squirming against his side, he muscled her up the long staircase onto the porch of another one of the cottages. Neala opened her mouth and managed a single scream—Grayson's name—before Will's fist slammed into her chin.

"Now you know how it feels," he hissed.

He kicked open the door and dragged her across the threshold, slamming the door behind him. After shoving her into a chair, he turned to grab the washstand, dragging it across to bar the door. The white ceramic bowl and pitcher tumbled to the floor and smashed into pieces.

Neala groggily righted herself in the straight-back chair, blinked away tears as she tentatively pressed her fingers against her throbbing chin. The room was dark, every shadow coiled to pounce.

Will struck a match, lit one of the gas lamps over the fireplace. "You shouldn't have tried to yell." Feeble light trickled across the room as he returned and stood over Neala. He wiped his hand across the back of his mouth, all the time staring reproachfully at her.

"And if I yell again? Will you hit me—or just use the knife?" She wriggled her jaw. Like her knuckles, it throbbed in protest but nothing seemed to be broken. She hoped she would never be called upon to hit anybody else, including Will. "I don't plan to cooperate anymore, Will."

"You never have shown much common sense, have you?"

he muttered, staring down at her. Yellow light deepened the brooding cast of his mouth beneath the false mustache; beads of sweat pearled across his forehead. "You shouldn't *warn* me that you don't plan to cooperate. You're like a child, Neala, with no awareness of danger. You think you can taunt me into making a mistake. Only you're the one making a mistake."

Shaking his head, he thrust his hands inside his jacket pocket, then stood there, swaying slightly. "Never mind. He knows we're here," he muttered. "I have to think." He moved across to the barricaded door, shoved the table again as though to test its effectiveness. "I have to think about what I'm going to do," he repeated. "With both of you."

Unnerved, Neala sat motionless, straining to listen for Grayson while reality punched her as though she were bread dough. She *was* an idealistic ninny, a foolish, reckless dunderhead. She had actually deluded herself into believing in her powers of persuasion, that her desire for people to act reasonably would be honored, that her innocence would shield her from mortal harm. Even when she lay trussed to the bed with a gag in her mouth, in the darkest reaches of her mind she had still believed that, despite God's desertion, she could somehow wriggle her way out on her own.

Because He had not answered her prayers the way she wanted, she had given up on God—and committed the grievous sin of presumption, by assuming His power and authority, claiming it for herself to wield as she saw fit. Oh, she hadn't sinned on purpose, like Will, nor at the time even realized her presumption. But ignorance of her folly did not displace the sin of it. 'Twas a miracle she wasn't already dead.

God, dear God. Forgive me. I didn't mean to… Don't allow Grayson to die because of me.

A single tear of utter humbleness trickled down her cheek. *Lord? Please, will You help us out of this mess?* Not that she deserved it, but because…because even when she'd turned her back on God, He loved her enough to stay with her. All along, even though she hadn't "felt" Him, even though she had cast her faith into the darkness and set out on her own path— her own *wrong* path, God had remained close by. The Almighty ruler of the universe loved her enough to hurt with her, to wait patiently for her to open her heart back up, and believe in the power of His love.

She should have been a better witness to Grayson, when she'd possessed the opportunity.

Even as she mentally prostrated herself before the Almighty, for the first time in her entire twenty-three years she grasped the extent of her gullibility and her…yes, her pride, along with her almost irrational predisposition to assume everything would work out all right because she'd always tried to be an obedient Christian.

But she'd learned her lesson at last. And the message burned to ash a lifetime of misconceptions.

Sometimes God allowed things to go terribly wrong, even with devout Christians, not because He didn't care, or because He was bent upon punishment—but because He had given mankind the gift of freedom of choice. And most of the time, people seemed to choose wrongly. Even those who claimed Christ as Savior and Lord.

Welcome to the human race, Neala Shaw.

Footsteps clattered up the porch outside.

Chapter Twenty-Seven

"Lipscomb!" Grayson's voice roared through the door panels as though they were made of thin cotton. "There's nowhere you can run. Nowhere you can hide. Give it up, man." There followed a brief pause. Then Grayson added, "Don't you think there's been enough killing? Let Neala go. You don't want to kill her—I don't want to kill you. Open the door."

Neala slowly slid forward to the edge of the chair, then wobbled to her feet. Heartbeat thrumming in her ears, she took one step, then another. One more second, and she would make a dash for the door, try to shove the table out of—

"Don't move," Will warned. His eyes were black with violent emotion. He glared first at Neala, then the window behind her, finally at the door. "Don't," he repeated, only this time the word emerged more as a plea than a threat.

"I'll give you ten more seconds, Lipscomb. Or should I call you by your real name—William Crocker?"

"My real name will be William Shaw!" he burst out in a maniacal scream, yanking the curly black wig from his head and flinging it into a corner. Next he attacked the mustache, clawing and ripping it from his upper lip. He seemed to have

forgotten Neala altogether when he stomped over to the door
and commenced pounding on the wood with his fists. "William
Shaw," he bellowed. "William Shaw. *William Shaw!* I've
planned for this my whole life, and you will not stop me now!"

The tirade ceased as suddenly as it had erupted. Chest
heaving, he slewed back around and faced Neala, paralyzing
her with the unadulterated fury blazing from the black pits of
those eyes.

He was going to kill her after all. Frozen in place, Neala
twined her fingers together and fought the spike of terror that
locked her throat. *Grayson… God, take care of Grayson.* When
Will shifted she jolted as though he'd stabbed her through the
heart, but he…Why, he wasn't even looking her way any
longer. Instead his gaze seemed fixed upon the room's only
window.

What if he tried to escape through that window?

The prospect jarred the panic loose, cudgeled it into resolve.
She was neither drugged, nor bound, and she categorically
refused to stand here like an ice block while Will squirmed
through that window. As long as there was breath in her body,
she would do what she could to—

Stand still, and wait upon the Lord. *The Lord will fight for
you; you need only to be still.*

The verse winked into her mind, like a firefly dancing in
the night. Awareness suffused her veins, saturated her with a
yearning to believe. To—*know.* She felt as though she'd been
transported into a bright, soundless vacuum where nothing
existed but Neala, and the longing. She held her breath—and
did not move. *Are You… Are You here?* Tingling warmth spread
from the crown of her head downward.

Knowledge rife with expectation joined the firefly dance.
The time had arrived for her to choose: she could try to stop Will
through her own efforts—or she could obey the instruction she

had just been given, trust the One Who had illuminated her mind.

Stand still…for it is by faith you stand firm. Once again the words of Scripture flashed through her mind, unbidden but as real as the flickering light keeping the darkness at bay in this small room. Neala forced her feet to stay glued to the floor. *All right, Lord. I'm, ah, waiting for You to do something.*

Her suspended sense of time shattered when Will screamed out, "I know you're still out there! Where are you? Don't you play games with me! I'll kill her, I mean it." He yanked out the knife and started across the room toward Neala.

Terror-roughed chills skated down her spine. Did God intend her to be the sacrificial lamb?

Will lifted the knife, and from somewhere more knowledge poured over her, through her, galvanized her limbs, pushed her forward. Instead of running, she met Will in the middle of the room. "Put that knife away, Will Crocker!" The words gushed forth in a torrent. "You told me you were tired of killing, you even asked me to marry you! Now look at what you're doing! Marriage requires mutual love, and you don't begin to know what that means. Love doesn't take. It gives. It doesn't threaten—it protects."

"You don't understand anything." Will thrust the knife in front of Neala's face, its point inches away from her nose. "Back off, Faulkner!" he yelled. "If I don't hear you leave, I'll slit her throat. By the time you break in her blood will be spilling all over the floor."

"No," Neala told him calmly, utterly at peace. "No, Will. You don't want to do that."

"Don't tell me what—"

There was no warning. With the explosive force of a summer deluge, the door splintered open, flinging the wash-stand to the floor. Will lifted the knife over his head. Neala automatically raised her arms to protect her throat. But instead of stabbing her, Will jerked around and hurled the knife toward the man charging through the doorway like a runaway bull moose. The point missed Grayson's ear by a whisker and thudded harmlessly into the ruined door post.

"Grayson!" Neala screamed.

She launched herself at Will, grabbing his arm and hanging on with all her strength until Will's elbow jammed into her midriff. Gasping, Neala fell to her knees, then rolled aside in a tumble of skirts and petticoats.

Grayson, weapon drawn, savage intent darkening his face, started across the room. Even as Will grabbed a poker from the fireplace, Gray's leg kicked out, his foot connecting with Will's wrist. The poker spun into the air, landing with a clatter on the floor and out of immediate reach.

Will feinted sideways, swiveled toward the door, but before he managed two steps Gray had holstered the gun and latched onto Will's shoulders. He toppled the other man like a tiger attacking its prey, slamming him to the floor and following him down.

Neala staggered to her feet, then darted across to tug the knife out of the wood. "I've got his knife, Grayson!" she called breathlessly.

Grayson didn't acknowledge her, and after a horrified glance Neala realized that he was as out of control as Will, and most likely would kill the other man with his bare hands if someone didn't bring him to his senses. After a reproachful glance heavenward, Neala approached the thrashing bodies, hands outstretched. Oh…the knife. Hastily she folded it up and thrust it inside her skirt pocket.

For a moment she hovered, terrified because she might distract Grayson and allow Will to get the upper hand; even more terrified that if she stayed out of the way, Grayson would be the one committing murder. Galvanized by the ugly possibility, she sucked in a sustaining breath, steeled herself—and Grayson pinned Will facedown, wrapping his forearm around the other man's neck.

Pulse thumping in her ears, Neala stepped closer and stretched out a hand to brush the bunched muscles of Grayson's shoulder. Her gaze collided with Will's.

His face was mottled a dusky-red, and his eyes were bloodshot and wild, yet his expression reached inside Neala and twisted her heart like a dishrag.

"Grayson." She stepped closer, rested her hand more firmly on his shoulder. "Grayson, stop. You're killing him. Stop. I'm all right. I'm—"

The words died in her throat when Grayson whipped his head sideways. "He hurt you. For over a year he's tried to kill you. Now he's going to pay." He uttered the words with pitiless matter-of-factness.

"If you kill him, you'll be the one paying." She shifted her hand to skim her fingertips across his cheekbone. "And so will I. Grayson…don't. I—I love you. Please don't kill him."

She hadn't intended the words, had in truth not realized how much she did love him, until she watched him choking the life out of another human being and knew, deep inside her soul, that if he succeeded the man she loved would die as well.

The strange fluttering drifted over her again, into her, settled her pulse to a slow, deep throbbing and her heart to racing. Love…casts out fear…love forgives…keeps no record of wrongs. God's love endures forever…His love for His children never fails… Love…gives people strength and hope and grace and—

Determination.

"Grayson! Let him go and listen to me! You big lunk, *I love you!* So you better look at me and say something about that."

A shudder rippled through his body. Then, almost as though he were plowing his way through a mud hole, Grayson released the chokehold on Will and sat back. For a moment he didn't move, then slowly rolled off the other man. Will coughed, wheezed in air, and made a feeble attempt to rise before he collapsed to sprawl unmoving on the floor.

Grayson's head lifted until the blue eyes focused on Neala.

"I love you, too," he murmured in a rusty-sounding voice. Tears glittered, and he lifted the hand that had been choking Will to swipe at the moisture, never looking away from Neala. "You have a bruise on your chin, and your cheek." A muscle twitched at the corner of his mouth. "There's a cut on your neck, and your wrists are—"

"Fine," Neala hurriedly interjected, the lightness dancing around her until she thought she might float away with it. "Grayson, I'm all right. You came for me."

A crooked sliver of a smile briefly appeared. "I shouldn't have had to." He shuddered. "Neala…Neala…" His eyes closed briefly, and when they reopened they were full of more tears. "Of course I came. Did he…hurt you? I mean—hurt you worse than I can see?"

Will stirred. Gray calmly planted a knee in the small of his back, his gaze never leaving Neala.

"I'm not hurt anywhere that matters. I'm fine. Fine." In the blink of an eye she erased twenty-four hours of pain and humiliation, eighteen months of uncertainty and fear. The past had lost all power to haunt her, and therefore no longer mattered. She reached and touched his cheek, where a tear left a dusty trail of moisture. "I never thought I'd see you cry."

Incredibly, a blush stained his cheekbones. He searched her face, and with a tenderness that reduced Neala to a puddle, gently ran one finger over the bruises, then tangled in a lock of curling hair that had spilled over her forehead. "I've cried," he admitted in a husky whisper. "Especially when I thought I'd never see you again."

"I'm sorry for everything I did."

One eyebrow arched quizzically. "I'll remind you of that—later."

With the lithe grace that still amazed Neala, he levered himself up, then hauled Will to his feet and shoved him down in the chair. "Unless you feel up to a second bout, stay there."

Shoulders bowed, Will ducked his head and didn't respond. Defeat clung to him like layers of caked mud. His lethargy pinched Neala's conscience—though only a little.

"Come here, love," Grayson then ordered her in a very different tone.

Still floating in that otherworldly cloud, Neala took two steps. Suddenly shy, she dropped her gaze to her shoes. Heat crept into her cheeks.

"We have a mountain of unfinished business," Grayson murmured, his warm hand tipping her chin. "But just to set the record straight—" He slid a steely glance down at Will, then brushed Neala's lips in a light but mesmerizing kiss. "This woman belongs to me," he announced with the authority of a desert sheikh, which bothered Neala not a bit. "You're alive only because of her. Don't tempt me to alter that condition by doing something stupid. Like moving."

"Grayson…perhaps you should tie him up?"

Grayson smiled down at her, drew her close to his side, and before her dazzled eyes the gun appeared in his hands. "I think you might be right," he murmured. "Trouble is…I don't have any rope handy."

Giddily they grinned at each other. "I know where we can find some," Neala said. "If you like, I can fetch—"

"Move away from my son!" A pale, gaunt woman stepped across the broken doorway. She lifted a small but deadly pistol—and pointed it straight at Neala. "You scheming, lying jezebel, how dare you poison my son against me!"

For Gray, time seemed to evaporate, sucking him into the past with a punch that left him disoriented. *A woman, with a weapon aimed at someone he loved.*

"I know your reputation, Mr. Faulkner. So if I see your fingers so much as twitch, I'll pull the trigger." Mrs. Crocker flicked a malevolent glare his way. "I'll shoot her, and you, too. Both of you are liars. Full of deceit."

"Momma!" Will struggled to his feet. "Momma, don't. It's over. Don't do this."

"It's not over." She jerked her chin toward Neala. The gun didn't waver. "Where is it? Where's the clan crest, whelp of a faithless philanderer? I've waited for this moment for over fifty years. Where is it?" The question cracked like a whip. "I know you have it. William told me he'd discovered it in your room. That he'd held it in his hands."

The clan crest? Obviously she was aware of its value, and was willing to commit murder over it. Gray was disillusioned, but unsurprised. Beside him Neala shifted her weight as though she might try to distance herself. Gray wasn't about to allow even a few inches between them. He curved his hand about her waist, drew her closer to his side, and felt the subtle relaxation of her body.

"You want Grandfather's crest badge?" she asked Will's mother. "I'll give it to you, but you'll have to let us go so I can retrieve it. I…left it somewhere. Let us go, and I p-promise to give it to you. By right it belongs to your son."

"No!" Will cried out. "I don't want it anymore. I'm tired." His voice cracked. "I'm tired, Momma."

"Neala, I don't think you should—"

"I don't believe you." Mrs. Crocker stepped closer, her expression murderous. "Yer jes' trying to trick me, same as you tricked my son." Her shaking finger moved to the trigger of what looked to be an old Colt .22 pocket revolver.

The skin at the back of Gray's neck crawled, but he didn't dare go for his own weapon. He might enjoy a reputation as the fastest draw on both sides of the Mississippi, but speed mattered not a bit when confronted by an irrational woman with a loaded revolver, whose heart was poisoned with decades of festering hate. "Mrs. Crocker, put the gun down. Then we can talk, and you—"

"Don't talk to my mother like that," Will interrupted.

Some of his bluster had returned, but Gray noted the caution stiffening his body. His gaze shifted between Neala, his mother and the Colt .22 ferociously gripped in her shaking hand. "Momma," he continued hoarsely, "Neala's not the problem. It's the man. Grayson Faulkner's the one who deserves to be shot like a cornered rat. Keep the gun trained on him, while Neala and I fetch the crest badge."

"No! You won't go anywhere with her." Her pallid face crumpled, much as Gray had witnessed in the hotel. "William…how could you think of marrying this creature?"

"Because…" Will inched around Gray, just out of reach. "Because I—because I thought if we married, I'd have the name as well as the crest, Momma. But she refused, and I don't care about anything now. Don't you see? Nothing mat-ters."

"I see you've forgotten everything my momma and I taught you all your life, that's what I see."

Her mouth worked; a tremor quaked through her bony frame and for an instant the gun wavered. But even as Gray's muscles bunched to reach for his own weapon, the deadly little revolver was leveled at Neala again.

"You never should have been born," she spat. "If my mother had taken care of things, my father and that treacherous female who stole him would have burned in a lake of fire. Now God's justice will be served at last. Me and my son, we'll finally get what's ours."

"Your mother started the fire at my grandparents' boarding-house!" Neala exclaimed. "Everyone thought it was just a story, but it wasn't, was it? Your mother was Letitia Rutledge."

Her lips flattened into a thin white line. "You ain't fit to say her name."

"Madam," Gray inserted in a deceptively smooth tone, "if you shoot Neala, I promise you won't live long enough to enjoy holding that crest badge in your murderous hands."

"Grayson...wait." Neala grabbed his left hand and squeezed. "Mrs. Crocker, Will's right. I promise you, I'm not going to marry your son." She glanced up at Grayson, her gaze vaguely apologetic. "I'm sort of hoping to marry Mr. Faulkner, if he'll have me."

"No! Not *him!*" Will flung himself between Gray and Neala, grappling for Gray's Smith & Wesson at the same moment his fist swung toward Gray's cheekbone.

Reflexively, Gray jerked sideways so the blow only grazed his chin. Desperate to protect Neala, he pivoted, thrusting her behind him with one arm while with the other he wrestled Will for control of his weapon. Vaguely he was aware of Mrs. Crocker screeching like a steam kettle, of Neala scrambling out of the way, of Will yelling and cursing.

The air exploded with an earsplitting roar.

Chapter Twenty-Eight

God...Oh, God. Please. Don't let her... No...

Wild with fear, Gray planted his palm against Will's face and shoved, wrenched himself free and staggered across toward Neala. She hadn't fallen, she was still standing. She was alive. Standing on her own two feet, not spiraling into a boneless heap on the floor with blood gushing forth. But beneath the tumble of dust-coated curls her face was stripped of color, blank as a corpse.

"Neala?" Somehow Gray managed to say her name. He couldn't feel his feet or his knees.

Behind him, Mrs. Crocker burst into loud gulping sobs.

Slowly Neala turned toward him, lifted a shaking hand to her face. "I—why, I'm okay," she whispered, and blinked. The awful blankness vanished. More frantically she ran both hands over her face, head, and neck. Then she looked across at Mrs. Crocker. "You missed," she said.

Gray wrapped her in a hug that caused her to squeak in protest. "Sorry," he choked out. "Let me see, let me make sure." As he murmured the words he was running his hands down her arms, her back, her side. "Easy, love. It's all right. You're all right."

He couldn't think over the relief, couldn't translate into action the potential for danger that still existed.

Somewhere within his resurrected conscience he managed a garbled prayer of thanks.

Her arms crept up and around him in a tentative embrace. "I felt the bullet go by," she noted in a pedantic little voice. "Neither Will nor Mrs. Crocker is as good a shot as you are. Did I tell you that Will was the hunter who shot at me last spring?"

The gun. Will. Gray's stomach leaped into his throat as her words jabbed him back to reality. "Get behind me, darling."

"What about—"

He kissed her hard, and shoved her behind him once more. "Stay behind me," he repeated as he slipped the Smith & Wesson from the holster. A swift survey of the room marginally relaxed his muscles; Will's attention had been diverted to his mother—not Gray and Neala. He seemed to be trying to persuade her to hand over the Colt .22.

Mrs. Crocker refused to relinquish the gun, twisting and turning, batting at Will's hands. She screamed a sewer full of abuse at her son, terms of endearment usually reserved for babies, invectives and pleas to rid the earth of all Shaws. From where Gray stood, Will's mother had completely shed herself of sanity.

A slender hand tapped his shoulder. "Perhaps I should try to help," Neala ventured.

The hairs at the back of his neck seemed to ignite into flames. Without turning his head, he clamped his free hand over Neala's. "Stay out of the way," he commanded with far too much harshness. He couldn't help it. Terror burned his gut like live coals. If Mrs. Crocker managed to free herself, if she regained control of the pistol…

"I'll keep them distracted. You slip out the door. Please,

Neala. Please, love. I can't bear the thought of seeing someone else I love die, not like this."

Because he couldn't help himself, for one precious moment Gray turned to Neala, leaving his back exposed. But he had to look at her, had to know that she understood. Had to fill himself with her love, because these might be their last moments together. Chest tight, he scraped together a semblance of a smile. Reverently he skimmed one finger along her temple, down her damp cheek, to the point of her chin. "This will be the last time I ever want you out of my sight. I promise," he said, inwardly tensed for the agonizing impact of a bullet.

Neala searched his face, her eyes huge, liquid with unspoken words. "All right, Grayson." Her hand crept up to rest over his heart. "I will always love you," he thought she whispered.

The screaming abruptly stopped.

Ears still ringing, Gray shifted his attention to the two Crockers even as his hand urgently pushed Neala toward the door. Will was talking to his mother in a low, strained voice, most of the words inaudible; he looked as though he were embracing her in a hug. Mrs. Crocker hung limply in his arms, but at least she was silent.

The sinister little Colt .22 pocket revolver was nowhere in sight.

Prickles feathered the back of Gray's neck again, this time more insistently. He adjusted his grip on his Smith & Wesson, at the same time moving in front of Neala as she edged toward the door.

Will didn't even turn his head their way, but the mumbled words now drifted clearly across the otherwise silent room. "…and I know this is hard for you. But right now I don't know what else to do. I tell you I'm tired of the killing. I'm just…worn out."

"I…nothing to live for," Mrs. Crocker returned plaintively,

her words muffled since her face was pressed against Will's chest. "You've betrayed...left me nothing. I've lost you. Lost...only thing...ever mattered to me."

Gray bent until his lips brushed Neala's ear. "Duck outside and run for the main hotel. I'll keep them distracted. The staff should already have telephoned the sheriff's office."

"All right, Grayson." Neala's hand shifted until her fingers twisted in the collar of his shirt. "But I don't like it. You better be careful yourself."

"Faulkner!" Will called out. "It would be best if you left." A portentous silence thickened before he added leadenly, "Take Neala with you. I'm—I'm not going anywhere."

And he was a three-tailed raccoon. "Not a chance, Will. You and your mother are—"

Mrs. Crocker erupted with an inhuman shriek, wrenched free of Will, then slapped his face, hard. Staggering, he side-stepped and before anyone could react, she snatched the revolver out of her son's hands and darted around him to the front door, blocking the way.

"I won't let you give up like this! You're nothing but a coward! A weak-minded coward and you'll roast for what you've done to me! All of you will!"

She lifted the gun, pointed it straight at Neala.

"Momma! No! *No!*"

Gray's finger tightened on the trigger—and Will leaped in front of him and Neala. Once more the crack of a gunshot ripped through the room.

Only... Only Gray felt nothing. No molten pain, no spurt of warm blood soaking his shirt. He stared down at his gun. He hadn't taken the shot, he knew he hadn't. What—?

Almost in slow motion, Will sank to his knees, his gaze upon his mother. Both hands clutched his chest. "No more killing," he whispered.

Eyes wild, Mrs. Crocker stared down at her son. *"William?"*. Mouth quivering, she took a step forward. "William?"

Will shuddered. A moan leaked from his half-open mouth and he lifted one of his hands in front of his face. Bright red blood dripped from fingers curled like claws.

Gray heard Neala gasp. Taking no chances, however, he kept his weapon trained on Mrs. Crocker and didn't move toward the fallen man. "How bad is it?" he asked Will.

"Not sure…" He started to sway.

"No… My son. My son…" Mrs. Crocker dropped down, threw her arms around Will. "I'm sorry, baby. I'm so sorry. Please don't leave me, William. It will be all right. I promise. You'll marry her, it will be all right. You'll be William Shaw… William?"

Eyes glazing, Will slid free of his mother's arms to lie motionless on the floor. Gray quickly knelt and with more force than gentleness snatched the gun from Mrs. Crocker's unresisting hand. Rising, he holstered his own gun, shucked the remaining bullets from the pocket revolver, then flung it through the open door, out into the darkness. For the first time in hours he managed a deep breath.

When he turned back around, Neala was crouched by Will, her hands pressing a snowy-white handkerchief against his chest. Within seconds the handkerchief was soaked with blood.

Like Lot's wife, frozen into a pillar of salt at the sight of something too unbearable to imagine, Mrs. Crocker stared at the tableau of her son and the woman she had come to destroy.

Grayson crossed the room, knelt by Neala. His arm went around her shoulders and she rested her head against him. Tears stood in her eyes.

"He saved both our lives," she murmured.

Eyes cloudy, Will wheezed a single rattling breath. "Tired…

of the killing," he repeated. His head rolled so that his gaze fell upon his mother. "S-sorry."

His mother didn't respond.

Neala touched his cheek. Will slowly focused back on her face. "Thank you, Will. Thank you, for saving both our lives."

Something came and went in the dull brown eyes. When Neala leaned down, her face almost brushing Will's, it took the last of Gray's remaining control not to haul her back and away into the safety of his embrace. But something beyond his ability to comprehend wrapped around his arms, gently but authoritatively pressing him to stillness.

Even when Neala brushed a fleeting kiss to Will's brow.

"Your name should have been Shaw," she told him then. "Grandfather was wrong. Please forgive him, Will." A shudder rippled through her body, and Gray watched in utter bafflement as her face seemed to soften, while at the same time light infused her in ethereal radiance. He could not tear his eyes away. "You see, I'm forgiving you for everything you did, that brought death and grief to my family." The tears flowed freely down her cheeks. "I forgive you, Will."

But Will shook his head in a single renunciatory gesture. His lips moved soundlessly. The dark hopelessness in his eyes deepened until his lids drifted down. A final breath sighed past his lips.

Gray forced himself to look across at Mrs. Crocker, who hadn't moved, hadn't blinked. She exhibited no sign whatsoever that her son had just died, by her hand, much less that she remained a threat to Neala, or himself. "Mrs. Crocker?"

No response. Still cautious, Gray slipped his hand beneath Neala's elbow. "Come along, love," he said, and helped her to her feet. "It's over now. It's all over."

"Yes." She swallowed noisily. "Grayson…he saved our lives. But he—but he…"

"I know."

The strange sensation tugged at him again, an uncomfortable weight of, well, of *knowing* that demanded acknowledgment, only Gray couldn't seem to find the words. "I don't want to end up like Will," was what came forth, almost on its own volition. He held Neala a little ways from him and cupped her face in his hands. "I want to feel forgiveness," he whispered. "And…I want to give it. To you. To my—" he blinked hard "—to my own mother, as well as…them."

The smile Neala gave him took his breath away. "Oh, I think we'll both be surprised," she murmured, "how easily we'll slip into the miracle of grace."

He couldn't help it. Despite a dead body at their feet and a catatonic woman who may or may not have been aware of her surroundings, Gray dipped his head and pressed a kiss to his beloved's lips. Life seemed to leap between them. Life—and a love that had triumphed over evil, over death.

Aunt Bella doubtless would have plenty of spiritual applications. For the first time in his life, Gray realized he looked forward to hearing every one of them.

Hands entwined, he and Neala turned to Mrs. Crocker. Neala squeezed Gray's hand, then freed herself to gently tug Mrs. Crocker to her feet, guiding her away from the body of her son. Grayson grabbed a bedspread and draped it over the corpse.

A moment later, he ushered the two women around the wreckage of the door and onto the gallery of the cottage. Shining from the deep black night sky, the rising moon cast a brilliant white light above the gentle silhouettes of the mountains. A single moonbeam streamed through the trees onto the grounds, almost, Gray thought in a fanciful turn of mind, as though it were lighting the way.

Aunt Bella, he promised his distant aunt, I think your prayers for me have finally been answered.

When Mrs. Crocker reached the bottom of the long set of stairs, she roused, looked around dazedly, then burst into heaving, uncontrollable sobs.

And Grayson Faulkner, misogynist and hater of female tears and histrionics, swung up into his arms the woman he had almost killed—the woman he could have killed without compunction—and carried her across the lawn toward the main hotel. Beside him, her step jaunty and her head up, Neala commenced a running discourse on God, peace and God's Presence in their lives even when they couldn't feel it, see it, or believe it.

And Gray could only nod in agreement.

Chapter Twenty-Nine

Isabella Chilton Academy
October 1890

Departing rain clouds scudded across the eastern sky, blown toward the ocean by a frosty northwestern wind. Bundled in cloaks and hats, a small party of mourners gathered in the midst of a small copse of ancient trees, their leaves tipped in gold and scarlet. Tucked beneath a massive chestnut, a new granite headstone marked the single grave where William Crocker had been laid to rest.

"Still say he deserved naught but a pauper's grave," Liam Brody grumbled. "As for this fancy-dancy headstone…"

"He saved my life, and Grayson's," Neala responded with a coaxing smile for the crusty stable master. "I couldn't bury him in the family cemetery, but it didn't seem, well, fair, condemning him to a pauper's grave."

"Well, I can't promise no' to spit on the grave, when there's nobody else about."

Beside her, Grayson chuckled. Across from them, Miss

Isabella cleared her throat, and Liam subsided, but Neala watched the two men exchange nods of masculine accord.

"I think this spot is most appropriate," she said. "After all, these woods are where Grayson and I met for the first time."

She sneaked a footstep closer to her fiancé, basking in his warmth and the newfound peace that had erased the lines scoring his forehead over the past few months. Inside her gloves, she pressed the fingers of her left hand together to better savor the unfamiliar weight of her betrothal ring. "If Will hadn't been shooting at me," she continued, "who knows if Grayson and I would ever have shared more than a passing acquaintance?"

"Are you going to hold that over me the rest of our lives?" Grayson leaned to brush his lips to her temples in a feathery caress, then glanced across at his aunt. "Why don't you go ahead and say some words over the grave? The wind's picking up."

Expression thoughtful, Miss Isabella repositioned a strand of silver-gray hair the wind had tugged loose. Then she lifted her Bible and thrust it out, over the grave, to Grayson. "I think it would be far more appropriate for you to be the one to say some words."

After a stunned moment, Grayson reached and took the Bible, muttering something unintelligible. He clutched it awkwardly, and an endearing blush crept up his neck. Then he took a deep breath, and the corner of his mouth kicked up. "I can see this business of talking to God isn't going to come easy," he confessed. "Frankly, I'd rather just recite the Lord's Prayer and be done with it. But—" he looked down at Neala so tenderly her eyes stung "—I've ignored, denied, or given lip service long enough. So—" red stained his cheeks "—let's, ah, pray."

He bowed his head and closed his eyes. Neala couldn't

help but dart a quick look at the other bystanders, her heart squishing to a puddle as every one of them obediently bowed their heads.

"God…ah, I don't understand much about You yet," Grayson began, "but I've come to believe that understanding isn't necessary for…for knowing that You're God—and I'm not. And that faith in You makes me a better man, but not a saint. A stronger man, not a weaker one. And…" Neala heard him swallow hard "…and a man who wants to honor his promises, not just today when it's easy, but for all the days I have left on the earth. So if Your Son can forgive all the bad things I've ever done, I need to forgive Will Crocker, for the bad things he did. Because, in the end, he did a good thing, God. He did a good thing."

Neala instinctively lifted her hand to cup the clan crest, pinned securely on her cloak. While her faith in God and family had faltered, Grayson's had taken root and sprouted. As she listened to his halting yet heartfelt prayer, she realized all over again that her husband-to-be had protected not only her life—but her heritage. It was because of Grayson that she'd been able to forgive her grandfather, seeing him with a clearer—and more understanding—eye.

On the other hand, she could scarcely comprehend that what she had assumed all of her life were colored chips of glass were in fact priceless gemstones.

Grayson's voice deepened, snapping Neala's attention back on his words.

"In a bizarre kind of way, in the end, I think I understand how Will felt," he said, then paused.

When Neala heard him swallow, she couldn't resist an upward peek. Her eyes filled, because Grayson's eyes were still closed tightly—but a single tear had tracked a damp path down his hard-boned cheek. When he opened his mouth, she hastily dropped her head.

"I don't know all the right words yet," Grayson finished huskily. "Just…help me to be the man, and the husband, I need to be. And…well…thanks."

For several long moments, silence hovered over the small group.

Then, "Amen," Liam boomed out, the Irish brogue ringing a benediction.

"Amen," Miss Isabella echoed, and the other mourners followed suit, clustering around her to speak to Neala and Grayson. Neala was surprised to see Jocelyn Tremayne hovering behind the other students. Her solemn face spoke of a haunting sorrow deeper than words; Neala wondered with a guilty pinch if this simple graveside service had reawakened the young widow's grief over her dead husband. Or if Neala and Grayson's obvious happiness filled her with loneliness instead of shared joy. She would have gone to her, but Abigail approached, hands outstretched.

"I'm so happy for you," she said, the genuine warmth of the words belied by her own sadness that, like Jocelyn's, lurked deep behind her smile.

Neala wrapped her in a fierce hug. "We'll be nearby, remember. The site Grayson found for our house is just on the other side of these woods. Scarcely an hour's walk on a pretty day."

Miss Isabella laid a hand on her nephew's shoulder. "Since they'll be living here at the Academy while the house is being built, this is as good a time as any to say welcome home. And that I'm as proud of you as if you were my own son."

"I used to wish I was," Grayson replied gruffly. "After Pamela Crocker, though, I think maybe I can look a little more kindly on my own."

"That Mrs. Crocker's a horrid woman," Nan Sweeney put in, ever the dramatist. "Are you sure there's no risk of her escaping from that asylum in Georgia? What if she did, and tracks you and Neala down, and—"

"Nan," Miss Isabella interrupted, but Gray shook his head.

"It's all right, Aunt Bella. Besides, even though you'd never admit it, I'm sure you've thought the same. I know, I know. You don't worry, you pray." He winked, and Miss Isabella's face pinked up like a rosy-cheeked infant. "I promise you, Mrs. Crocker is no longer a threat to anyone but herself. I talked to the sheriff in White Sulphur Springs, before we boarded the train. He confided that she'd pretty much gone round the bend. Wouldn't speak to anybody—anyone alive, that is. But she did talk to her mother, and Will, like they were there in the room with her. Sheriff said he'd never seen anything like it." A muscle in his jaw twitched. "Two generations who allowed hate to deteriorate into madness. It's unnerving, realizing the effect parents have on their children's lives."

"Mmm. I'll remind you of that sentiment," Miss Isabella remarked pointedly, "when you and Neala have your first-born. And remind you how even prodigal sons such as yourself can be restored, with a lot of prayer and a bit of God's grace."

"And a bit of soul-searching on my part," Grayson muttered. "You've made your point, Aunt Bella. No more lectures, please."

"Have you set a wedding date?" Abigail asked shyly.

"We're waiting to see if we can find Adrian first," Neala said. "And…I want to finish my studies here at the Academy."

"I'll have two-dozen chaperones to contend with," Grayson joked. "Our courtship was a lot more satisfying at the Old White, when I had you mostly to myself."

"Well, don't be thinking the pair of you can slip off without me knowing about it." Liam slapped a hand on Grayson's shoulder. "Not that I'll be doing anything, mind you. I'll just be knowing."

More laughter rippled through the group. Then, as though by some prearranged signal, one by one, faces turned away and people drifted off, heading for the warmth of the Academy, until only Miss Isabella remained with Neala and Grayson.

"Don't dally too long," she said. "There's a bite to this wind, and rain in the air."

Neala started to speak, but the headmistress lifted a hand. "You both need to say a private farewell." She studied them a long moment before her gaze rose to the brilliant forest canopy. "While you're about it, perhaps you can bid farewell to a number of preconceptions and misconceptions as well. There's more to marriage, my dears, than avowals of undying love."

For a few moments after Miss Isabella departed, Neala and Grayson stood together in peaceful silence.

"You probably ought to know that I don't think I'd be here, like this, if Will had done to her what he did to Mrs. Wilkes," Grayson eventually admitted.

"I wouldn't blame you." Neala approached the headstone and lightly laid her hand on cold granite. "Grayson, do you wish you'd killed Mrs. Crocker?"

He came to her, stripped off his gloves and dropped them to the ground, then cupped her face in his bare hands. "No. But I would have, if she'd shot you." The warmth of his fingers reached deep inside Neala, calm and caressing. "I didn't want to kill Mrs. Crocker. I'm glad I didn't have to. My finger was on the trigger, pulling it back to fire. But—something stopped me, the same way you stopped me from choking Will. I know now that 'something' was God. And it occurred to me that one of the reasons I couldn't bring myself to pull the trigger was because of the day my best friend died, and I killed a woman."

He set her a little ways from him to search her face. "If what happened in Philadelphia had never occurred, I don't think I would have held back with Mrs. Crocker."

Cautiously Neala nodded.

"For over a year now that whole tragedy has been eating away at me, in a way killing the last of my humanity. I couldn't see any sense to it, couldn't get out from under the awful *unfairness* of it." A frustrated sound escaped his throat. "I didn't know what to do. So I blamed God."

"Did you know that I gave up on God after Will murdered Mrs. Wilkes?"

"What?"

Smiling a little, Neala nodded. "She was sort of my camel's straw. All my life, I'd tried to be a good person, even after everyone in my family died, or left me. I blamed myself for Mrs. Wilkes's death. By the time Will abducted me, I didn't care about anything. I didn't even care about dying, because I never expected to see you again. I felt abandoned, by everyone, including the Lord."

She was watching Grayson closely enough to catch the muscle twitch in his jaw. "I also felt I deserved it," she added contritely, "because I'd deceived you."

"It's over," Grayson put in roughly. "I don't want to talk about it, not now. Not ever."

"Okay. But does it help, knowing that I felt God had abandoned me?"

"No. You should have known better, about both of us."

"Are you going to rub my nose in it the rest of our lives?" Neala mimicked the words he'd spoken to her earlier.

"Only the first ten or fifteen years." His hands slid inside her cloak, up her arms until his thumbs could caress her throat. "Don't ever leave me," he whispered. Then his mouth covered hers.

A gust of wind shoved them, splattering their faces with the first drops of rain. Grayson wrapped her in another bear hug and turned so that his body protected her from the weather. "I figured something else out, about God," he confessed against her temple.

Neala murmured an unintelligible sound of encouragement, and with a long, peaceful sigh Grayson continued. "I figured out that Marty and Mrs. Wilkes didn't die because God turned a blind eye. They died because two bitter, twisted people killed them. I can accept—now—that God allows senseless deaths not because He doesn't care, but because He gave mankind the freedom to choose."

"I tried to explain as much to Will." Neala burrowed deeper into Grayson's protective bulk after a raindrop splashed onto her nose. "He wouldn't listen."

"Mmm. I'm not sure he knew how."

A lump formed in her throat. "I know."

As though he could read her mind, Grayson jostled her a bit. "A senseless tragedy last year in Philadelphia turned out to be the catalyst I needed to do the right thing last week at White Sulphur Springs." He pressed another kiss to her temple, then one to the corners of both eyes. "Something good came from something awful." His voice thickened. "It still doesn't make much sense, because I don't believe God deliberately engineered circumstances so that Mrs. Wilkes and the woman who killed Marty would die. But I feel different inside now. At peace with myself, with everything that's happened, the bad and the good."

Laughing a little, he clasped her shoulders, then took a couple of backward steps, until he was leaning against the trunk of a massive chestnut. "If you don't kiss me again I'm liable to start babbling like a circuit-riding preacher."

"I love listening to your babbling almost as much as I love kissing you," Neala told him, her own throat aching. To satisfy them both she stretched on her toes to plant a kiss at the corner of his mouth, where the lips were curved in a smile. "You might be interested to know there's a verse, in the New Testament. The Book of Romans. It captures what you're saying perfectly. We'll have to read it together. Someplace…dry."

More raindrops splattered them, and the wind set the trees around them to swaying. They exchanged another kiss, then turned to face William's grave one last time.

"Goodbye, William," Neala said, then because the urge welled up and spilled over, she dropped to her knees and bowed her head while rain began to fall in a steady patter. "Lord, help us to remember always, that even when life is tossing its worst our way, that You're still beside us. And no matter how afraid we are, or angry, or hurting, or grieving over things we can't understand, that if we choose to trust You with our lives, You will always plant flowers in our hearts, instead of thorns."

Beside her, she felt Grayson kneel as well, felt his arm wrap around her shoulder in a firm, comforting grip.

"Help us to choose to look for the flowers, Lord. Amen."

Grayson helped her to her feet. For a moment they stood, staring down at the grave.

"How about," he finally said, "if we plant some flowers on his grave, next spring?"

"I think that would be a good thing to do," Neala said. "How about…forget-me-nots?"

Hand in hand, they turned their faces and their steps toward the Academy. All around them rain and cold wind blew, dulling the brilliant fall foliage and darkening the sky. Likely they would be soaked before they reached shelter, but neither Neala nor Grayson cared.

"We're in for a lecture," Grayson commented.

"Not," Neala returned with a conspiratorial grin, "if we

hide out in the stable with Liam until the storm passes. He installed one of Mr. Bell's telephones there, this past summer. It connects to the main house, so he can call Miss Isabella and let her know we're safe and sound."

"Just what I need. A cantankerous Irishman for a chaperone."

"Did I mention that he and Mr. Pepperell spend every Friday evening playing chess—in Mr. Pepperell's cottage?"

"Ah. And today's Friday, isn't it? So you think that, after he telephones the main house to assure everyone of our safety, he'll trot right on out in the storm to play chess, leaving us alone in the stables?"

Neala swiped a hank of damp, wind-tossed curls out of her face. "Absolutely. Liam loves his chess game. Besides—" she blinked raindrops away as she grinned up at her beloved "—the entire school has been praying that you and I would realize we're a perfect match. Abby told me, when we returned last week."

Grayson paused to tug her cloak tighter and pull the hood over her head. "Then by all means, let's head for the barn. I'm still fairly new at practicing my Christian faith, but even I know God has a fondness for stables."

Their laughter rang through the rain and the wind, which whisked it upward toward heaven.

* * * * *

Dear Reader,

Thanks for stepping into the story of Neala Shaw and Grayson Faulkner as they struggle not only with a relentless murderer, but also their relationship with each other. Neala's faith in an all-loving God lacks depth because until now it has never been tested. Gray spurns God's presence in his life altogether. But even from opposite viewpoints they also struggle with baffling spiritual questions asked by every human being in times of grief and despair, regardless of religious beliefs.

As a Christian for half a century now, I've asked such questions myself. Some of the answers I've come to believe as truth are interwoven into the spiritual themes of *Legacy of Secrets*. Through the humble vehicle of this novel, perhaps you can learn along with Neala and Gray—and me—that God *will* speak to you…but you have to learn how to hear His voice. And to trust His love even when you can't hear Him.

As always, it is my hope that my books bring hope to your heart and—even if only for a brief moment—a smile to your face.

Joy to you,

Sara Mitchell

QUESTIONS FOR DISCUSSION

1. Neala lost not only her family, but her home and most of her possessions. How did Neala's faith help her cope during those difficult times? How do you think you would cope if this happened to you?

2. Family relationships throughout childhood contribute to the way we interact with other people as adults. In what ways are Gray and Neala's childhoods similar? How did they differ?

3. Gray and Neala meet in a most unusual fashion—he thinks he's rescuing her, she thinks he's shooting at her. How did you meet your spouse? Was it a conventional or unconventional meeting? How did this affect your relationship later on?

4. Isabella Chilton's Academy helps women who have no family and teaches them how to support themselves as well as how to be a good wife. This represented a more progressive mode of thinking in 1890s America, where much of society still viewed women as the "gentler sex." Have things changed in 2008? How have they not?

5. Even though Neala had a brother, Adrian, her grandfather decided to make her his heir and gave her the Shaw family crest badge. If you were Neala's brother, would you have reacted as he did? Why or why not?

6. Neala runs off from the Academy to White Sulphur Springs thinking she will protect her friends if she leaves.

Was this smart? Should Neala have stayed and tried to confront her stalker?

7. Concerned for her safety, Grayson goes to White Sulphur Springs and acts as Neala's bodyguard. Though Mrs. Wilkes is their chaperone, they spend a lot of time alone together. Was this proper for a couple in 1890s West Virginia? How important was it for unmarried ladies to keep their reputations scandal free?

8. In North Carolina, Gray and Neala uncover the truth about her grandfather: he left his fiancée at the altar and eloped with another woman. Have you ever discovered that one of your relatives did something legally or morally reprehensible? What happened? Did it change your attitude toward them in any way?

9. Will Crocker and his mother have a very odd relationship. How did she make him the man he became? Should he have left her and gone out on his own? Stayed behind? Why?

10. Were you surprised that another person was murdered by the stalker at the White Sulphur Springs resort? Why or why not?

11. Very often, Neala runs away from Gray's protection, and straight into harm's way. Do you think she makes logical decisions regarding her safety, or is she reacting emotionally? Is she relying on God for guidance? What would you do in her situation?

12. When Neala's stalker is revealed, were you surprised by

the revelation, or had you already guessed the identity? What clues gave it away?

13. At the end of the book Neala's stalker ends up saving her and is killed in her stead. Was this surprising or expected? Could the book have ended some other way? How?

Colorado, June 1882

"You know the story of Cain and Abel?"

"I do."

"Patrick was Abel. I'm Cain."

Daniela Baxter gaped at the man in the doorway. Unshaven and bleary-eyed, he looked enough like Patrick to be his brother. She and Patrick were engaged to be married. She'd expected her fiancé to greet her with a smile. Instead, she'd been assaulted by this stranger's sneering question about Cain and Abel.

Dani knew better than to judge by appearances, but the stranger had declared himself to be Cain, the brother who'd surrendered to sin. Even so, God hadn't left Cain. Cain had abandoned God.

"Patrick's dead."

Dani blinked. "I must be at the wrong house."

The man studied her. "Who are you?"

"Daniela Baxter. I'm his fiancée."

His gaze stayed hard, but his voice softened like hot caramel. "I'm sorry, miss. Patrick died five days ago."

Gasping, Dani clutched her reticule. It held her only picture of the man she loved. She yearned to be a mother, both to his girls and the babies to come.

"I'm Beau Morgan. Patrick's brother."

Patrick had mentioned his brother just once. *He's not a man I'd trust with my girls. I made a will before Beau went crazy. As soon as we're married, I'll change it. I want you to adopt the girls.*

Beau stood with his arms crossed and his feet spread wide. If he'd been wearing boots, Dani might have been intimidated. Instead, she saw a hole in his sock. She suspected his life was in the same sorry shape and prayed he'd leave Patrick's daughters in her care.

"Patrick asked me to adopt the girls," she said.

Mr. Morgan raised one brow. "And would he want you to have the farm, too?"

"I suppose." She needed a way to support the girls.

"Miss Baxter, you're either naive or a con artist."

Dani gaped. "How dare you!"

"No, how dare *you?* You waltz in here and announce you want my nieces and the farm. I have an obligation to my nieces and I intend to meet it. A train leaves in the morning. I want you on it."

"Absolutely not. I promised Patrick—"

"I know what you promised." His voice turned gentle. "I also know what it's like to be grief stricken. It leaves you numb, but only for a while. Once the shock passes, you wake up screaming. It'll eat you alive if you let it."

Peering into his eyes, she saw a kinship born of suffering. Who had Beau Morgan mourned?

If he felt the connection, it didn't show. "But I'm prepared to offer a compromise. I'll move to the barn while we sort things out. You get room and board in exchange for keeping house."

She wanted to say yes, but she had to protect her reputation as well as the children. "I'd prefer the hotel if the girls can stay with me."

"I can't allow it. You're too naive."

Dani bristled. "I've just traveled a thousand miles—"

"And I've traveled ten thousand." He raised his chin. "Have you ever seen a pack of wolves?"

She'd heard howling near her father's farm, but the wolves had stayed out of sight. "No."

"I have," he said. "The kind with two legs."

"Castle Rock seems safe to me."

His eyes glittered. "It was before I got here."

REQUEST YOUR FREE BOOKS!

2 FREE INSPIRATIONAL NOVELS
PLUS 2
FREE
MYSTERY GIFTS

Love Inspired.
HISTORICAL
INSPIRATIONAL HISTORICAL ROMANCE

YES! Please send me 2 FREE Love Inspired® Historical novels and my 2 FREE mystery gifts (gifts are worth about $10). After receiving them, if I don't wish to receive any more books, I can return the shipping statement marked "cancel". If I don't cancel, I will receive 4 brand-new novels every other month and be billed just $4.24 per book in the U.S. or $4.74 per book in Canada, plus 25¢ shipping and handling per book and applicable taxes, if any*. That's a savings of over 20% off the cover price! I understand that accepting the 2 free books and gifts places me under no obligation to buy anything. I can always return a shipment and cancel at any time. Even if I never buy another book, the two free books and gifts are mine to keep forever. 102 IDN ERYA 302 IDN ERYM

Name	(PLEASE PRINT)	
Address		Apt. #
City	State/Prov.	Zip/Postal Code

Signature (if under 18, a parent or guardian must sign)

Mail to Steeple Hill Reader Service:
IN U.S.A.: P.O. Box 1867, Buffalo, NY 14240-1867
IN CANADA: P.O. Box 609, Fort Erie, Ontario L2A 5X3

Not valid to current subscribers of Love Inspired Historical books.

Want to try two free books from another series?
Call 1-800-873-8635 or visit www.morefreebooks.com

* Terms and prices subject to change without notice. N.Y. residents add applicable sales tax. Canadian residents will be charged applicable provincial taxes and GST. This offer is limited to one order per household. All orders subject to approval. Credit or debit balances in a customer's account(s) may be offset by any other outstanding balance owed by or to the customer. Please allow 4 to 6 weeks for delivery. Offer available while quantities last.

Your Privacy: Steeple Hill Books is committed to protecting your privacy. Our Privacy Policy is available online at www.SteepleHill.com or upon request from the Reader Service. From time to time we make our lists of customers available to reputable third parties who may have a product or service of interest to you. If you would prefer we not share your name and address, please check here. ☐

LIH08

Love Inspired.
HISTORICAL

TITLES AVAILABLE NEXT MONTH

Don't miss these two stories in May

THE ROAD TO LOVE by Linda Ford
During the depths of the Depression, widow Kate Bradshaw
was struggling to raise her children and hold on to her farm.
Then Hatcher Jones came by. His kindness warmed her
heart, and she longed to make the troubled drifter see that
his wandering had brought him home at last.

THE BOUNTY HUNTER'S BRIDE by Victoria Bylin
Mail-order bride Dani Baxter was left to raise three little
girls when her intended suddenly died. She was determined
to keep his small family together. But her deceased fiance's
brother Beau Morgan wasn't about to let her go it alone.
Together they could make this family whole again.

LIHCNM0408